The Cock-House at Fellsgarth

by

Talbot Baines Reed

The Cock-House at Fellsgarth
by Talbot Baines Reed

ISBN: 978-93-63057-17-3

Published by

DOUBLE 9 BOOKS

2/13-B, Ansari Road
Daryaganj, New Delhi – 110002
info@double9books.com
www.double9books.com
Tel. 011-40042856

ABOUT THE AUTHOR

Talbot Baines Reed was an English author of boys' fiction who lived from April 3, 1852, to November 28, 1893. He created a type of school stories that lasted until the middle of the 20th century. The Fifth Form at St. Dominic's is one of his most well-known works. He often and regularly wrote for The Boy's Own Paper (B.O.P.). Most of his writing was first published there. Reed became a well-known typefounder through his family's business. He also wrote the standard work on the subject, History of the Old English Letter Foundries. John Reed was a colonel in Oliver Cromwell's army during the English Civil War. The Reed family came from him. Their home was in Maiden Newton, which is in the county of Dorset. They moved to London at the end of the 18th century. Andrew Reed (1787–1862), Talbot Reed's grandpa, was a minister in the Congregational Church and the founder of many charitable organizations, such as the London Orphan Asylum and a hospital for people who could not get better. He was also a well-known hymn writer. His "Spirit Divine, attend our prayers" can still be found in many hymnals today. Talbot Baines Reed grew up in a happy family where Charles Reed was very religious and thought that tough outdoor games were the best way to raise boys.

CONTENTS

Chapter One
Green and Blue

First-night at Fellsgarth was always a festive occasion. The holidays were over, and school had not yet begun. All day long, from remote quarters, fellows had been converging on the dear old place; and here they were at last, shoulder to shoulder, delighted to find themselves back in the old haunts. The glorious memories of the summer holidays were common property. So was not a little of the pocket-money. So, by rule immemorial, were the contents of the hampers. And so, as they discovered to their cost, were the luckless new boys who had to-day tumbled for the first time headlong into the whirlpool of public school life.

Does some one tell me he never heard of Fellsgarth? I am surprised. Where can you have been brought up that you have never heard of the venerable ivy-clad pile with its watch-tower and two wings, planted there, where the rivers Shale and Shargle mingle their waters, a mile or more above Hawkswater? My dear sir, Fellsgarth stood there before the days when Henry the Eighth, (of whom you may have possibly heard in the history books) abolished the monasteries and, some wicked people do say, annexed their contents.

There is very little of the old place standing now. A piece of the wall in the head-master's garden and the lower buttresses of the watch-tower, that is all. The present building is comparatively modern; that is to say, it is no older than the end of the Civil Wars, when some lucky adherent to the winning side built it up as a manor-house and disfigured the tower with those four pepper-castors at the corners. Successive owners have tinkered the place since then, but they cannot quite spoil it. Who can spoil red brick and ivy, in such a situation?

Not know Fellsgarth! Have you never been on Hawkswater then, with its lonely island, and the grey screes swooping down into the clear water? And have you never seen Hawk's Pike, which frowns in on the fellows through the dormitory window? I don't ask if you have been up it. Only three persons, to my knowledge (guides and natives of course excepted), have done that. Yorke was one, Mr Stratton was another, and the other—but that's to be part of my story.

First-night, as I have said, was a specially "go-as-you-please" occasion at the school. Masters, having called over their roll, disappeared into their own quarters and discreetly heard nothing. Dames, having received and unpacked the "night-bags," retired elsewhere to wrestle with the big luggage. The cooks, having passably satisfied the cravings of two hundred and fifty hungry souls, and having removed out of harm's way the most perishable of the crockery, shrugged their shoulders and shut themselves into the kitchens, listening to the noise and speculating on the joys of the coming term.

What a noise it was! Niagara after the rains, or an express train in a tunnel, or the north wind in a gale against the Hawk's Back might be able to beat it. But then Fellsgarth was not competing; each of the fellows was merely chatting pleasantly to his neighbours. It was hardly a fair trial. And yet it was not bad for the School. When Dangle, who owned the longest ear in the school, could not hear a word which Brinkman, who owned the loudest voice, shouted into it, it spoke somewhat for what Fellsgarth might do in the way of noise if it tried.

The only two persons who were not actively contributing to the general clamour were the two new boys who sat wedged in among a mass of juniors at one of the lower tables. They may have considered that the beating of their hearts was noisy enough. But people in this world are slow at hearing other people's hearts beat. No one seemed to notice it.

It is due to the stouter of these two young gentlemen to say that the beating of his heart, and the general state of amaze in which he found himself, did not interfere greatly with his appetite. He had brought that accomplishment, if no other, from home, and not being engaged like those around him in conversation, he contrived to put away really a most respectable meal. Indeed, his exploits in this direction had already become a matter for remark among his neighbours.

"It's all right," said one of the juniors, who answered to the name of D'Arcy; "his buttons are sewn on with wire. They'll hold."

"I suppose he's made of gutta-percha," observed another. "He'll stretch a little more before he's done."

"I say, what a bill he's running up! By the way, what do they charge for this kind of pudding?"

"It's a dear kind—and nothing like as good as the sort we get for regular. I never could understand why they make fellows shell out for what they eat first-night."

"It *is* a swindle," said D'Arcy, solemnly. "I've had to make a very light meal, because I've only half a crown, and I'm afraid there won't be much change left out of that."

The new boy was just laying butter on a roll, and preparing to close the proceedings of the meal with a good square turn of bread and butter. But as D'Arcy's words fell on his ears he suddenly stopped short and looked up.

"I say," said he, "isn't this dinner charged in the house bill then?"

D'Arcy laughed derisively.

"Well, you most be a muff. Don't you know school doesn't begin till to-morrow? They give you dinner to-night, but you're not obliged to eat it."

The new boy took a gulp of water, which he calculated would be gratis under any circumstances, and then gasped—"I say, I didn't know that."

D'Arcy looked solemn. "Jolly awkward," said he; "what have you had?"

Whereupon Master Ashby, the new boy, entered on a detailed confession, which D'Arcy, evidently an expert at mental arithmetic, "totted up" as he went along.

"How many times pudding did you say?" he asked towards the end, "Twice and a bit."

"Three and ten; I dare say he won't be stiff about the bit, three and ten; and that roll and butter—"

"I've not eaten them."

"No, but you've touched them. You'll be charged, unless you can get a fellow to take them off your hands."

"Will *you* have them?" asked Ashby.

Whereupon there was a laugh at *D'Arcy's* expense, which annoyed that young gentleman.

"I don't want your second-hand grub. You'd better take it round and see what you can get for it."

Ashby looked at the bread, and then glanced round the table.

"No," said he, "I'll have it and pay for it, if it comes to that."

"That'll be four bob."

Ashby gave a gulp of despair.

"I've not got so much."

"Then you'll get in a jolly row."

"Could you lend me one and six, I say?" asked the new boy.

Again D'Arcy got the worst of the laugh.

"Didn't you hear me say I'd only just got enough to pay for my own? But I tell you what; you can hide under the table. You're not known."

Ashby looked round, and felt about with his foot under the table to ascertain what room there might be there. Then he flushed up. "No, I shan't," said he; "I'd get into the row instead."

As his eye travelled round and marked the curious smile on every face it suddenly dawned upon him that he had been "done." His first sensation was one of immense relief. He should not have to pay for his dinner after all! His second was a cunning device for getting out of the dilemma.

"I thought you'd begin to laugh soon," said he to D'Arcy. "I knew you couldn't keep it up."

D'Arcy turned very red in the face and glared at this audacious youngster in deserved wrath.

"What do you mean, you young ass? You know you've swallowed it all."

"He swallowed all the grub anyhow," said another.

"No, I've not," said Master Ashby. "I'd have another go-in now. I knew he'd have to laugh in the end."

It was hopeless to deal seriously with a rebel of this sort. D'Arcy tried to ride off on the high horse; but it was not a very grand spectacle, and Ashby, munching up the remains of his roll, was generally held to have scored. The relief with which he hailed the discovery of his mistake was so genuine, and the good spirits and appetite the incident put into him were so imperturbable, as to disarm further experiment at his expense, and he was left comparatively free to enjoy the noise and imbibe his first impression of Fellsgarth in his own way.

The other new boy, meanwhile, was not altogether without his difficulties.

Fisher minor, to which name this ingenuous young gentleman answered, would probably have been the first to pour contempt on the verdure of his companion. He had come up to Fellsgarth determined that, in whatever respect he failed, no one should lightly convict him of being green. He had wormed out of his brother in the Sixth a few hints of what was considered the proper thing at Fellsgarth, and these, with the aid of his own brilliant intellect and reminiscences of what he had read in the books, served, as he hoped, both to forewarn and forearm him against all the uncomfortable predicaments into which the ordinary new boy is apt to fall.

It must be confessed that as he sat and listened to the noise, and marked how little Fellsgarth appeared to recognise his existence, he felt a trifle uneasy and nervous. He wasn't sure now that he knew everything. All these fellows seemed to be so thoroughly at home, and to know so exactly what to do; he wished he could do the same.

He wished, for instance, he could spin a fork round with his first finger and thumb while he talked, as Yorke, the captain, was doing. He did once privately try, while he was not talking, but it was a dismal failure. The fork fell with a great clatter to the floor and attracted general attraction his way. He picked the weapon up with as easy an air as he could assume, whistling *sotto voce* to himself as he did it, so as to appear unconcerned.

"Look out, I say; you mustn't whistle at meal-times, it's bad manners," said a voice at his side.

He turned round and perceived a pleasant-looking youth of the species junior, in a red tie and wrist studs to match.

This youth evidently knew what was what at Fellsgarth; and a further glance at him convinced Fisher minor that he had met him in a good hour. For all dinner-time he had been exercised as to whether it was the thing to wear the jacket opened or buttoned. Yorke wore his buttoned, so did a good many of the Sixth; and Fisher minor had consequently buttoned up too. But his new friend, who was pronounced in all his ways and evidently an authority on etiquette, wore his open. Fisher minor therefore furtively slipped his fingers down and opened his coat.

"You're a new kid, I suppose," said he of the red necktie.

"Yes, I'm Fisher minor."

"What, son of Fisher the boat-builder? I didn't know he had one so old."

"No, oh no. That's my brother up there, talking to the Dux."

"The who? I don't see any ducks."

"I mean Yorke, you know, the captain."

"Why ever do you call him ducks? You'd better let him catch you calling him names like that. Oh, you're a brother of old Fisher? You look it."

Fisher minor was alarmed at the tone in which this observation was made. It seemed to imply that Fisher major was not quite all that could be desired, and yet the younger brother did not exactly know what it was in the elder which called for repudiation. However, he was spared the pain of deciding by a new voice on his other side.

"What's that, Wally? Does this kid say he belongs to Fisher? Oh, my stars, what form we're coming to!"

Fisher minor glanced round, and experienced a shock as he did so.

For the new speaker was so like the last that he was tempted to suppose the latter had suddenly changed seats and contrived to substitute a blue necktie for a red, and button his jacket during the feat. But when he looked back, the owner of the red tie was still in his place. After considerable wagging of his head, he was forced to admit that he was seated between two different persons.

"Why, he can't help that," said the gentleman addressed as Wally.

Fisher minor laughed feebly, and really wished his brother would pay a little more attention to the "form."

"Of course," said Wally, talking across to his twin brother, "fellows can't tell what asses they look until they're told. Don't you remember the chap last term who always wore his trousers turned up, till the prefects made him turn them down or go on the Modern side."

"Catch us taking any of your cast-off louts on our side," retorted the other brother, who evidently belonged to the slighted side; "yes—shocking bad form it was—and when he turned them down at last, they found seventy-four nibs, fifty matches, and nobody knows how many candle-ends."

All this time Fisher minor, with panic at his heart, was furiously trying to turn down his trouser-ends with his feet. What a lucky escape for him to get this warning in time! During the walk round the grounds he had turned his ends up, and had quite forgotten to put them down again when he came in. Now, no coaxing would get them down without manual assistance. He sat clawing with one foot after another, lacerating his shins and his garments in vain. At length in despair he dropped his fork again, and under cover of this diversion attempted to stoop and adjust the intractable folds.

In his flurry he naturally forgot the fork; so that when, after a minute and a half, he emerged without it into the upper world, his two companions were not a little perplexed.

"What have you been up to down there? Do you generally eat your grub under the table?" asked Wally. "All I can say is, it's the best place for him if he wears his hair like that," said the other in tones of alarm. "Young kid, I never noticed that before! Whatever induces you to part it on the right? Did you ever hear of a Fellsgarth fellow— Oh, I say, what a wigging you'll get! Look at me and Wally and Yorke and all of 'em. Whew! it makes one ill to see it! Just look round for yourself."

As more than half of those present appeared to have no parting at all, and most of the rest parted on the left, Fisher minor realised with horror that he had been guilty of a terrible solecism.

The alarm depicted in the faces of both the twins was proof enough that the matter was a critical one. It was no time for shuffling. He had had enough of that over his trouser-ends. He must throw himself on the mercy of his critics.

"I quite forgot—of course," said he hurriedly; "I—I—"

"Look here," said Wally, hurriedly shoving a pocket-comb into his hands; "you'd better go downstairs again and change it sharp, or you'll be spotted. Cut along."

So Fisher minor began with shame to look once more for his fork, and in doing so crawled well under the table, and sitting down proceeded nervously and painfully to open up a parting on the left side of his head. It was an arduous task, and not made easier by the unjustifiable conduct of the twins, who having got their man safe under hatches began to kick out in an unceremonious fashion and basely betray his retreat to their friends and neighbours.

"Pass him on!"

"WHAT'S THIS?" HE DEMANDED, LIFTING UP FISHER II.

"Ware cats!" was the cry, in the midst of which the luckless Fisher minor, finding a return to his old place effectually barred, and wearying of the ceremony of running a gauntlet of all the legs along the table before it was half over, made a hasty selection of what seemed to him the mildest pair within reach, and clutching at them convulsively, hung on for dear life.

The owner of the limbs in question was Ranger, a prefect of his house and more or less of a grandee at Fellsgarth. As he was unaware of the cause of the excitement around him, this sudden assault from below took him aback, and he started up from his chair in something as near a panic as a Fellsgarth prefect could be capable of. Naturally his parasite followed him.

To Ranger's credit, he took in the situation rapidly, and did not abuse his opportunities.

"What's this?" he demanded, lifting up Fisher minor, with his hair all on end and the pocket-comb still in his hand, by the coat-collar. "Who does this belong to?"

No one in particular owned the object in question.

"What are you?" asked the prefect.

"I'm Fisher minor; I got under the table, somehow."

"So I should suppose. Afraid of the draughts, I suppose."

"It was Wally and his brother put me there. I didn't mean—"

"Oh—Wally, was it? Here, young Wheatfield, you shouldn't leave your property about like this. It's against rules. Here, hook on, and don't go chucking it about any more."

"All serene," said the twin. "Come along, kid. Done with my comb? You look ever so much better form now; doesn't he, you chaps? How came you to lose your way downstairs?"

Fisher minor owned himself utterly unable to account for the misadventure, and discreetly remained silent until the signal was given to return thanks and separate every boy to his own house.

As he was wandering across the court, very dismal and apprehensive of what more was in store for him, a lean youth with a pale face and very showily attired accosted him.

"Hullo, kid, are you a new chap?"

"Yes," replied Fisher minor, eyeing the stranger suspiciously.

"What side are you on?"

Fisher stared interrogatively.

"Well, then, are you Modern or Classic?"

"I don't know, really," said Fisher minor, wishing he knew which he ought to proclaim himself. Then making a bold venture, he said, "I believe Modern."

"Good job for you," said the youth; "saves me the trouble of kicking you. Can you lend me a bob? I'll give it you back to-morrow as soon as I've unpacked."

It did strike Fisher minor as queer that any one should pack shillings up in a trunk, but he was too pleased to oblige this important and fashionable-looking personage to raise any question.

"Yes. Can you give me change out of a half-crown? Or you can pay me the lot back to-morrow, I shan't be wanting it till then," said he.

"All serene, kid; I'm glad you are our side. I shall be able to give you a leg-up with the fellows. Whose house are you in?"

"Wakefield's, the same as my brother."

"What—then you must be a Classic! They're all Classics at Wakefield's. Why can't you tell the truth when you're asked, instead of a howling pack of lies?"

"I didn't know, really, I thought—"

"Come, that's a good one. Any idiot knows what side he's on at Fellsgarth."

Fisher minor was greatly confused to stand convicted thus of greenness.

"You see," said he, putting on a little "side" to cover his shame, "I was bound to be stuck on the same side as my brother, you know."

"Nice for you. Not a gentleman among them. All paupers and prigs," said this young Modern, waxing eloquent. "You'll suit them down to the ground." Considering that Fisher minor had just lent the speaker half a crown, these taunts struck him as not exactly grateful. At the same time he writhed under the reproach, and felt convinced that Classics were not at all the "form" at Fellsgarth.

"Why," pursued the other, pocketing his coin in order to release his hands for a little elocution, "we could boy 'em up twice over. The workhouse isn't in it with Wakefield's. There's not a day but they come cadging to us, wanting to borrow our tin, or our grub, or something. There, look at that chap going across there! He's one of 'em. Regular casual-ward form about him. He's the meanest, stingiest lout in all Fellsgarth."

"Why," exclaimed Fisher minor, looking in alarm towards this prodigy of baseness, "why, that's—that's Fisher, my brother!"

The Modern youth's jaw fell with a snap, and his cheeks lost what little colour they had.

"What? Why didn't you tell me! Look here, you needn't tell him what I said. It was quite between ourselves, you know. I must be cutting, I say. See you again some day."

And he vanished, leaving Fisher minor considerably more bewildered, and poorer by a cool half-crown, than he had been five minutes ago.

Chapter Two
Lamb's Singing

Wakefield's house, as Fisher minor entered it under his brother's wing, hardly seemed to the new boy as disreputable a haunt as his recent Modern friend had led him to expect. Nor did the sixty or seventy fellows who clustered in the common room strike him as exactly the lowest stratum of Fellsgarth society. Yorke, the captain, for instance, with his serene, well-cut face, his broad shoulders and impressive voice hardly answered to the description of a lout. Nor did Ranger, of the long legs, with speed written in every inch of his athletic figure, and gentleman in every line of his face, look the sort of fellow to be mistaken for a cad. Even Fisher major, about whom the younger brother had been made to feel decided qualms, could hardly have been the hail-fellow-well-met he was with everybody, had he been all the new boy's informant had recently described him.

Indeed, Fisher minor, when presently he gathered himself together sufficiently to look round him, was surprised to see so few traces of the "casual-ward" in his new house. True, most of the fellows might be poor—which, of course, was highly reprehensible; and some of them might not be connected with the nobility, which showed a great lack of proper feeling on their part. But as a rule they held up their heads and seemed to think very well of themselves and one another; while their dress, if it was not in every case as fashionable as that of the temporary owner of Fisher minor's half-crown, was at least passably well fitting.

Fisher minor, for all his doubts about the company he was in, could not help half envying these fellows, as he saw with what glee and self-satisfaction they entered into their own at Wakefield's. They were all so glad to be back, to see again the picture of Cain and Abel on the wall, to scramble for the corner seat in the ingle-bench, to hear the well-known creak on the middle landing, to catch the imperturbable tick of the dormitory clock, to see the top of Hawk's Pike looming out, down the valley, clear and sharp in the falling light.

Fisher minor and Ashby, as they sat dismally and watched all the fun, wondered if the time would ever come when they would feel as much at home as all this. It was a stretch of imagination beyond their present capacity.

To their alarm, Master Wally Wheatfield presently recognised them from across the room, and came over patronisingly to where they sat.

"Hullo, new kids! thinking of your mas, and the rocking-horses, and Nurse Jane, and all that? Never mind, have a good blub, it'll do you good."

Considering how near, in strict secrecy, both the young gentlemen addressed were to the condition indicated by the genial twin, this exhortation was not exactly kind.

They tried to look as if they did not mind it, and Fisher minor naturally did his best to appear knowing.

"I don't mind," said he, with a snigger; "they're all milksops at home. I'd sooner be here."

"I wouldn't," put in the sturdy Ashby. "I think it's horrid not to see a face you know."

"There you are; what did I say! Screaming for his mammy," gibed Wally.

"And if I was," retorted Master Ashby, warming up, "she's a lot better worth it than yours, so now!"

Master Wally naturally fired up at this. Such language was hardly respectful from a new junior to an old.

"I'll pull your nose, new kid, if you cheek me."

"And I'll pull yours, if you cheek my mother."

"Booh, booh, poor baby! Who's cheeking your mother? I wouldn't cheek her with a pair of tongs. Something better to do. I say, are both you kids Classics?"

"Yes," they replied.

"I thought you must be Moderns, you're both so precious green. All right, there'll be lamb's singing directly, then you'll have to sit up."

"What's lamb's singing?" said Ashby.

"Don't you know?" replied Wally, glad to have recovered the whip hand. "It's this way. Every new kid has to sing in his house the first-night. You'll have to."

"Oh," faltered Ashby, "I can't; I don't know anything."

"Can't get out of it; you must," said the twin, charmed to see the torture he was inflicting. "So must you, Hair-parting."

Fisher minor was too knowing a hand to be caught napping. He had had the tip about lamb's singing from his brother last term, and was prepared. He joined in, therefore, against Ashby.

"What, didn't you know that, kid? You must be green. *I* knew it all along."

"That's all right," said Wheatfield. "Now I'm going. I can't fool away all my evening with you. By the way, mind you don't get taking up with any Modern kids. It's not allowed, and you'll get it hot if you do. My young brother," (each twin was particularly addicted to casting reflections on his brother's age) "is a Modern. Don't you have anything to do with him. And whatever you do, don't lend any of them money, or there'll be a most awful row. That's why we always call up subscriptions for the house clubs on first-night. It cleans the fellows out, and then they can't lend any to the Moderns. You'll have to shell out pretty soon, as soon as Lamb's singing is over. Ta, ta."

This last communication put Fisher minor in a terrible panic. He had evidently committed a gross breach of etiquette in lending that Modern boy (whose name he did not even know) a half-crown; and now, when the subscriptions were called for, he would have to declare himself before all Wakefield's a pauper.

"I say," said he to Ashby, dropping the patronising for the pathetic, "could you ever lend me half-a-crown? I've—I've lost mine—I'll pay it you back next week faithfully."

"I've only got five bob," said Ashby; "to last all the term, and half a crown of that will go in the clubs to-night."

"But you'll get it back in a week—really you will," pleaded Fisher minor, "and I'll—"

But here there was a sudden interruption. Every one, from the captain down, looked towards the new boys, and a shout of "lamb's singing," headed by Wally Wheatfield, left little doubt as to what it all meant.

"Pass up the new kids down there," called one of the prefects. Whereupon Fisher minor and Ashby, rather pale and very nervous, were hustled up to the top of the room, where sat the grandees in a row round the table on which the sacrifice was to take place.

For the benefit of the curious it may be explained that "lamb's singing," the name applied to the musical performances of new boys at Fellsgarth on first-night, is supposed to have derived its title from the frequency with which these young gentlemen fell back upon "Mary had a little lamb" as their theme on such occasions.

"Isn't one of them your minor?" asked Yorke of Fisher senior.

"Yes," said the latter rather apologetically; "the one with the light hair. He's not much to look at. The fact is, I only know him slightly. They say at home he's a nice boy."

"Does he spend much of his time under tables, as a rule?" asked Ranger, recognising the lost property which had hung on to his legs at dinner-time. "If so, I'll take the other one for my fag."

"He's bagged already," said Denton. "Fisher and I put our names down for him an hour ago."

"Well, that's cool. If Fisher wanted a fag he might as well have taken his own minor."

"Fisher major knew better," said the gentleman in question. "It might raise awkward family questions if I had him."

"Wouldn't it be fairer to toss up?" suggested the captain. "Or I don't mind swopping Wally Wheatfield for him; if you really—"

Ranger laughed.

"No, thank you, I draw the line at Wally. I wouldn't deprive you of him for the world. I suppose I must have this youngster. Let's hear him sing first."

"Yes, lamb's singing. Now, you two, one at a time. Who's first? Alphabetical order."

Ashby, with an inward groan, mounted the rostrum. If anything could have been more cruel than the noise which greeted his appearance, it was the dead silence which followed it. Fellows sat round, staring him out of countenance with critical faces, and rejoicing in his embarrassment.

"What's the title!" demanded some one.

"I don't know any songs," said Ashby presently, "and I can't sing."

"Ho, ho! we've heard that before. Come, forge ahead."

"I only know the words of one that my con—somebody I know—sings, called the *Vigil*. I don't know the tune."

"That doesn't matter—out with it."

So Ashby, pulling himself desperately together, plunged recklessly into the following appropriate ditty; which, failing its proper tune, he manfully set at the top of his voice, and with all the energy he was capable of, to the air of the *Vicar of Bray*—

> The stealthy night creeps o'er the lea,
> My darling, haste away with me.
> Beloved, come I see where I stand,
> With arms outstretched upon the strand.
>
> The night creeps on; my love is late,
> O love, my love, I wait, I wait;
> The soft wind sighs mid crag and pine;
> Haste, O my sweet; be mine, be mine!

This spirited song, the last two lines of which were aught up as a chorus, fairly brought down the house; and Ashby, much to his surprise, found himself famous. He had no idea he could sing so well, or that the fellows would like the words as much as they seemed to do. Yet they cheered him and encored him, and yelled the chorus till the roof almost fell in.

"Bravo," shouted every one, the captain himself included, as he descended from the table; "that's a ripping song."

"That sends up the price of our fag, I fancy," said Denton to his chum. "Your young brother won't beat that."

"Next man in," shouted Wheatfield, hustling forward Fisher minor. "Now, kid, lamm it on and show them what you can do."

"Title! title!" cried the meeting.

Now, if truth must be told, Fisher minor had come to Fellsgarth determined that whatever else he failed in, he would make a hit at "lamb's singing." He had made a careful calculation as to what sort of song would go down with the company and at the same time redeem his reputation from all suspicion of greenness; and he flattered himself he had hit upon the exact article.

"Oh," said he, with an attempt at offhand swagger, in response to the demand. "It's a comic song, called *Oh no*."

It disconcerted him a little to see how seriously everybody settled down to listen, and how red his brother's face turned as he took a back seat among the seniors. Never mind. Wait till they heard his song. That would fetch them!

He had carefully studied not only the song but the appropriate action. As he knew perfectly well, there is one invariable attitude for a comic song. The head must be tilted a little to one side. One eyebrow must be raised and the opposite corner of the mouth turned down. One knee should be slightly bent; the first finger and thumb of one hand should rest gracefully in the waistcoat pocket, and the other hand should be free for gesture.

All these points Fisher minor attended to now as carefully as his nervousness would permit, and felt half amused at the thought of how comic the fellows must think him.

"Do you—" he began.

But at this point Ranger unfeelingly interrupted, and put the vocalist completely out.

"Did you say 'Oh no' or 'How now'?"

"Oh no," repeated the singer.

"You mean h-o-w n-o-w?"

"Oh no; it's o-h n-o."

"Thanks—sorry to interrupt. Fire away." Fisher tried to get himself back into attitude, and began again in a thin treble voice;—

Do you think I'm just as green as grass! Oh no!

Do you take me for a silly ass! Oh no! Do you think I don't know A from B! Do you think I can't tell he from she! Do you think I swallow all I see?

Oh no—not me! He was bewildered by the unearthly silence of his audience. No one stirred a muscle except Wheatfield, who was apparently wiping away a tear. Was the song too deep for them, or perhaps he did not sing the words distinctly, or perhaps they *had* laughed and he had not noticed? At any rate he would try the next verse, which was certain to amuse them. He looked as droll as he could, and by way of heightening the effect, stuck his two thumbs into the armholes of his waistcoat and wagged his hands in time with the song.

Do you think I lie abed all day?

Oh no! Do you guess I skate on ice in May?

Oh no! Do you think I can't tell what is what? Do you think I don't know pepper's hot? Or whereabouts my i's to dot?

Oh no, no rot!

As he concluded, Fisher minor summoned up enough resolution to shake his head and lay one finger to his nose in the most approved style of comedy, and then awaited the result.

Fellows apparently did not take in that the song was at an end, for they neither cheered nor smiled. So Fisher minor made an elaborate bow to show it was all over. The result was the same. A gloomy silence prevailed, in the midst of which the singer, never more perplexed in his life, descended from the table and proceeded to look out for the congratulations of his admirers.

"Beautiful song," said Wally, still mopping his face.

"I never thought I could be so touched by anything. We generally get comic songs on first-night."

"This *is* a comic one," said Fisher minor.

"Go on," said Wheatfield; "tell that to D'Arcy here—he'll believe you—eh, D'Arcy?" D'Arcy looked mysterious.

"It's no laughing matter, young Wheatfield," said he, in a loud whisper, evidently intended for the eager ears of Fisher minor. "I heard Yorke just now ask Denton if he thought Fisher's minor was all there. Denton seemed quite cut up, and said he hadn't known it before, but it must be a great family trouble to the Fishers. It accounted for Fisher major's frequent low spirits. You know," continued D'Arcy confidentially, "I can't help myself thinking it's a little rough on Fisher major for his people to send a minor who's afflicted like this to Fellsgarth. They might at least have put him on the Modern side. He'd have been better understood there."

This speech Fisher minor listened to with growing perplexity. Was D'Arcy in jest or earnest? He seemed to be in earnest, and the serious faces of his listeners looked like it too. Had the captain really made that remark to Denton? Suppose there *was* something in it! Suppose, without his knowing, he was really a little queer in his head! His people might have told him of it. And Fisher major, his brother—even he hadn't heard of it! Oh dear! oh dear! How was he ever to recover his reputation for sanity? Whatever induced him to sing that song?

Poor Fisher minor devoutly wished himself home again, within reach of his mother's soothing voice and his sisters' smiles. *They* understood him. These fellows didn't. *They* knew he was not an idiot. These fellows didn't.

Further reflection was cut short by a loud call to order and cheers, as Yorke, the captain, rose to his feet.

Every one liked Yorke. As captain of the School even the Moderns looked up to him, and were forced to admit that he was a credit to Fellsgarth. In Wakefield's, his own house, he was naturally an idol. Prodigious stories were afloat as to his wisdom and his prowess. Examiners were reported to have rent their clothes in despair at his answers; and at football, rumour had it that once, in one of the out-matches against Ridgmoor, he had run the ball down the field with six of the other side on his back, and finished up with a drop at the goal from thirty yards.

But his popularity in his own house depended less on these exploits than on his general good-nature and incorruptible fairness. He scorned to hit an opponent when he was down, and yet he would knock down a friend as soon as a foe if the credit of the School required it. A few, indeed, there were whose habit it was to sneer at Yorke for being what they called "a saint." The captain of Fellsgarth would have been the last to claim such a title for himself; yet those who knew him best knew that in all he did, even in the common concerns of daily school life, he relied on the guidance and help of a Divine Friend, and was not ashamed to own his faith.

The one drawback to his character in the eyes of certain of his fellow-prefects and others at Wakefield's was that in the standing feud between Classics and Moderns he would take no part. He demanded the allegiance of all parties on behalf of the School, and if any man refused it, Yorke was the sort of person who would make it his business to know the reason why.

Now as he got up and waited for the cheers to cease, no one could deny that he wasn't as fine a captain as Wakefield's could expect to see for many a day. And for the first time some of those who even feared him realised with a qualm that this was the last "first-night" on which he would be there to make the usual speech.

"Gentlemen," he said, "we are all glad to be back in the old place," (cheers). "At any rate I am," (loud cheers). "On first-night, as you know, we always combine business with pleasure. We have just had the pleasure," (laughter, in the midst of which Fisher minor pricked up his ears and wondered if his song wasn't going to be appreciated after all). "The lambs have bleated and done their level best, I'm sure," (renewed laughter, and cries of "How now?"). "Now for the business. Gentlemen, the house clubs demand your support." (Fisher minor turned deadly green as he remembered the Modern boy and his half-crown. He looked round wildly for Ashby, but Ashby was standing between Wally and D'Arcy, and the proximity was not encouraging for Fisher's purpose. The idea occurred to him of appealing to his brother. But Fisher major, pen in hand, sat at the receipt of custom, and he dare not approach). "We hope there will be no shirking. Every fellow in the house is expected to back up the clubs. If the House clubs are not kept up to the mark, the School clubs are sure to go down," (cheers). "We don't ask much. The seniors pay 5 shillings, the middle-boys 3 shillings 6 pence, and the juniors 2 shillings 6 pence." (Fisher minor glanced frantically in the direction of the door, and began to edge that way.) "Now, gentlemen, one word more. You know, last term, there was a lot of bad blood between Classics and Moderns," (great cheers and three groans for the Moderns). "Of course it's open to any idiot who likes to make a fool of himself, and quarrel with anybody he likes. He's welcome to do it up to a certain point, if it gives him pleasure. But I want to say this—and I'd say it if the whole of the school was here—that if these rows once begin to interfere with the honour of the School in sports or anything else, as they nearly did last term, the fellows who indulge in them will be dropped on pretty heavily, no matter what side or what house they belong to."

The captain looked so uncommonly like meaning what he said, that D'Arcy, who had already made an appointment to fight Lickford, a Modern boy, at the Three Oaks before breakfast to-morrow, quailed under his eye, and wondered if he could with dignity "scratch" the engagement.

A general movement towards the table at which Fisher major sat with his pen and account-book followed the captain's speech. Of all the company present, only one failed to enrol himself. He was a new boy called Fisher minor, who, evidently worn out by the fatigues of the day and unversed in the etiquette of first-night, had sought the dame at a somewhat early hour, and received her permission to go to bed.

Such at least was that lady's version when Fisher major, having missed his minor, made inquiries respecting his absence.

"Best thing he could do, to make himself scarce, after such a performance," said the elder brother to Denton, who accompanied him.

"Yes, indeed, I envy Ranger his fag. It's a lucky thing we bagged the other one in time."

"The young donkey couldn't be in better hands," said Fisher; "but I say, Den, didn't the captain come down rather heavy with his thunder to-night? What does it all mean?"

"Bows, I expect," said Denton. "He's not going to stand what went on last term, and I'm jolly glad of it. We must back him up."

"If he means I'm not to feel inclined to kick Dangle whenever I see him, I can't promise him much."

"Dangle's a good quarter-mile man, and a good long-stop. If your kicking him prevents his playing for the School, you'll have to mind your eye, my boy. That's what he means."

"Oh!" grunted Fisher major, "I suppose the rows will begin to-morrow, when we elect the officers for the School clubs. Those fellows are sure to want to stick their own men in."

"At any rate you're safe enough for treasurer, old man. But come, I'm dead sleepy to-night. Time enough for rows to-morrow and the next day."

Chapter Three
Canvassing

When Fisher major woke early next morning he had the curious sensation of something on his mind without knowing what it was.

He was not out of sorts. The private supper of which he and Denton and Ridgway had partaken last night in Ranger's study had been wholesome, if miscellaneous. Ranger's people had given him a hamper to bring back, containing a good many good things—cake, biscuits, potted meats, jam, Worcester sauce, pickles, coffee, and other groceries intended to diversify the breakfasts of the half. By some error of judgment this valuable article of luggage had come from town in the van, where it had apparently been placed at the very bottom of the baggage. The consequence was, that when it came to be opened, its several ingredients were found to have got loose, and fused together in a most hopeless way. Jam, and pickles, and Liebig's extract, and moist sugar were indistinguishable. The only thing seemed to be to attack the concoction *en masse*, without needless delay, and to that end Ranger had summoned the assistance of his friends and neighbours. Fisher major was unable to attribute any part of the weight on his mind to this perfectly wholesome and homely refreshment.

What was it? It was not Denton. He had come back as loyal and festive as ever, threatening to work hard this half, and determined to have Fisher major as his guest at the rectory on the lake for the Christmas vac.

Nor was it the captain's speech last night that bothered him. True, it was not altogether conciliatory to those, who, like Fisher major, were resolved to have no truce with the enemy. Of course it was the right thing for Yorke to say. But Yorke knew, as well as anybody, that the Classics meant to keep their house Cock-House at Fellsgarth.

Nor was it the accounts; although Fisher minor had to own to himself he was not a grand hand at finance, and that if he was appointed treasurer of the School clubs, as well as of his House clubs, he would have his work cut out for him to keep both funds clear and solvent.

What then was it? His young brother? He supposed it must be. The young donkey had made a bad beginning at Fellsgarth—which was bad enough. But had the elder brother done quite the decent thing in half disowning him, and letting him run on his fate in the way he had? A little brotherly backing up, a word or two of warning, and, if needs be, a little timely intimidation, might have made all the difference to the youngster, and would not have done the senior much harm.

Yes; it was this precious minor of his who was on Fisher major's mind. It was too late, of course, to pick up the milk already spilled. But it might be worth while to give him a word of admonition as to his future conduct.

With this view he sent Ashby (who, with all the alacrity of a brand-new fag, punctually presented himself for orders before getting-up bell had ceased ringing) to summon Fisher minor to his brother's room.

"Well, kid," said the elder brother, commencing his toilet, "how did you get on? Sleep well?"

"Middling," said Fisher minor. "Some of the fellows had put pepper on the blankets, and it got into my eyes—that's all."

"It's a good job they did nothing worse."

"Well," said Fisher minor, who was evidently in a limp state, and had not at all enjoyed his night, "they *did* tease a good deal."

"Humph—who did!"

"Well, there was that boy they call—"

"Stop," said Fisher major, turning round fiercely in the middle of brushing his hair; "do you mean to say you don't know that it's only cads who sneak about one another?"

"But you asked me."

"Of course I did, and made sure you wouldn't let out. I hope they'll give you a few more lively nights, to teach you better."

The young brother's lips gave an ominous quiver at this unfeeling speech, and he horrified Fisher major by betraying imminent symptoms of tears.

"Look here, Joey," said the senior, rather more soothingly, "you've made a jolly bad start, and that can't be helped. The mistake you made is in thinking you know everything, whereas you're about as green as they make them. Why ever do you pretend not to be? Look at that other new kid—the other one who sang. He's green too; but, bless you, it's no crime, and all the fellows take to him because he doesn't put on side like you. Why, that song you sang—oh, my stars!—what on *earth* put that rot into your head?"

This finished up poor Fisher minor. The recollection of his performance last night was more than he could stand, and he began to whimper.

"Come, old chap," said Fisher major, kindly, patting him on the shoulder; "perhaps it's not all your fault. I suppose I ought to have given you a leg-up, and prevented you making a fool of yourself. You'll get on right enough if you don't swagger. And in any case, don't blubber."

"I shall never get on here," said the new boy. "All the fellows are against me. Besides—I didn't know it was wrong; and—oh, Tom?—I lent a fellow half a crown, and now I've nothing to pay for the clubs!"

Fisher major laughed.

"I thought from your tones you were going to confess a murder, at least. You'd better look alive and get the half-crown back."

"That's just it. I lent it in the dark to a—a Modern chap; and I don't know his name."

"Upon my honour, Joey, you are a— Well, it's no good saying what you are. I hope you'll see your money again, that's all."

Fisher minor groaned.

"Would you ever mind lending me half-a-crown for the clubs, just this once?" he pleaded.

"Very convenient arrangement. I suppose I shall have to. At least I'll mark you as paid; and if you've not got back what you've lent your friend before I have to shell out, I shall have to pay it for you."

"Thanks, Tom; you're an awful brick," said the younger brother, brightening up rapidly. "I say, I wish I could be your fag. Couldn't I?"

"Ranger's bagged you—you'll get on better with him than me. He won't stand as much nonsense as I might. There! he is calling. Cut along, and don't go making such an ass of yourself again. You'll have to get on the best you can with your fellows; I can't interfere with them unless they break rules, you know. You can come in here, of course, any time you like, and if you want a leg-up with preparation, and Ranger's busy, you may as well do your work here."

After this Fisher major felt a little easier in his conscience, and was able to face the tasks of the day with a lighter mind than if he had had the care of his minor upon it all the time.

The school work of the day was not particularly onerous. Dr Ringwood, the head-master, held a sort of reception of the Sixth, and delivered, as was his wont, a little lecture on the work to be taken up during the ensuing half, interspersed with a few sarcastic references to the work of the previous half, and one or two jokes, which scoffers like Ridgway used to say must have cost him many serious hours during the holidays to develop.

"Aristophanes," said the head-master, after calling attention to the particular merits of the Greek play to be undertaken, "did not write solely for the Sixth form of a public school. I am afraid some of you, last term, thought that Euripides did. He will require more than usual attention. I am sure he can easily receive it. I would not, if I were you boys, be too chary this term of extra work. Some of you are almost painfully conscientious in your objection to overdo a particular study. Aristophanes is an author with whom liberties may safely be taken in this respect. The test of a good classical scholar, remember, is not the work he is obliged to do, but what he is not obliged to do—his extra work; I advise you not to be afraid to try it. The Sanatorium has been unusually free of cases of over-pressure lately. A quarter of an hour's extra work a day by the Sixth is not at all likely to tax its capacity," etcetera.

This was the doctor's pleasant style, delivered with a severe face and downcast eyes.

Then ensued a little lecture to the prefects on their duties and responsibilities, which was respectfully listened to. To judge by it, such a thing as any rumour of dissensions between rival sides and houses in the school had never reached his ears. And yet the knowing ones said the doctor knew better than the captain himself everything that went on in Fellsgarth, and could at any moment lay his hand on an offender. But he preferred to leave the police of the place to his head boys; and on the whole it was perhaps better for the School that he did.

To a larger or less degree the other forms, Classic and Modern, were lectured in similar strains by their respective masters. The new boys among the junior division were, perhaps, the only ones who listened attentively to what Mr Stratton, the young, cheery athlete who presided over their studies, had to say. And even the irrespectful admiration was a good deal distracted by the babel of voices which was going on all round them.

"Never mind him," said D'Arcy; "he's a kid of a master, and don't know any better. It's all rot. Bless you, we get the same thing—"

"D'Arcy," said the master, suddenly, "I was recommending the value of extra work, especially for clever boys. Perhaps you will try the experiment with fifty lines of Virgil by this time to-morrow."

"There you are," said D'Arcy, appealing to his neighbours; "didn't I tell you he talked rot? Did you ever hear such a stale joke as that?"

The two new boys were tremendously impressed by this sudden swoop of vengeance, and gazed open-mouthed at the master for the rest of the class, stealing only now and again a hasty glance at D'Arcy to see how he was bearing up against his sore afflictions.

D'Arcy, to do him justice, appeared to be bearing up very well. He was, in truth, engaged in a mental calculation as to how, during the coming term, he could most economically "job" out the impositions which usually fell to his share. If his countenance now and then brightened as he met the awe-struck gaze of the two new boys, it was because in them he thought he discerned a lively hope of solving the problem creditably to himself and not unprofitably to them.

"Come along," said he as soon as the class was released; "let's get out into the fresh air and have a cool. Hullo, Wally," as the owner of that name trotted up, "what's up?"

"Up?" said Wally in tones of injured innocence; "one would think you didn't know it was School club elections on in an hour, and all the chaps to whip up! If the Moderns turn up in force, it'll be touch-and-go if they don't carry every man. I can't stop now—mind you bring those kids."

And off he went with all the importance of captain's fag on his electioneering tour.

"Wally's right," said D'Arcy. "It'll be a close shave to carry our men. You see, kids," added he condescendingly, "it's just this way. The Moderns are going to try to carry the clubs to-day, and if they do, the whole of us aren't going to stand it, and there'll be such a jolly row in Fellsgarth as— well, wait till you *see*."

This sounded very awful. Fisher minor would have liked to know what sort of clubs were to be carried, but did not like to ask. Ashby, however, more honest, demanded further particulars.

"I don't know what you mean," said he.

"Don't suppose you do. Whose fault is that? All you've got to do is to yell for our side and vote for our men."

That seemed simple enough, if D'Arcy would *only* vouchsafe to tell them when to begin.

"Come along," said the latter. "We've half an hour yet to canvass. You know Wally's and my study?"

"Yes."

"All right; now you," pointing to Ashby, "you hang outside that door. That's the Modern minors' class. Collar one of them as they come out, or two if you can; and fetch 'em up to my room. You," pointing to Fisher minor, "go and prowl about the kids' gymnasium and fetch any one with a blue ribbon on his hat, as many as you can bag. I'm going to see if I can find some of 'em near the tuck-shop. Kick twice on my door and say 'Balbus,' so that I shall know it's you. Go on; off you go. Don't muff it, whatever you do, or it'll be your fault if Fellsgarth goes to pot."

Ashby, whose uncle was an M.P., had had some little experience in general elections, but he never remembered canvassing of this kind before. However, D'Arcy had an authoritative air about him, and as the School was evidently in peril, and there was no suspicion of practical joking in the present case, he marched off sturdily to the Modern minors' class-room, and sheltering himself conveniently behind the door, waited the turn of events.

He had not to wait long. He could hear the master announcing the lesson for preparation, and the general shuffle which precedes the dismissal of a class. Then his heart beat a little faster as he distinguished footsteps and heard the unsuspecting enemy approaching his way.

Now Ashby, although a new boy, was *man* enough to calculate one or two things. One was that his best chance was either to attack the head or the tail of the procession; and secondly, that as the head boys in a form are usually those nearest the front, and conversely, the lowest are usually nearest to the door, the smallest boys would probably be the first to come out. For all of which reasons he decided to make his swoop at once, and if possible abscond with his booty before the main body arrived on the scene.

The event justified his shrewdness. The moment the door opened, two small Moderns scampered out clean into the arms of the expectant kidnapper, who before they had time so much as to inquire who he was or what he wanted, had a grip on the coat-collar of each, and was racing them as hard as their short legs could carry them across the grass.

"Let go, you cad!" squeaked one, presently. "What we you doing!"

"It's only fun," said Ashby, encouragingly; "come along."

The other prisoner was more practical. He tried to bite his captor's hand, and when he failed in that, he tried to kick. But though he succeeded better in this, the pace was kept up and the grip on his collar, if anything, tightened. Whereupon he attempted to sit down. But that, though it retarded the progress, was still insufficient to arrest it. The pace dropped to a quick walk, and in due time, greatly to Ashby's relief, the portal of Wakefield's was reached.

Here, of course, all was safe. If any of the few boys hanging about had been inclined to concern themselves in the affair, the colour of the ribbon on the victims' hats was quite sufficient reason for allowing the law to take its course; and Ashby, who began to grow very tired of his burden (which insisted on sitting down on either side all the way upstairs), arrived at length at Messrs D'Arcy and Wally's door without challenge.

He had no need to knock, or say "Balbus," as the room was empty. The other canvassers had evidently not yet returned.

With a sigh of relief he deposited his loads on the carpet and locked the door.

"Let us go, you cad!" yelled the prisoners. "What do you want bringing us here into this place for?"

"Fun," said Ashby. "You'll know presently."

"If you don't let us out, we'll yell till a master comes."

"Will you?—we're used to yelling here. Yell away; it'll do you good."

To the credit of the two "voters" they did their best, and made such a hideous uproar that Ashby began to grow uneasy, and was immensely relieved when presently he heard outside a sound as of coals being carelessly carried up the staircase. Some one was evidently coming up with a good load.

Ashby was prudent enough not to open the door till an irregular double kick and a breathless cry of "Balbus, look sharp," apprised him that another of the electioneering agents had returned. He then cautiously opened the door, and in tumbled D'Arcy, gasping, yet triumphant, under the weight of three fractious youngsters.

"Bully for us," said he, surveying the harvest. "Five for our side. Jolly well done of you, kid—you're a stunner. Two of mine are new kids—they came easy enough; but the other's a regular badger."

The badger in question seemed determined to maintain his reputation, for he flew upon his captor, calling upon his fellow-prisoners to do the same. All but the new boys obeyed, and the two "canvassers" were very hard put to it for a while, and might have fared yet worse, had not D'Arcy astutely hung out a flag of truce. "Look here," said he; "I never knew such idiots as you Modern kids are. Here I've done my best to be friends and invited you to a spread in my room; and now you won't even let me go to the cupboard and get out the black currant jam and cake."

"You're telling crams; that's not why you brought us here. You're a howling—"

The Cock-House at Fellsgarth | 33

"Yes, really," said D'Arcy, in quite a friendly tone, "Cry *pax* for one minute, and if I don't hand out the things you may go; honour bright. I've a good mind to kick you out without giving you anything."

The caged animals sullenly fell back and eyed the cupboard which D'Arcy leisurely opened. A row of half a dozen pots on a top shelf, a segment of a plum-cake, and something that looked very like honey in the comb, met their greedy eyes.

"There you are," said D'Arcy. "What did I tell you! They belong to Wally; he'll be here directly. You'll be all right—all except *you*," said he, singling out his principal assailant. "You don't know how to behave, like these other kids. I shall advise Wally not to waste any of his stuff on you."

"I didn't know it was a feast," said the youth, much softened. "I thought you were only humbugging; really I did."

"I've a good mind to do what you think. You'd better mind your eye, I can tell you—I wish Wally would come. There's five o'clock striking—I'll go and look for him. Ashby, you see if he's in the library; you kids, stay here, and lock the door, and don't let anybody in but Wally. Do you hear? If you do, you'll get it pretty hot for being out of your house. And look here, if Wally doesn't come by half-past, you can help yourselves."

"Thanks awfully," said the party.

"Mind! honour bright you don't touch a thing till the clock strikes the half. When you've done, stay here till one of us comes to fetch you, and we'll see you safe out. Don't go without, as our chaps are awfully down on Moderns this term, and you'll get flayed alive. If they've seen you come in, they'll try to get at you, be sure; so lock yourselves in, whatever you do, and don't make the room in too great a mess. Come along, Ashby; let's look for Wally."

"Cut hard," said he, as soon as they stood outside, and had heard the lock within duly turned. "We've only just time to get over; that's five votes lost to their side! Real good business! I wonder where the other new kid is? He was bound to make a mess of it. That's why I sent him to the gymnasium; it's closed to-day."

"Hooray for the Cock-House!" shouted Ashby, as, side by side with his now admiring patron, he entered the School Hall, where the ceremony of club elections was just beginning.

At the door they encountered Wheatfield.

"Such games!" whispered D'Arcy, clapping him joyously on the back. "We've got five Modern kids boxed up in our room, waiting for the clock to strike the half-hour before they have a tuck in at our empty jam-pots."

"Ha, ha!" said Wheatfield; "splendid joke!" and vanished.

D'Arcy's countenance suddenly turned pale as he gripped his companion by the arm.

"What's the matter?" inquired Ashby, alarmed for his friend's health. "What's up?"

"It's all up! We're regularly done. My, that *is* a go!"

"Whatever do you mean?"

"Why, you blockhead, didn't you see that was the wrong Wheatfield— not Wally, but the Modern one! And now he's gone to let those chaps out, and we're clean done for!"

"Whew! what is to be done?" groaned Ashby, almost as pale as his friend.

Chapter Four
A Close Election

Ever since certain well-meaning governors, two years ago, had succeeded in forcing upon Fellsgarth the adoption of a Modern side, the School had been rent by factions whose quarrels sometimes bordered on civil war. When people squabble about the management of a school outside, the boys are pretty sure to quarrel and take sides against one another inside.

The old set, consisting mostly of the Classical boys, felt very sore on the question. It was a case of sentiment, not argument. If boys, said they, wanted to learn science and modern languages, let them; but don't let them come fooling around at Fellsgarth and spoiling the reputation of a good old classical school. There were plenty of schools where fellows could be brought up in a new-fangled way. Let them go to one of these, and leave Fellsgarth in peace to her dead authors.

The boys who used such arguments, it is fair to say, were not always the most profound classical scholars. Most of them, like D'Arcy and Wally Wheatfield, had a painful acquaintance with the masterpieces of old-world literature in the way of impositions, but there their interest frequently ended. The upper Classical boys, however, though not so noisily hostile, had their own strong opinions about the new departure; and when it was discovered that the new Modern side had not only alienated one or two of their old comrades, but, so far from being apologetic, were disposed to claim equal rights with, and in certain cases superior privileges to, the old boys, the relations became strained all round.

As it happened, the Modern set consisted of a number of moderate athletes who could not be wholly ignored in the School sports, and had no intention of being ignored. And to add to their crimes they numbered among them a good number of rich boys, who boasted in public of their wealth with a freedom which was particularly aggravating to the Classical seniors, who were for the most part boys to whose parents money was an important consideration.

As has been said, the rivalry had been growing acute all last term, and but for Yorke's determined indifference, it might long ago have come to a rupture. Now, every one felt that at any moment the peace might be broken, and civil war break out between the two sides at Fellsgarth.

The School clubs offered a rare opportunity for an exhibition of party feeling, for they were the common ground on which every one was bound to meet every one else on *level* terms.

By an old rule, every member of the House clubs was a member of the School clubs and had the privilege of electing the committee and officers for the year. It was this business which brought together the crowd that flocked into the Hall to-day; and it was in view of this critical event that Mr D'Arcy had carefully shut up five voters of the other side in his study until the election should be over.

"Whatever's to be done?" asked Ashby, with blank countenance.

"Nobody but a born idiot would begin to ask riddles just now!" retorted D'Arcy surlily. "Shut up; that's what's to be done."

"I expect it will be all right," persisted the dogged Ashby, venturing on a further remark. "They won't let him in, if he's not Wally; or if they do, they'll go for him."

"I hope they will. Anyhow we've done our best. Stick near the door. We may be able to bundle a few of 'em out before the voting comes on. Look out, Yorke's speaking. Yell as hard as you can."

Whereupon Ashby lay his head back and yelled until D'Arcy kicked him and told him it was time to shut up.

Yorke was moving a resolution that the captains, vice-captains, secretaries, and treasurers of each house should form the School sports committee, whose business it would be to arrange matches, keep the ground, make rules, and generally organise the athletics of Fellsgarth. He hoped every one would agree to this.

Clapperton, the Modern captain, and head of Forder's house, rose to second the motion.

"Howl away!" said D'Arcy, nudging his *protégé*. Whereupon Ashby held on to a desk and howled till the windows shook.

"That'll do," shouted D'Arcy in his ear after a moment or two, and Ashby, thankful for the relief, shut off steam and awaited his next orders.

Clapperton was a big, smirking fellow, rather loudly dressed, with a persuasive voice and what was intended to be a condescending manner. Some fellows could never make out why Clapperton did not go down in Fellsgarth. He tried to be civil, he was lavish with his pocket-money, and always disclaimed any desire to quarrel with anybody. And yet no one oared for him, while of course the out-and-out champions of the rival side hated him. He seconded with pleasure the motion of "his friend Yorke,"—("Cheek!" exclaimed D'Arcy, *sotto voce*; "what business has he to call our captain his friend!") This was the old rule of Fellsgarth, and a very good rule. It meant hard work, but he was always glad to do what he could for the old School. (It always riled the Classics to hear a Modern talking about "the old School," and their backs went up at this.) He had been on this committee two years now, and had had the pleasure in a humble way of helping the clubs through one or two of their financial difficulties, and he should be glad to serve again. He seconded the motion.

It was a trial to one or two who had listened to see that the names were being put to the vote by Yorke *en bloc*, without giving them the chance of voting against anybody. Never mind, their chance for that would come!

The next business was the election of captain of the clubs; and of course Yorke was chosen by acclamation. No one dared oppose him. Even "his friend Clapperton," who had the pleasure of proposing him, was sure every one would be as glad as he would to see "his fellow-captain" (oh, how the Classics squirmed and ground their teeth at the expression!) at the head of the clubs.

The pent-up feelings of D'Arcy and those of his way of thinking found some relief in the demonstration which accompanied the carrying of this resolution. It was too good a chance to be lost, and for three minutes by the clock the Classics stood on their feet and cheered their champion, glaring defiantly as they did so at the Moderns, who having held up their hands and cheered a little, relapsed into silence and left the noise in the hands of the other side.

Then followed the election of vice-captain, which of course had to go to Clapperton. This time the Moderns had their demonstration amid the silence of the Classics, who thought they had never in their lives seen fellows make such asses of themselves.

It was twenty minutes past the hour, and D'Arcy and Ashby were both getting uncomfortable and impatient. What did these Modern idiots want to waste the time of everybody by standing there and bellowing! It was scandalous.

"Shut up—go on to the next vote," they cried, but in vain. The Moderns were going to have their full share, if not a little more, of the row, and to stop them before their time was hopeless.

"Disgusting exhibition, isn't it?" said D'Arcy; "never mind. Hullo, I say, there's some one at the door. It's those chaps!"

No, it was only Fisher minor, who, having waited meekly all this time outside the deserted gymnasium, now ventured, like a degenerate Casabianca, to desert his post and come and see what was going forward in the Hall.

As he tried to enter, a Modern boy, seeing by his ribbon that he was on the wrong side, put his foot against the door and tried to turn him back. But his little plot dismally failed. For D'Arcy and Ashby, shocked and horrified witnesses of this scandalous act of corruption, came to the rescue with a hubbub which even made itself heard above the shouting.

"Let him in!—howling cheat!—he's trying to shut out one of our side! Ya-boo! That's the way you elect your men, is it! Come in, Fisher minor. Let him in, do you hear? All right; come on, you fellows, and kick this Modern chap out for a wretched sneak—(that'll be seven off their side, counting Wheatfield; and one more to us—bully!) Yah, cheats! turn 'em out!"

Amid such cries of virtuous indignation, Fisher minor was hauled in, and his obstructor, by the same *coup de main*, excluded. Fisher minor might have had his head turned by this triumphal entry, had he not recognised in the ejected Modern boy the gentleman to whom he had lent his half-crown on the previous evening. Any reminder of yesterday's misfortunes was depressing to him, and his joy at finding himself on the right side of the door now was decidedly damped by the knowledge that his half-crown was on the wrong. However, there was no time for explanations, as the shouting had ceased, and an evidently important event was about to take place. This was the appointment of treasurer, for whom each of the rival sides had a candidate; that of the Classics being Fisher major, and that of the Moderns Brinkman of Forder's house, a particular enemy of the other side, and reputed to be rich and no gentlemen.

Both candidates were briefly proposed and seconded by boys of their own side, and both having declared their intention of going to the vote, a show of hands was demanded.

The excitement of our young friends at the end of the Hall while this tedious operation was in progress may well be imagined. The captain had sternly ordained silence during the voting; so that all they could do was to hold up their hands to the very top of their reach, and keep a wild look-out that they were being counted, and that none of the enemy was in any way, moral or physical, circumventing them. As for Fisher minor, he simply trembled with excitement as he cast his eyes round and calculated his brother's chances. He could not comprehend how any one could dare not to vote for Fisher major; and absorbed in that wonder he continued to hold up his hand long after the two tellers had agreed their figure, and the captain had ordered "hands down."

"Fisher major, one hundred and twenty-seven votes; now, hands up for Brinkman."

"Whew!" said D'Arcy, fanning himself with his handkerchief; "it'll be a close shave. I say, we'd better lean up hard against the door. It'll keep out the draughts."

"They've got it, I'm afraid," said Ashby, looking round at the forest of hands; "we hadn't as many as that."

"I say, that cad Brinkman is voting for himself," said some one.

"What a shame! My brother didn't. He's too honourable," said Fisher minor.

"Hullo! 'How now'—you there?" cried Wally.

Whereupon, amid great laughter, Fisher minor retired modestly behind the rest.

The counting seemed interminable, and every moment, to the guilty ears of Ashby, there seemed to be a sound of footsteps without. At last, however, the cry, "hands down," came once more, and you might have heard a pin drop.

"Fisher major, one hundred and twenty-seven votes; Brinkman, one hundred and twenty-two. Fisher is elected."

Amid the terrific Classic cheers which greeted this announcement, D'Arcy and Ashby exchanged glances.

Those five voters, waiting patiently in Wally's room for the clock to strike the half-hour, would have turned the scale!

Ashby wished the majority had been greater or less. But he tried to be jubilant, and in response to D'Arcy's thumps on the back yelled and roared till he was black in the face.

As he did so, he caught sight through the window of a small procession of five or six boys emerging from the door of Wakefield's house and starting at a trot in the direction of Hall.

"I say," shouted he in D'Arcy's ear, "here they come!"

D'Arcy abruptly ceased shouting and descended from his form.

"Come and squash up near the front," said he, hurriedly; "more room, you know, up there."

"Hoo, hoo! nearly licked that time," shouted a Modern youth near the door, as they moved forward. "Served you right!"

"Never mind, we'll take it out of you, next vote," retorted D'Arcy. "Come on, kid; squash up." Then a happy thought struck him. The boys immediately near the door were mostly Moderns. What a fine bit of electioneering, if he could get them to shut out their own men! So he shouted, "Look out, our side! Mind they don't keep out any of our chaps. Just the sort of dodge they'd be up to."

Whereupon the Moderns set their backs determinedly against the door and wagged their heads at one another, and were obliged to D'Arcy for the tip.

"That'll do for 'em," said that delighted schemer; "they won't let 'em in, you bet. Look out—they're going to vote for secretary now."

The Classical side candidate for this important office was Ranger, almost as great an idol in his house as the captain himself. His Modern opponent was Dangle, a clever senior, reputed to be Clapperton's toady and man-of-all-work. It was felt that if he were secretary, there would be a strong Modern bias given to the clubs, which in the opinion of the Classic partisans would be disastrous.

The show of hands had been taken for Ranger, and every one was silent to hear the figures, when a hideous clamour arose at the door, with shouts of—

"Open the door I let us in. Cheats! Fair play!"

To D'Arcy's satisfaction, as from the safe shelter of a front place he peered down that way, the Moderns held their post at the door and refused to let it open. For a minute it looked as if they would succeed; when suddenly the irate Wally appeared on the scene, followed by Fisher minor, and shouting, "Cheats! cads! Let our fellows in!" went for the obstructionists.

"Stupid ass!" growled D'Arcy. "It's all up now. Why couldn't he have let them be?"

A short and sharp *mêlée* followed. The Classics were reinforced rapidly, and the Moderns, seeing their plot detected and fearing the intervention of the seniors, sullenly raised the blockade, and allowed the door to open.

Whereat in tumbled Percy Wheatfield with five young Moderns at his heels—the very five who had been waiting for the clock to strike in Wally's study.

"What do you mean by keeping us out!" demanded Percy of his brother, who chanced to be the first person he encountered.

"What are you talking about?" retorted Wally, extremely chagrined to discover who it was he had been helping. "We were the chaps who let you in! It was your own cads who were keeping you out. Ask them."

"We thought you were Classics," said one of the offenders, letting the cat out of the bag.

"Oh, you beauty! Wait till I get some of you outside," bellowed the outraged Percy.

"Order! Shut up, you kids down there!" was the cry from the front.

"Shut up, you kids down there!" echoed D'Arcy and Ashby on their own account.

"Ranger one hundred and twenty-three. Hands up for Dangle; and if the youngsters down there don't make less noise, I'll adjourn the meeting," said the captain. This awful threat secured silence while the counting proceeded. D'Arcy's face grew longer and longer, and Wally at the back began to breathe vengeance on the world at large.

"Hands down."

The captain turned and said something to Clapperton; and Fisher major, who overheard what was said, looked very glum. Every one knew what was coming.

"Ranger one hundred and twenty-three votes, Dangle one hundred and twenty-four. Dangle is—"

The shouts of the Moderns drowned the last words, and the captain had to wait a minute before he could finish what he had to say.

"The votes are very close," said he. "If any one would like, we can count again."

"No, no!" cried Ranger. "It's all right. I don't dispute it."

"That concludes the elections," said the captain.

And amid loud cheers and counter-cheers the meeting dispersed.

The prefects of Wakefield's house met that evening in Yorke's study to talk over the events of the afternoon.

The captain was the only person present who appeared to regard the result of the elections with equanimity.

"After all," said he, "though I'm awfully sorry about old Ranger, it seems fairer to have the officers evenly divided. There's much less chance of a row than it we were three to their one."

"That's all very well," said Fisher, whose pleasure in his own election had been completely spoiled by the defeat of his friend, "if we could count on fair play. You know Dangle as well as I do. I'd sooner resign myself than have him secretary."

"What rot!" said Ranger. "You'd probably only give them another man. No, we shall have to see we get fair play."

"And give it, too," said the captain.

"They simply packed the meeting," said Dalton, "and fetched up five juniors at the very end, who turned the scale. If our fellows had done the same, we should have been all right."

"I don't see the use of growling now it's well over," said Yorke; "the great thing is to see we get the best men into the teams, and that they play up."

"We hardly need go outside Wakefield's for that," said Fisher major; "they've not a man worth his salt in a football scrimmage."

"Look out that they haven't more than we have, that's all," said the captain, gloomily. "I tell you what, you fellows," added he, with a touch of temper in his voice, "if our house is to be Cock-House at Fellsgarth, we can't afford to make fools of ourselves. The School's a jolly sight more important than any one house, and as long as I'm captain of the School clubs I don't intend to inquire what house a man belongs to so long as he can play. We can keep all our jealousy for the House club if you like; but if it's to be carried into the School sports we may as well dissolve the clubs and scratch all our matches at once."

"I wonder if Clapperton is giving vent to the same patriotic sentiments to his admirers," said Ridgway, laughing. "Fancy him, and Dangle, and Brinkman conspiring together for the glory of the School."

"Why not!" said the captain, testily. "Why won't you give anybody credit for being decent outside Wakefield's?"

"I'm afraid old Yorke hardly gives any one credit for being decent in it. For pity's sake don't lecture any more to-night, old man," said Dalton. "I'll agree to anything rather than that."

"There's just one more thing," said Yorke, "which you may take as lecture or not as you like. Clapperton said something about helping out the clubs with money. Fisher major, you are the treasurer; don't have any of that. Don't take more than the regular subscription from anybody, and don't take less. If there's a deficit let's all stump up alike. We don't want anybody's charity."

This sentiment was generally applauded, and restored the captain in the good opinion of every one present. After all, old Yorke's bark was always worse than his bite. He wasn't going to be put upon by the other side, however much he seemed to stick up for them.

Ranger waited a few minutes after the others had gone.

"Look here, Ranger," said the captain, "you must back me up in this. You can afford to do it, because you've been beaten. I only wish you were in my place. I know you hate those fellows, and are cut up to have lost the secretaryship."

"I'm not going to break my heart about that," said Ranger.

"Of course not. You're going to do what will be a lot more useful. You're going to work as hard for the School as if you were secretary and captain in one; and you're going to back me up in keeping the peace, aren't you?"

"Would you, if you were in my shoes?" said Ranger.

"I might find it hard, but I almost think I should try. And if I had your good temper, I should succeed too."

Ranger laughed.

"I didn't think you went in for flattery, Yorke. Anyhow, I believe you are right. I'll be as affectionate as I can to those Modern chaps. Ugh! good night."

After the day's excitement Fellsgarth went to bed early. But no one dreamed, least of all the heroes of the exploit themselves, how much was to depend during the coming months on those five small voters who had waited patiently in Wally Wheatfield's study that afternoon to hear the clock strike 5:30.

Chapter Five
Percy Wheatfield, Envoy Extraordinary

The misgivings of the Classics were justified. The Moderns did not accept their victory at Elections with a meekness which augured harmony for the coming half.

On the contrary, they executed that difficult acrobatic feat known as going off their heads, with jubilation.

For many terms they had groaned under a sense of inferiority, partly imagined but partly well founded, in their relations with the rival side. The Classics had given themselves airs, and, what was worse, proved their right to give them. In its early days the Modern side was not "in it" at Fellsgarth. Its few members were taught to look upon themselves as altogether a lower order of creation than the pupils of the old foundation, and had accepted the position with due humility. Then certain rebellious spirits had arisen, who dared to ask why their side wasn't as good as any other? The answer was crushing. "What can you do? Only French, and book-keeping and 'stinks'"—(the strictly Classical nickname for chemistry). "You can't put a man into the cricket or football field worth his salt; your houses are rowdy; your men do nothing at the University; two out of three of you are not even gentlemen." Whereupon the Moderns went in desperately for sports, and claimed to be represented in the School clubs. They maintained that they were as good gentlemen as any who talked Latin and Greek; and to prove it they jingled their money in their trouser-pockets, and asked what the Classics could do in that line. The Classics could do very little, and fell back on their moral advantages. By degrees the new side grew in numbers, and made themselves heard rather more definitely. They put into the field one or two men who could not honestly be denied a place in the School teams; and they began to figure also among the School prefects. The present seniors, Clapperton and his friends, carried the thing a step further, and insisted on equal rights with their rivals in all the School institutions. To their surprise they found an ally in Yorke, who, as we have already said, hurt the feelings of many of his admirers by his Quixotic insistence on fair play all round.

The proceedings yesterday had been the most recent instance of the flow in the tide of Modern progress at Fellsgarth. Reinforced by an unusual influx of new boys, they had aimed at, and succeeded in winning, their level half of the control of the School clubs; and Yorke had looked on and let them do it!

No wonder they went off their heads as they discoursed on their triumph, and no wonder they already pictured themselves masters of Fellsgarth!

It never does occur to some people that the mountain is not climbed till the top is reached.

"Really, you know," said Brinkman, "I felt half sorry for those poor beggars; they did look so sick when Dangle was elected."

"It's my opinion," said Clapperton, "you'd have been in too, if all our fellows had turned up. I saw four or five of our youngsters come in at the last moment."

"Yes—by the way," said Dangle, "that ought to be looked into. It's fishy, to say the least of it, and would have made all the difference to Brinkman's election."

"Do you know who the fellows were?" asked Clapperton.

"I believe your fag was one of them."

"Percy Wheatfield? Catch him being shut out of anything. But I'll ask about it. Fancy poor Yorke's feelings if we were to demand a new election!"

"I tell you what," said Dangle, "I don't altogether understand Yorke. He tries to pass off as fair, and just, and all that sort of thing; but one can't be sure he's not playing a game of his own."

"We shall easily see that when it comes to choosing the football fifteen against Rendlesham. I mean to send him in a list of fellows on our side. It's only fair we should have half of them our men."

"Half fifteen is seven and a half," said Fullerton, a melancholy senior who had not yet spoken; "how will you manage about that?"

"Shut up, you ass!"

"I only asked," said Fullerton. "It doesn't matter to me, I don't mind going as the half man, if you like. If you send seven names you'll be in a minority in the fifteen, and if you send eight you'll be in a majority. It doesn't matter to me a bit."

"Just like Fullerton. Always asking riddles that haven't got an answer," said Dangle.

"I wonder how Fisher will manage the treasurership," said Brinkman, who was evidently sore at his defeat. "I shouldn't have thought accounts were much in his line."

"He can't have very hard work doing his own," said Clapperton, laughing, "but that's not his fault, poor beggar. Only I think it would be much better to have a fellow for treasurer who wasn't in a chronic state of being hard up."

"I suppose you mean," said Fullerton, who had a most awkwardly blunt way of putting things, "he'd have less temptation to steal. I hope Fisher's not a thief."

"What an idiot you are, Fullerton!" said Clapperton; "whoever said he was?"

"I didn't. I only asked what you thought. It doesn't much matter to me, except that it wouldn't be creditable to the School."

"Of course it wouldn't; it's hardly creditable to our side to have a jackass in it," said Clapperton.

"Oh, all right—I'll go. I dare say you'll get on as well without me."

The others presently followed his example, and Clapperton, left to himself, proceeded to draw up his list.

"Dear Yorke," he wrote, "You will probably be making up the fifteen for the Rendlesham match shortly. Please put down me, Brinkman, Dangle, Fullerton, West, Harrowby, and Ramshaw major, to play from our side. This will give your side the odd man.

"Yours truly,—

"Geo. Clapperton."

This important epistle accomplished, he shouted for his fag to come and convey it to its destination.

It was not till after several calls, on an increasing scale of peremptoriness, that Master Percy condescended to appear. When he did, he was covered with dust from head to foot, and his face, what could be seen of it, was visibly lopsided.

"Why don't you come when you're called? Whatever have you been up to—fighting?"

"Rather not," said Percy, "only boxing. You see, it was this way; Cottle brought a pair of gloves up this term, and young Lickford had an old pair; so we three and Ramshaw have been having an eight-handed mill. It was rather jolly; only Ramshaw and Lickford had the old gloves on, and they've all the horse-hair out, so Cottle and I got it rather hot on the face. But we took it out of them with our body blows—above the belt, you know—not awfully above. I couldn't come when you called, because we were wrestling out one of the rounds. It's harder work an eight-handed wrestle than four hands. Just when you called first, I nearly had Cottle and Lickford down, but you put me off my trip, and Ramshaw had me over instead."

"All very interesting," said Clapperton, "but you'll have to come sharp next time or I shall trip you up myself. Take this note over to Yorke. Stop while he reads it, and if there's any answer, bring it; if not, don't wait."

"Can't Cash take it? We're not nearly finished."

"No. Cut off, sharp!"

"Awful shame!" growled the messenger to himself, as he departed. "I hate Clapperton; he always waits till I'm enjoying myself, and then routs me out. I shan't stand it much longer. What does he want with Yorke! Perhaps it's a challenge. Yes, by the way, very good chance! I'll see what that cad Wally's got to say about those kids I found in his room yesterday. Nice old games he gets up to; Wally's all very well when he's asleep, or grubbing, or doing impositions, but he's a sight too artful out of school, like all those Classic kids. One's as bad as another."

As if to emphasise this sentiment, a Classic kid at that moment came violently into collision with Master Percy's waistcoat.

It was Fisher minor, who had once more caught sight in the distance of the mysterious borrower of his half-crown, and was giving chase.

"Where are you coming to, you kid. You've nearly smashed a button. I'll welt you for that."

"I beg your pardon, Wally, I—"

"Wally—what do you mean by calling me Wally?" exclaimed Percy.

"Well, Wheatfield, I beg your pardon; I was in a hurry to catch a fellow up and I didn't see you."

"Didn't you? Well, you'll feel me. Take that."

Fisher minor meekly accepted the cuff, and, full of his half-crown, essayed to proceed. But Percy stopped him.

"You're that new kid, Fisher's minor, aren't you?"

It astonished Fisher minor, that the speaker, whom he supposed he had seen only ten minutes ago, should so soon have forgotten his name.

"Yes, but I say, Wally, I mean Wheatfield—"

"Humph—I suppose you held up both hands for your precious brother yesterday."

"No, only one. I was nearly late, though. I waited an hour at the gymnasium, you know, and no Modern chaps came out at all."

Percy began to smell rats.

"Waited at the gymnasium, did you? Who told you to do that?"

"Oh, you know—it was part of the canvassing."

"Oh, *you* were in that job, were you, my boy? All serene, I'll—"

"I say," cried Fisher minor, turning pale, "aren't you Wally Wheatfield? I thought—"

"Me Wally? what do you take me for? I'll let you know who I am. You're a beauty, you are. Some of our chaps'll tell you who I am, Mr Canvasser. Now, look here, you stop there till I come back from Yorke's. If you move an inch—whew! you'll find the weather pretty warm, I can tell you. Canvassing? You'll get canvassed, I fancy, before you grow much taller."

And off stalked the indignant Percy, promising himself a particularly pleasant afternoon, as soon as his errand to the captain was over.

Yorke was at work, with his lexicon and notebooks on the table, when the envoy entered.

"Well, is that you or your brother?" inquired he.

"Not my brother, if I know it," said Percy.

"That's not much help. He says exactly the same when I put the same question to him."

"He does, does he? I owe Wally one already, now—"

"Thanks—then you're not Wally. What do you want?"

"This note. Clapperton said I was to wait while you read it, and bring an answer if there was one."

Yorke read the note, and smiled as he did so. Percy wished he knew what was in it. He didn't know Clapperton could make jokes.

"Any answer?" he demanded.

"Yes—there's an answer," said the captain.

He took out a list of names from his pocket, and compared it with that on Clapperton's letter. Then he wrote as follows:—

"Dear Clapperton,—The fifteen against Rendlesham is already made up as follows," (here followed the list). "You will see it includes six of the names you sent. We must play the best team we can; and I think we shall have it.

"Yours truly,—

"Cecil Yorke."

"There's the answer. Take it over at once."

"I like his style," growled Percy to himself. "He don't seem to have a 'please' about him. Catch me hurrying myself for him; I've got this precious canvasser to look after."

And he returned at a leisurely pace to the rendezvous.

No Fisher minor was there!

That young gentleman, when left to himself, found himself in a perspiration of doubt and fear. He had made a most awkward blunder, and confessed the delinquencies of his comrades to the very last man they would wish to know of them. That was bad enough; but, to make things worse, he was to be let in for the blame of the whole affair, and, with Master Percy's assistance, was shortly to experience warm weather among the Moderns.

Happy thought! He would not stay where he was. He would retire, as the Latin book said, into winter quarters, and entrench himself in the stronghold of Wally and D'Arcy and Ashby. If he *was* to get it hot, he would sooner get it from them than from the barbarians in Forder's.

With which desperate conclusion, and once more devoutly wishing himself safe at home, he made tracks, at a rapid walk, to Wally's room. His three comrades were all there.

"What's up?" said they as he entered, with agitated face.

"Oh, I say, it's all because you and your brother are so alike. I met him just now; and—he's heard about that canvassing, you know, and I thought you'd like to know."

"You mean to say you blabbed?" said Wally, jumping to his feet.

"It's your fault," said D'Arcy. "I've made the same mistake myself. Why can't you grow a moustache or something to distinguish you?"

"Why can't you get your brother to be a Classic! then it wouldn't matter—either of you would do," suggested Ashby.

Ashby was beginning to feel quite at home in Wakefield's.

"I'll let some of you see if it won't matter," retorted Wally. "If they've got wind of that affair the other side, there'll be a fearful row. They'll want another election. Oh, you young idiot! That comes of trusting a new kid, that sings comic songs, and parts his hair the wrong side, with a secret. D'Arcy's nearly as big an ass as you are yourself, to trust you."

After this Philippic, Wally felt a little better, and was ready to consider what had better be done.

"He's bound to come here, you chaps," said he. "You cut. Leave him to me—I'll tackle him."

Fisher minor considered this uncommonly good advice, and obeyed it with alacrity. The other two followed less eagerly. They would have liked to stay and see the fun.

As Wally expected, his affectionate relative, being baulked of his prey outside, came to pay a fraternal visit.

"What cheer?" said he. "I say, have you seen a kid called Fisher minor? The new kid, you know, that we had a lark with at dinner on first-night."

"Oh, that chap. Bless you, he messes in our study. What about him?"

"I want him. I want to say something to him."

"I'll tell him."

"All right. He's come and told you, has he? and you're hiding him? Never mind; I'll bowl him out, the beauty. I know all about that little game of yours, yesterday, you know!"

"What little game?"

"As if you didn't know! Do you suppose I didn't find five of 'em shut up here yesterday, being kept out of the way at Elections?"

"Yes; and do you suppose if it hadn't been for me they'd have got into the Hall at all? Don't be a beast, Percy, if you can help. They stayed here of their own accord. No one kept them in. I say, have some toffee?"

"Got any?"

"Rather. A new brew this morning. I say, you can have half of it."

"Thanks, awfully, Wally."

"You see—oh, take more than that—these new kids are such born asses, they boss everything. You should have heard that Fisher minor at lamb's singing the other night—like the toffee? I say, don't be a sneak about those chaps. You'd never have got them in without me. I backed you up, and got the door open. I say—would you like a Turkish stamp? I've got one to swop—but you can have it if you like."

"Thanks, old man. Yes, new kinds are rot. Well, ta, ta—better make it up, I suppose. I say, I shan't have time to write home to-day. You write this time, and I'll do the two next week."

"All serene, if you like. Here, you're leaving one of your bits of toffee. Ta, ta, old chappie."

And these great twin brethren, whose infirmity it was always to be fond of one another when they were together, and to scorn one another when they were apart, separated in a most amicable fashion.

"Well?" asked the three exiles, putting in their heads as soon as the enemy had gone.

"Choked him off," said Wally, fanning himself. "Jolly hard work. But he came round."

Percy, meanwhile, having suddenly remembered his errand, hastened back to the house. As he did so he observed notices of the fifteen for the Rendlesham match posted on Wakefield's door, on the school-board, and at Forder's. He solaced himself by writing in bold characters the word "beast" against each of the names which belonged to a Classic boy, and discovered, when his task was done, that he had inscribed the word nine times out of fifteen on each notice. Whereupon he made off at a run to his senior's.

"Well," said Clapperton, evidently anxious, "didn't I tell you to come back at once! Any answer?"

"Yes, this," said Percy, producing the captain's letter. "I say, Yorke grinned like anything when he read yours."

"Did he?" replied Clapperton, opening the envelope.

Evidently Yorke in his reply had not been guilty of a joke, for the face of the Modern captain was dark and scowling as he read it.

"Cool cheek," muttered he. "Dangle was right, after all. You can go, youngster."

"All right. I say, they've got the fifteen stuck up on the boards—six of our chaps in it. We ought to lick them this year."

But as Clapperton did not do him the favour of heeding his observations, he retired, and tried vainly to collect his scattered forces to conclude the eight-handed boxing match, which had been so unfeelingly interrupted an hour ago.

Clapperton, to do him justice, could not deny to himself that the team selected by the captain was the best fighting fifteen the School could put into the football field. But, having advanced his claim for half numbers, his pride was hurt at finding it almost contemptuously set aside. It would never do for him to climb down now.

The Moderns, after all, had a right to have their men in; and he had a right to assume they were better players than some of the selected Classics. It was easy to work himself into a rage, and talk about favouritism, and abuse of privilege, and all that. His popularity in his own house depended on his fighting their battles, and he must do it now. So he wrote a reply to Yorke.

"Dear Yorke,—I do not agree with you about the fifteen. I consider the men on our side whom you have omitted are better than the three I have marked on your list. If we are to make the clubs a success, we ought to pull together, and let there be no suspicion, however groundless, of favouritism.

"Yours truly, Geo. Clapperton."

To this letter, which he sent over by another junior, more expeditious than his last, he received the following reply:—

"Dear Clapperton,—Sides have nothing to do with it. If the best fifteen names were all on your side, I should have to select them. But they are not. The fifteen I have chosen are undoubtedly the best men we have, and the team most likely to win the match. I suppose that is what we play for.

"Yours truly,—

"Cecil Yorke."

This polite correspondence Clapperton laid before his friends. The general feeling was that the Moderns were being unfairly and disrespectfully used.

"It's the old story over again," said Dangle. "If we don't look after ourselves, nobody else will."

"At any rate, as long as he's captain, I suppose he has the right to pick the team," said Fullerton. "I shouldn't be particularly sorry if he were to leave me out. It wouldn't matter to me."

"Who cares whether it matters to you? It matters to our side," said Brinkman, "and we oughtn't to stand it."

Chapter Six
Rollitt

Rollitt of Wakefield's was a standing mystery at Fellsgarth. Though he had been three years at the school, and worked his way up from the junior form to one of the first six, no one knew him. He had no friends, and did not want any. He rarely spoke when not obliged to do so; and when he did, he said either what was unexpected or disagreeable. He scarcely ever played in the matches, but when he did he played tremendously. Although a Classic, he was addicted to scientific research and long country walks. His study was a spectacle for untidiness and grime. He abjured his privilege of having a fag. No one dared to take liberties with him, for he had an arm like an oak branch, and a back as broad as the door.

All sorts of queer stories were afloat about him. It was generally whispered that his father was a common workman, and that the son was being kept at school by charity. Any reference to his poverty was the one way of exciting Rollitt. But it was too risky an amusement to be popular.

His absence of mind, however, was his great enemy at school. Of him the story was current that once in the Fourth, when summoned to the front to call-over the register, he called his own name among the rest, and receiving no reply, looked to his place, and seeing the desk vacant, marked Rollitt down as absent. Another time, having gone to his room after morning school to change into his flannels for cricket, he had gone to bed by mistake, and slept soundly till call-bell next morning. "Have you heard Rollitt's last?" came to be the common way of prefacing any unlikely story at Fellsgarth; and what with fact and fiction, the hero had come to be quite a mythical celebrity at Fellsgarth.

His thrift was another of his characteristics. He had never been seen to spend a penny, unless it was to save twopence. If fellows had dared, they would have liked now and then to pay his subscriptions to the clubs; or even hand on an old pair of cricket shoes or part of the contents of a hamper for his benefit. But woe betide them if they ever tried it! The only extravagance he had ever been known to commit was some months ago, when he bought a book of trout-flies, which rumour said must have cost him as much as an ordinary Classic's pocket-money for a whole term.

To an impressionable youth like Fisher minor it was only natural that Rollitt should be an object of awe. For a day or two after his arrival, when the stories he had heard were fresh in his memory, the junior was wont to change his walk to a tip-toe as he passed the queer boy's door. If ever he met him face to face, he started and quaked like one who has encountered a ghost or a burglar. After a week this excess of deference toned down. Finding that Rollitt neither hurt nor heeded him, he abandoned his fears, and, instead of running away, stood and stared at his man, as if by keeping his eye hard on him he could discover his mystery.

It was two or three days after Elections that Fisher minor, having discovered by the absence of everybody from their ordinary haunts that it was a half-holiday, took it into his head to explore a little way down the Shargle Valley. He believed the other fellows had gone up; and he thought it a little unfriendly that they should have left him in the lurch.

He was not particularly fond of woods, unless there were nuts in them; or of rivers, unless there were stones on the banks to shy in. Still, it seemed to be half-holiday form at Fellsgarth to go down valleys, so he went, quite indifferent to the beauties of Nature, and equally indifferent as to where this walk brought him.

A mile below Fellsgarth, as everybody knows, the Shargle tumbles wildly into the Shayle, with a great fuss of rapids and cataracts and "narrows" to celebrate the fact; and a mile further, the united streams flow tamely out among reeds and gravel islands into Hawkswater.

Fisher minor had nearly reached the junction, and was proceeding to speculate on the possibility of picking his way among the stones towards the lake, when he caught sight of a boat in the middle of the rapid stream. It was tied somewhat carelessly to the overhanging branch of a tree, which bent and creaked with every lurch of the boat in the passing rapids. Standing in the stern as unconcerned as if he was on an island in a duck-pond, was Rollitt with his fishing-rod, casting diligently into the troubled waters.

For the first time the junior enjoyed an uninterrupted view of the object of his curiosity. He found it hard to recognise at first in the eager, sportsmanlike figure, with his animated face, the big shambling fellow whom he had so often eyed askance in the passages at Wakefield's. But there was no mistaking the shabby clothes, the powerful arms, the broad, square back. Rollitt the sportsman was another creature from Rollitt the Classic, and Fisher minor was critic enough to see that the advantage was with the former.

There was no chance of being detected. Rollitt was far too busy to heed anything but the six-pounder that struggled and plunged and tore away with his line to the end of the reel. Had all Fellsgarth stood congregated on the banks, he would never have noticed them.

Ah! he was beginning to wind in now, gingerly and artfully, and the fish, sulking desperately among the stones, was beginning to find his master. It was a keen battle between those two. Now the captive would dive behind a rock and force the line out a yard or two; now the captor would coax it on from one hiding-place to the next, and by a cunning flank movement cut off its retreat. Then, yielding little by little, the fish would feign surrender, till just as it seemed within reach, twang would go the line and the rod bend almost double beneath the sudden plunge. Then the patient work would begin again. The man's temper was more than a match for that of the victim, and, exhausted and despondent, the fish would, sooner or later, have to submit to the inexorable.

How long it might have gone on Fisher could never tell; for once, when victory seemed on the point of declaring for the angler, and the shining fins of the fish floundered despairingly almost within his reach, a downward dash nearly wrenched the rod from his hands and sent him sprawling on to the thwarts. The sudden lurch of the boat was too much for the ill-tied rope, and to Fisher's horror the noose gave way and sent boat and fisherman spinning down the rapids at five miles an hour.

Rollitt either did not notice the accident or was too engrossed to heed it. He still had his fish, though as far off as before, and once more the tedious task of coaxing him out of his tantrums was to begin over again. It was useless to shout. The roar of the water among the stones above and over the rocks below was deafening, and Fisher's piping voice could never make itself heard above it. He tried to throw a stone, but its little splash was lost in the hurly-burly of the rapids. It was hopeless to expect that Rollitt would see him. He had no eyes but for his rod.

The last glimpse Fisher minor caught of him as the boat, side-on, swirled round the turn towards the falls below, he was standing on the seat, craning his neck for a glimpse of his prize, and winding in gingerly on the reel as he did so. Then he disappeared.

With a groan of panic the small boy started to follow. The boulders were big and rough, and it was hard work to go at ordinary rate, still more to run. Happily, however, after a few steps he stumbled upon a path which, though it seemed to lead from the river, would take him, he calculated, back to it above the falls at the end of the bend in which the boat was. It was a tolerable path, and Fisher minor never got over ground so fast before or after. A few seconds brought him out of the wood on to the river-bank, where the stream, deepening and hushing, gathers itself for its great leap over the falls.

Had the boat already passed, and was he too late! No; there it came, sidling along on the swift waters, the angler still at his post, leaning over with his landing-net, within reach at last of his hard-earned prize. What could Fisher minor do! The stream was fairly narrow, and the boat, sweeping round the bend, was, if anything, nearer the other side, where the banks were high. His one chance was to attract the anglers attention. Had that angler been any one but Rollitt, it might have been easy.

Arming himself with a handful of stones, Fisher minor waited till the boat came within a few yards. Then with a great shout he flung with all his might at the boat.

The sudden fusillade might have been unheeded, had not one stone struck the angler's hand just as he was manoeuvring his landing-net under the fish. In the sudden start he missed his aim and looked up.

"Look out!" screamed Fisher. "You're adrift! Catch the branch!"

And he pointed wildly to the branch of an ash which straggled out over the water just above the fall.

Rollitt took in the situation at last. He cast a regretful glance at the fish as it gave its last victorious leap and vanished. Then, standing on the gunwale and measuring his distance from the tree, he jumped. For a moment Fisher minor thought he had missed; for the branch yielded and went under with his weight. But in a moment, just as the boat with a swoop plunged over the fall, he rose, clutching securely and hauling himself inch by inch out of the torrent. To Fisher, who watched breathlessly, it seemed as if every moment the branch would snap and send the senior back to his fate. But it held out bravely and supported him as he gradually drew himself up and finally perched high and dry above the water.

Fisher minor's difficulties now began. Having seen his man safe he would have liked to run away; for he was not at all sure how Rollitt would take it. Besides, he wouldn't much care to be seen by fellows like Wally or D'Arcy walking back in his company to Fellsgarth. On the other hand, it seemed rather low to desert a fellow just when he was half-drowned and might be hurt. What had he better do? Rollitt decided for him.

He came along the bough to where the boy stood, and dropped to the ground in front of him.

"Thanks," he said, and held out his hand.

Fisher was horribly alarmed. The tone in which the word was spoken was very like that which Giant Blunderbore may have used when dinner was announced. However, he summoned up courage to hold out his hand, and was surprised to find how gently Rollitt grasped it.

"I didn't mean to hurt you with the stones," he said.

"You didn't. Come and look for the boat, Fisher minor."

"He knows my name then," soliloquised the minor, beginning to recover a little from his panic. "I hope nobody will see me."

The boat was found bottom upwards—a wreck, with its side stove in, entangled in a mass of flotsam and jetsam which had gathered in one of the side eddies below the waterfall.

"Haul in, Fisher minor," growled Rollitt, surveying the wreck.

With difficulty they got it ashore and turned it right side up.

"Rod, flies, net, all gone," said Rollitt, half angry; "and fish too."

"It was such a beauty, the trout you hooked. I wish you'd got it. You nearly had it too when you had to jump out," ventured Fisher.

Rollitt looked down almost amiably at the speaker. Had the boy studied for weeks he could not have made a more conciliatory speech.

"Can't be helped," said the senior. "Might have been worse. Thanks again. Come and see Mrs Wisdom."

Mrs Wisdom was a decent young widow woman in whom the Fellsgarth boys felt a considerable interest. Her husband, late gamekeeper at Shargle Lodge, had always had a civil word for the young gentlemen, especially those addicted to sport, by whom he had been looked up to as a universal authority and ally. In addition to his duties at the Lodge, which were very ill paid, he had eked out his slender income by the help of a boat, which he kept on the lower reach below the falls, and which was, in the season, considerably patronised by the schoolboys. When last season he met his death over one of the cliffs of Hawk's Pike, every one felt sympathy for the widow and her children, who were thus left homeless and destitute. An effort was made, chiefly by the School authorities, to get her some laundry work, and find her a home in one of the little cottages on the School farm, near the river; while the boys made it almost a point of honour never to hire another boat down at the lake if Mrs Wisdom's was to be had.

Last week the boat had been brought up to the cottage on a cart, to be repainted for the coming season, and while here Rollitt had begged the use of it for this particular afternoon to fish from in the upper reach.

"Take care of her, Master Rollitt," said the widow; "she's a'most all I've got left, except the children. My John, he did say the upper reach was no water for boats."

"I'll take care," said Rollitt.

As the two boys now walked slowly, towards the cottage, Fisher minor could see that his companion's face was working ominously. He mistook it for ill-temper at the time, for he did not know Mrs Wisdom's history, or what the wreck meant to her.

She was at her door as they approached, and as she looked up and saw their long faces, the poor woman jumped at the truth at once.

"Don't say there's anything wrong with the boat, Master Rollitt. Don't tell me that."

Rollitt nodded, almost sternly.

"It went over the fall," said Fisher, feeling that something ought to be said. "Rollitt only just got out in time."

"Over the fall! Then it's smashed," cried she, bursting into tears. "It was to keep our body and soul together this season. Now what'll become of us! Oh, Master Rollitt, I did think you'd take care of my boat. It was all I had left—bar the children. What'll *they* do now?"

Rollitt stood by grimly silent till she had had her cry and looked up.

"I'm sorry," said he, in a voice that meant what it said. "What was it worth?"

"Worth? Everything to me."

"What would a new one cost?"

"More than I could pay, or you either. My John gave five pound for her—and oh, how we scrimped to save it! Where's it to come from now!" and she relapsed again into tears.

Rollitt waited a little longer, but there was nothing more to add; and presently he signalled Fisher to come away.

He was silent all the way home. The junior did not dare to speak to him—scarcely to look up in his face. Yet it did occur to him that if any one had a right to be in a bad temper over that afternoon's proceedings it was Mrs Wisdom, and not Rollitt.

As they neared the school, Fisher minor began to feel dreadfully compromised by his company. Rollitt's clothes were wet and muddy; his hands and face were dirty with his scramble along the tree; his air was morose and savage, and his stride was such that the junior had to trot a step or two every few yards to keep up. What would fellows think of him! Suppose Ranger were to see him, or, still worse, the Modern Wheatfield, or—

At this moment fate solved his problem. For just ahead of him, turning the corner of Fowler's Wall, was the cadaverous individual who owed him half a crown.

"Oh, excuse me, Rollitt," said he, "there's a fellow there I want to speak to. Good-bye."

Rollitt did not appear either to hear the words or notice the desertion, but stalked on till he reached Wakefields'. The house seemed to be empty. Evidently none of the other half-holiday makers had returned. Study doors stood open; an unearthly silence reigned in Wally's quarters. Even the tuck-shop was deserted.

The only person he met was Dangle, the clubs' secretary, who had penetrated into the enemy's quarter in order to confer with his dear colleague the treasurer as to calling a committee meeting, and was now returning unsuccessful.

"Ah, Rollitt," said he, "tell Fisher major, will you, I want to see him as soon as he comes in. I'd leave a line for him, but I don't know his room."

Whether Rollitt heard or not, he had to guess. At any rate he hardly felt sanguine that his message would be delivered.

As for Rollitt, he shut himself into his study with a bang, and might have been heard by any one who took the trouble to listen, pacing up and down the floor for a long time that evening. He did not put in an appearance in the common room, and although Yorke sent to ask him to tea, he forgot all about the invitation, and even if he had remembered it, would have forgotten whether he had said Yes or No.

The next morning—Sunday—just as the chapel bell was beginning to ring, Widow Wisdom was startled by a loud knock at her door.

"Oh, Master Rollitt," said she, and her eyes were red still, "is the boat safe after all?"

"No; but I've got you another. Farmer Gay's was for sale on the lake—I've bought it. It's yours now."

"Farmer Gay's—mine? Oh, go on, Master Rollitt, how could *you* buy a boat any more than me? You've no money to spare, I know."

"It's yours—here's the receipt," said the boy, with almost a scowl.

"But, Master Rollitt—"

But Master Rollitt had gone to be in time for chapel.

Chapter Seven
Trial by Jury

Fisher minor's hopes rose high within him as he stalked his debtor across the School Green. Three times already he had encountered him, but fate had stepped in to prevent the collection of his dues. Now—

He had arrived at this stage when a voice at his side sent a cold shiver down his back.

"Hullo, kid, got you at last, then? That's what you call waiting where I left you, do you?"

"I didn't promise to wait," said Fisher. "You told me to."

"It's the same thing. Now you'll come along with me, my beauty."

Had Fisher minor been anything but a raw hand, it might have occurred to him that it would take Percy Wheatfield all his time to convey a boy his, Fisher's, size against his will into Forder's house. But such is the force of innocence on one side, and authority on the other, that the new boy laid down his arms, and followed his captor meekly into the enemy's citadel. Just as they were entering, a posse of the enemy appeared on the scene, consisting, among other supporters of the Modern cause, of Ramshaw, Cottle, Lickford, and Cash.

"Here's a game, Rammy," cried Percy. "Got him at last! This is the villain, this is the murdering, highway forger. Come on, you kid; you're in for it."

It did occur to Fisher minor at this juncture that a change of air might be refreshing. But it was too late now. The enemy had him fast. There was no getting out of the "warm weather" which had been promised him.

"Come on—we'll have a regular Old Bailey of it," cried Percy. "Go and tell the fellows, and collar some witnesses, do you hear; and tell the hangman he'll be wanted in half an hour."

This promise of judicial dispatch was not consoling to the prisoner, who had grave doubts as to the impartiality of the tribunal before which he was to be arraigned. He wondered if Ashby, or D'Arcy, or any of his friends would appear among the witnesses.

The trial took place in the room jointly owned by Percy, Ramshaw, Cottle, and Lickford. A chair was planted on the bed for the accommodation of the judge. The fender was brought out in front of the chest of drawers for a witness-box; while Rix minimus, who officiated as jury, sat on a footstool on the table.

As for the prisoner, a dock was provided for him in the form of a wash-stand, out of which the basin had been removed to make room for his uneasy person in the vacant hole.

"Now, you chaps," said Percy, who had naturally appointed himself, in addition to his other offices, "usher of the court", "no larks. Shut up. This is a big job. This young cad cheated at Elections."

Here the door opened, and Dangle looked in.

"What on earth is all this row?" he said.

"A trial. I say, Dangle, will you be judge? It's a Classic kid that cheated at Elections."

"No, really, I didn't," said Fisher, painfully aware that so far, the trial was going against him.

Dangle, who fancied something might come of this, was condescending enough to say he didn't mind playing at judge, if they liked. Whereat, amid cheers, he was voted to the chair on the bed, where he sat rather precariously, and ordered silence in the court.

"Who is the prisoner?"

"Go on, kid, tell 'em your name," said Percy, encouragingly.

"Fisher minor—really I didn't do anything," said the prisoner.

"What's the charge?" said the judge.

"You see, it's this way," said Percy, forgetting to go inside the fender— "Bam, and Cot, and Lick and I were having a ripping eight-handed mill in here the other day—"

The prisoner thought over all his crimes, and could recall nothing that was even remotely connected with an eight-handed mill.

"Cot and Lick had got gloves with no horse-hair in them, you know, so they lammed it pretty hard; but Ram and I were just scrunching them up—"

"Crams! You never got near us. My nose wasn't hit once," said Cottle.

"No; but we had you in the ribs."

"Under the belt," ejaculated Lickford.

"No, it wasn't—I say, Dangle," said the witness, "it was just on his waistcoat pocket, and he says that's below the belt. If he likes to wear his belt round his neck, of course he gets hit under."

"And if you wear yours round your ankle, there's not much room for your bread-basket," retorted Cottle.

"And where does Fisher minor come in?" asked the judge; "was he in the middle of the mill?"

"No. You see, we were just in the middle of it, and these jolly cheats were beginning to cave in—"

"Ho, ho!—It would take a lot more than you to make us—"

"Order in the court—go on, Wheatfield."

"There you are—shut up, you chaps—beginning to cave in, when Clapperton yelled for me, and I had to go."

"Lucky job for you," growled Cottle. "You wouldn't have been able to go at all five minutes later."

Whereupon Percy appealed to the court to keep order.

"Fire away," said the judge, "that's nothing to do with the prisoner."

"Oh, hasn't it!—You see, Clapperton wanted me to take a letter to Yorke. It must have been a screamer, for Yorke yelled when he read it. I wanted him to let me finish our mill first, but—"

"Who, Yorke?"

"No, Clapperton. If there'd been time for another round—"

"Now, then, don't let's have any more of that mill," said the judge.

"That's just what they felt at the time, wasn't it, Lick?" ejaculated Cottle.

"Did we?—wait till you see, my beauty," said the witness. "I wish you wouldn't interrupt. Oh, so I had to go, and this kid came and caught me a jolly crack in the stomach."

"Which side of your belt?" inquired Lickford.

"The side you'll get it hot, my boy, next time I catch you," retorted Percy.

"That'll be under, you bet," said Lickford.

"I didn't mean to hurt you," said the prisoner, who began to hope that the charge against him was to prove much less serious than he had at first feared, "I apologise."

"Shut up, don't talk to me—talk to the jury."

As the jury at this moment was struggling manfully to protect his hassock from the depredations of Cash, who was anxious to investigate its interior, it was not much use addressing him; so Fisher subsided, and wished the hole of Percy's wash-stand had been at least so much easier in diameter as to allow him room to sigh.

"Fire away," said the judge, "we shall be all night at this."

"Well, you see," continued Percy, "it's this way. I've got a brother, you know, called Wally, a seedy Classic chap, and up to no end of low tricks."

"We know him," echoed the court generally.

"Not got such a rummy-shaped waist as his brother, though," whispered Cottle.

"All right, young Cottle, I'll take it out of you, you'll see."

"What'll you take! I keep mine outside," replied Cottle.

"Order in the court. Forge away, Wheatfield."

"I should like to know how I'm to forge away, with these two asses fooling about down here? Why can't you raise them to the bench to keep them quiet? Oh yes—well, you see, this kid, being new, and green, and about as high old an idiot as they make them—did you fellows see him on first-night? I say! oh my—"

"Look here, Wheatfield," said the judge, sternly, "if you aren't done in three minutes, I'll call the next witness."

"*He* wouldn't know anything about it, bless you," said Percy. "You see, it was like this—this kid thought I was Wally—what do you think of that?"

"Cheek. Jolly rough on Wally," remarked Cash. The witness looked at the interrupter, and tried to make out whether his remark was a compliment or the reverse. He decided that, as he had only three minutes left, he had better defer thinking the question out till afterwards.

"So, of course, he began to swagger about his big brother—"

"No, you asked me—" began the prisoner.

"Shut up," cried Percy, sternly, "how am I to get done in three minutes if—"

"Only two left now," said Ramshaw.

"Go on, Ram, I've not been a minute yet."

"Yes, you have—sixty-five seconds," said Ramshaw, who held his watch in his hand.

"I never did believe in those Waterbury turnips, they always stop when you—oh yes!—swaggered about his big brother and all those fellows over there, and blabbed out there'd been a regular plant among 'em to rig the Elections, and he and a lot of 'em had been out canvassing and bagged a lot of our kids and locked them out, and if it hadn't been for that, Brinkman would have pulled off the treasurership, and if it hadn't been for me getting wind of it, and going and fetching them out and bringing them into Hall in the nick of time, Ranger would have got the secretaryship, and our side would have been jolly well out of it, and I mean to say it's a howling swindle—and—hope—there'll—be—a—jolly—good—row   kicked—up—and—you—needn't—say—I—let—out—about   it—because—Wally—asked—me—to—keep—it—mum—and I—said—"

"Time's up," said Ramshaw. "No side?"

Whereupon the witness stopped short triumphantly, like an athlete who has just won his race by a neck.

"Come," said the judge, "this is getting interesting. Who's the next witness? Are any of our fellows who were collared here?"

"Rather—young Rix is one."

"Please, Dangle," said the prisoner, "I didn't touch anybody. I was—that is—"

"Don't tell crams," said Percy, "it's a bad habit."

"Rix had better go into the witness-box," said the judge.

"What about the jury?" asked that functionary.

"Oh, I'd keep the place warm," volunteered Percy.

Whereupon Rix quitted his hassock, and entered the fender.

"I and Slingsby got nailed by a Classic cad outside our form door. I kicked him on the shins, though," said he.

"What Classic cad!"

"Oh, I don't know; a new kid with sandy hair, a horrid lout. It was Wally's room we were taken to, and they fooled us about high tea and that sort of thing. The place was swarming with our chaps who had been collared."

"How many?" asked the judge. "Fifty?"

"Not quite so many; there were four or five."

"Next witness."

Another of the captives gave similar evidence. After which, Lickford deposed that he had seen the troop come in to Elections just in time to vote for Dangle.

"Yes; and who tried to keep us out, I'd like to know?" said Percy. "There you are, it was *you*!"

"I thought you were on the other side."

"Did you? I'm very glad Wally gave you a welting for it. I wish he'd do it again."

"He hits above the belt, that's how I know him from you," retorted Lickford.

"Order—what's the prisoner got to say!"

"Crams," said Percy, "it's no use asking him."

"Wait a bit," said the judge. "Fisher minor, how many of our chaps did you collar?"

"None, really," said the prisoner. "I waited by the gymnasium."

"Oh. What for?"

"Well, I was canvassing."

"What did you wait at the gymnasium for?" This was awkward. Fisher minor found himself getting into a tight corner, tighter even than the wash-stand. "I was told to."

"Who by? your brother, I suppose."

"Oh no. My brother wouldn't do such a thing."

"What sort of thing?"

"Why, try to collar fellows off the other side."

"Oh, that was your little game, was it? Whose idea was it? Yorke's?"

"Oh no. It was D'Arcy spoke to me."

"Oh, D'Arcy. And who spoke to him? Whose fag is he?"

"Ridgway's."

"And what did Ridgway tell him?"

"I don't think Ridgway told him anything. The only one I heard speak to him was Wally."

"Wretched young sneak!" said Percy. "I'll let Wally know that."

"Wally, he's Yorke's fag. Who else was there?"

"Only me and Ashby."

"Who does Ashby fag for?"

"My brother, Fisher major."

"I thought you said just now your brother wasn't in it. You'd better be careful, youngster."

For the life of him, Fisher minor, in his bewildered state, could not make out how Ridgway, and Yorke, and Fisher major all seemed to have got mixed up in the affair.

"You mean to say," said the judge, "you don't know what the orders to the fags were?"

"No, really—I only heard of it from D'Arcy."

"Your brother never said anything to you direct!"

"Oh no."

"Has he said anything since?"

"Oh no; that is, he only said it was a pity Ranger got beaten."

"Did he say how it happened?"

"He said if the five Modern chaps hadn't turned up at the last moment, he'd have won."

"Was he angry about it?"

"He was rather in a wax."

"Did he tell you you were an ass?"

"Not that time."

"Another time?"

"Yes, once or twice."

"'Cute chap, your brother," said Percy, aside.

"Shut up, Wheatfield. Now tell me this, young Fisher major," said Dangle, with an air of importance which intimidated the prisoner; "what was it your brother said about the election?"

"It wasn't to me, it was to Ranger, my senior. He said it was a regular sell, and he'd have given a lot to see you beaten, because he knew you couldn't play fair at anything, even if you tried."

Some of the court were rude enough to laugh at this very candid confession; but the judge himself failed to see any humour in it.

"Oh, that's what he said? And yet you mean to tell me, after that, that your brother had nothing to do with trying to get Ranger elected instead of me?"

"I suppose he had; but I'm sure he didn't mean to do anything fishy, any more than I did. I thought it was only a joke."

"You've a nice notion of a joke. That'll do, you can cut."

"What!" exclaimed Percy, aghast, "aren't you going to hang him?"

"No, I must go. You can finish the trial yourselves."

As soon as the judge had quitted the bench, Percy mounted it, and proceeded to sum up.

"You're a nice article, you are," said he, addressing the prisoner—"what do you mean by sneaking on my young brother, Wally, eh? You'll get it hot for that, I can tell you. You're to be hanged, drawn, and quartered; then you're to be kicked all round our side; then you're to be ducked in the river; then you're to kneel down and lick every chap's boots; then you're to be executed; then you're to be burnt alive; then you're to write out fifty Greek verbs; then you're— Hallo, who's there? Come in! what do you want?"

This abrupt curtailment of the prisoner's doom was occasioned by a modest tap at the door; probably some belated witness come to add his evidence to the rest, "Come in, can't you?" repeated Percy.

Whereupon the door opened with a swing, and in rushed Wally, D'Arcy, Ashby, and three or four other Classic fags. How they had got wind of the capture of their man it would be hard to say; but now they had come to fetch him.

The only thing visible in Percy's room for several minutes was dust— out of which proceeded yells, and howls, and recriminations which would have done credit to Pandemonium. As the cloud rolled by, the Classics might be seen in a firm phalanx, with their man in the middle, backing on to the door. Signs of carnage lay all around. Lickford was struggling, head downward, in the wash-stand. Cash was leaning up in a corner, with his hand modestly placed over his nose. Ramshaw and Cottle were engaged in deadly strife on the floor, each under the fond delusion that the other was a Classic; while the twin brothers, armed with the better pair of boxing-gloves, were having a friendly spar in the middle.

It was a victory all along the line for the invaders, and when, a moment afterwards, they stampeded in a body, and marched with shouts of victory down the passage, carrying the late prisoner among them, there was no mistake about the ignominious defeat of the besieged garrison.

That evening Fisher major received a polite note from his colleague, the secretary.

"Dear Fisher,—It is only right to tell you, that we have discovered that five of our fellows were prevented from voting at Elections by boys of your side, apparently acting under orders from their seniors. We don't profess to know who were at the bottom of it, but it is a fact that the election for treasurer would have gone differently but for this very shady trick. Clapperton and most of us are not disposed to claim a new election, now everything is settled, and you have already got in most of the subscriptions. But it makes us think that even the virtuous Classics at Fellsgarth are not absolutely perfect even yet—which is a pity.

"Yours truly,—

"R. Dangle."

This pleasant letter, Fisher major, raging, carried to the captain.

Yorke pulled a long face when he read it.

"There's no truth in it, surely?" said he.

"I can't answer for any foolery the juniors have been up to; but apart from that, it's a sheer lie, and the fellows deserve to be kicked."

"Much better offer them a new election," said the captain.

"What! They'll get their man in."

"My dear fellow, suppose they do. You'll still belong to Fellsgarth. They mustn't have a chance of saying they don't get fair play."

"Well, perhaps you're right. I don't care twopence about the treasurership, but I wouldn't like to be beaten by Brinkman."

"I hope you won't be, old man," said the captain.

Next morning, when fellows got up, they found the following notice on the boards:

"Elections.

"A protest having been handed in against the recent election for treasurer, notice is given that a fresh election will be held for this office on Friday next at 3.

"C.Y., Captain."

Chapter Eight
One too many

The seniors of Forder's house were by no means gratified at the captain's prompt reply to Dangle's accusation. Indeed, that active and energetic official had written to Fisher on his own responsibility, and was now a little hurt to find that his colleagues were half inclined to repudiate his action.

"Why ever couldn't you speak about the thing before you wrote like that?" said Clapperton. "We don't want another election."

"You weren't going to sit down meekly, and let those fellows cheat without saying a word, were you?" retorted Dangle.

"No—rather not. But that wasn't the way to do it. It would have paid us much better to stand on our dignity."

"In other words," said Fullerton in his melancholy voice, "to have a grievance, and nurse it well."

"You idiot!" said Clapperton. "I don't want you to tell me what I mean."

"I wasn't, I was telling the others," said Fullerton. "But I agree with you. If we have another election and get beaten, we shall be far worse off than if we were able to take heaven and earth to witness we had been wronged and were too noble to seek revenge."

If Fullerton could have translated Cicero as well as he translated Clapperton, what a good Classic he would have been!

"We'd better decline the new election at once," said Brinkman; "it concerns me more than anybody else; and I agree with Clapperton."

"Why ever not have the new election?" said Dangle. "We're bound to get our man in."

"Better decline it first," said Clapperton. "They'll be glad enough not to let it go to a trial, I expect."

"Hurrah for injured innocence," said Fullerton; "it's the best paying thing I know."

The result of this conference was, that Dangle went across after school next morning to the captain's study where Fisher and Ranger happened to be calling at the same time.

"Look here, Yorke," said the secretary, adopting his most civil tones, "you quite misunderstood my letter to Fisher major. We don't want another election. We'd just as soon let things stop as they are. It was rough on us, of course; but it divides the offices up more fairly to have them as they are."

"Thanks," said Yorke, "that's not good enough. We'll have another election on Friday."

Dangle's face fell.

"You're fools if you do," said he. "Those five votes will make all the difference."

"I don't care if they've five hundred," said Yorke.

"Oh, all right. You've no message about the cheats who kept our men out, have you? Probably they've been promoted to prefects!"

"You took care not to commit yourself to any names; but, as you wrote to Fisher major, you probably include him as one of the cheats. If so, I dare say he'll be glad to discuss the matter with you outside."

"I never said it was he," said Dangle hurriedly.

"But I know who it was."

"Three of our juniors, I understand?" said Yorke. "The fags of three of your prefects, yes."

"Fisher," said the captain, "will you fetch Ashby, D'Arcy, and Fisher minor here?"

The young gentlemen in question were not far away busily engaged in their joint study, with Wally's assistance, in getting up a stock of impositions, which should serve as a common fund on which to draw daring the term.

The idea was D'Arcy's.

"You see," he had said, "we're bound to catch it, some of as, and it's a jolly fag having to do the lines just when they're wanted. My notion is, if we just keep a little stock by us, it'll be awfully handy. Why, suppose young Ashby were to get fifty lines at morning school next Saturday, what about his chance of getting into the 58th fifteen?"

"It's the 6th fifteen, not the 58th," said Ashby.

"Well, there's not much difference."

"It would be jolly awkward," said Ashby.

"Yes; and you always do get potted just when it is jolliest awkward," said D'Arcy. "That's why it's such a tip to have your impots written before you get them. Penny wise, pound foolish, you know."

It was not at all clear what this valuable aphorism had to do with the subject in hand, but it impressed the two new boys considerably.

"And just fancy," continued Wally, driving home his chum's nails with considerable industry, "just fancy if young Fisher was to have to sit up here swotting over lines, just when his brother wants his vote in Hall on Friday! Why, one vote will make all the difference."

Fisher immediately called for pens, ink, and paper, which Wally and D'Arcy promptly supplied for him and Ashby, and a scene of unparalleled industry ensued. Even D'Arcy insisted on doing his share, which consisted of drawing niggers in various stages of public execution, labelled with the names of Clapperton, Dangle, and Brinkman, while Wally generally superintended and assisted, by playing fives against the wall.

"I say," said he presently, "I suppose it's all out about your precious canvassing. That beast Percy has gone and blabbed—after me giving him toffee too!"

"Never mind," said D'Arcy, "we rather took it out of them, I fancy, yesterday. They won't mess about with us in a hurry again."

"No, we did pull that off pretty well. I'm sorry for our seniors, you know. We did our best for them, and we shan't be able to give them the same leg-up on Friday."

"They ought to be pretty civil to us this term, anyhow," said Wally.

Whereupon Fisher major entered the room.

"Yorke wants D'Arcy, Ashby, and my minor. Come at once, he's waiting."

"Don't he want me?" said Wally, evidently afraid lest his services were going to be overlooked. "I was in it too, you know, Fisher."

"Were you? Oh, you'd better come too, then."

"Thanks."

And the four, disposing themselves meekly for their coming honours, followed, single file, into the captain's room.

"Wally wished to come too," explained Fisher. "He says he was in it."

It perplexed the four heroes to see Dangle there. What did he want! And why did the captain look so stern? And, oh, horrors, what was that switch on the table for?

Gradually it dawned upon them that the honours in store for them would fall rather thicker than they were prepared for; and Wally, for one, wished he had stayed at home.

"You youngsters," said the captain, "it is said that you four behaved unfairly last election, by keeping out five boys from voting. Is that true?"

"Yes," said Ashby.

"They were only Modern kids," explained D'Arcy.

"They wouldn't have got in for the second vote, if it hadn't been for me," remarked Wally.

"I didn't catch any boys; I couldn't find any," said Fisher minor.

"You see, Yorke," said D'Arcy, who began to realise that he was "boss of this show," "these two kids are new kids; they oughtn't to be licked; it's Wally and me."

"Me?" exclaimed the injured Wally; "I like your style, young D'Arcy; what did *I* do?"

"All right, it's me then, if you like!"

"I don't mind being in it, to give you a leg-up," said Wally, touched by the heroism of his friend, "but you might let a chap bowl himself out, you know."

"All right, Yorke, it was me and D'Arcy."

"You should say *I* and D'Arcy," said Ranger. "What, were *you* in it? Good old—"

"No, you young ass; it's bad grammar to say *me* and D'Arcy were in it."

"I never knew you were. It's the first we've heard of it; isn't it, you chaps?"

The chaps most emphatically agreed that it was.

"Let them be, Ranger," said the captain. "There'll be time enough for a grammar lesson after."

"Can't do it to-day, we've got syntax this afternoon," said D'Arcy.

"Now, you youngsters, look here," said the captain. "You may think you're very clever; but this sort of thing is cheating, and cheating is what cads do. We don't want any of it inside Fellsgarth. Dangle, here are the youngsters, and here is the switch; will you lick them, or shall I?"

"I don't want to lick them. Let them off," growled Dangle.

The hopes of the culprits rose for a moment, but they went down below zero when Yorke picked up the cane.

"Wheatfield, come here."

Wally held out his case-hardened hand and received half a dozen cuts, for which it is saying a good deal that they made the recipient dance.

D'Arcy followed, and received his six with meek indifference. If he had come first, he would probably have danced. But as Wally had done that, he stood firm.

Ashby received three cuts only, which astonished him dreadfully. It was his first acquaintance with the cane. He had never realised before what a venomous instrument it can be. Still, he bore it like a man.

Poor Fisher minor had a similar experience. With his brother looking on, and his messmates to watch how he bore it, he passed through the ordeal creditably. His three "Ohs" varied in cadence from anguish to surprise, and from surprise to mild expostulation, "Oh!" "Ehee!" "Ow!" after which he felt very pleased, on his brother's account, that he had not shed tears.

"Now cut," said the captain, "and if you're bowled out in that sort of thing again, you won't be let off so easy."

"Yorke's a beast," said Wally, when the shattered forces mastered once more in his study, "but he's a just beast. He gave it us all hot alike."

No one disputed the proposition.

"I thought he'd let you new kids off, but he didn't. It's just as well. It'll do you good, and make you sit up."

"Jolly sell for that cad Dangle," said D'Arcy. "He thought Yorke was going to shirk it."

"He can't say that now," said Ashby, rubbing the palm of his hand up and down his thigh.

Dangle, meanwhile, had returned to his quarters with the unsatisfactory report of his mission.

"Bother them!" said Clapperton. "They take advantage of us whenever there's a chance. Now they've offered a new election, and licked the youngsters, the wind is out of our sails."

"When it comes to the time, I shall decline to be nominated," said Brinkman.

"That won't be much good. You'll get some of our fellows voting for you whether you stand or not. And if some vote, all must."

"We shall have to see all our men turn up," said Dangle. "It was a tight enough shave for the secretaryship."

"Yes. If we don't carry it now, we'd much better have left it alone. I only wish we had."

"There's this to be said," said Dangle, anxious to make the best of his mistake; "if we do get three officers to their one, there should be no doubt about our getting properly represented in the fifteen next week."

"Ah—yes; we've still that bone to pick with them."

As the Friday approached, signs of excitement in the coming conquest were plainly visible. By tacit agreement the return match between Percy's adherents and Wally's was postponed till after the election. Absentees at the last election were diligently looked up by their respective prefects, and ordered to be in attendance. Minute calculations were made by the knowing ones, which decided within one or two what Brinkman's majority would be. Even in Wakefield's it was admitted that the Classic chance was a slender one.

"I wish it was all over," said Fisher major. "I'm getting sick of these precious accounts already, and shall be glad to hand them over."

"You won't lose them," said Dalton, "if we can help. You may have to vote for yourself, though."

"Catch me. I've come to the conclusion I wasn't born a treasurer, and I couldn't conscientiously vote for myself. I only wish I could back out."

"You can't do that now," said his friend. "Bless you, we can keep the accounts for you. We couldn't for Brinkman."

When morning school was over on the Friday, there was a general stampede for the Hall, where boys crowded up for good seats a quarter of an hour before the time, and enlivened the interval with cheers and demonstrations for their favourite candidate. Wally and his friends were particularly active in their corner, and addressed the meeting generally in favour of Fisher major.

"Back up, you Classic kids!" shouted Wally, standing on his seat and apostrophising a group of the Sixth who were standing near. "Fisher's your friend! Won the mile in 4-38; batting average 34.658742.3; bowling, 12 wickets an innings, and 3 runs an over. Never tells lies, or cheats. Always comes home sober and gives silver in the collection. He won't waste your money or cook your accounts, like some chaps; and he'll run the ball up the field, instead of sitting down in the middle of the scrummage like the Modern chaps to keep warm. Walk up! walk up! vote for Fisher and economy! Hooray for Fisher! Down with the swell mob!"

Amid such torrents of eloquence the cause of Fisher major was not likely to go by default.

Brinkman, too, was not without his champions, who, however, avoided set speeches and confined themselves to personalities and generalities, such as—

"Who cheats at Elections?"

"Oh, my hands, what a licking!"

"How now—not me!" (Here Fisher minor coloured up.) "Look out, you chaps, there's a Classic cad blushing."

"No! where? won't he want a rest after it!"

"Here comes Brinkman! Hooray for honesty and fair play! Hooray for the Moderns! Down with Wakefield's kids! Send 'em home to their mas!"

"Shut up there! Sit down, you youngsters."

Whereupon there fell a lull.

Fisher minor surveyed the scene with anxious trepidation. If his brother were to lose now, it would be his—Fisher minor's—fault. He would never be able to hold up his head again. How he wished he had a dozen votes!

"Strong muster," he heard some one say near him. "I expect every fellow's here."

"Except Rollitt."

"Of, of course," said the other, with a laugh, "no one ever expects him."

"Why not?" said Fisher minor to himself. "Why shouldn't Rollitt come and vote?"

He quite shuddered at the audacity of the idea; and yet, when he looked up to the front and saw his brother standing there, worried and uneasy, and realised that in a few minutes he was to stand his ordeal, the younger brother's courage rose within him, and he edged towards the door.

In due time Yorke arose. This time, amid the vociferous cheers of his own side, a few of the Moderns ventured to mingle howls. They soon discovered their mistake, for not even their own side was with them as a body. They were hooted down with execrations, and the result of this interposition was that the captain was cheered for twice the usual time.

"You fellows," said he, as soon as there was silence, "you probably understand from the notice why this meeting is called. The last election was very close, and I am sorry to say there was not fair play. I am still more sorry to say the offenders were juniors in Wakefield's," (terrific yells and hoots from the Moderns), "who ought to have known better, and who I hope are thoroughly ashamed of themselves," (terrific cheers, during which, D'Arcy, Wally, and Ashby, who had been standing on a form, modestly took seats and exchanged defiant signals with the youth of the Modern side through the chinks of the crowd). "They have had the licking they deserve," ("Not half of it!" and laughter), "as Dangle here, who was present at the time, will testify." (Dangle scowled at this reference—What right had the captain to score off him?). "Of course under the circumstances it was necessary to have a new election. Fisher here," (tremendous cheers, amidst which the culprits, considering that the storm had blown over, remounted their perches) "would scorn to be treasurer of the clubs, and everybody would scorn him too, if there was any suspicion of foul play about his election. He has resigned, like an honest man; and our business is now to elect a treasurer." (Cheers and "Vote for Fisher major" from Wally.)

Dalton rose and proposed his friend Fisher major, which Ranger briefly seconded.

Dangle thereupon proposed Brinkman. He was sorry the School was being put to the trouble of this new election. They hadn't wanted it on their side; and his friend had been very reluctant to stand. But of course, as the election was to take place, he hoped Brinkman would win by a majority which would show the School what Fellsgarth thought about the foul play which had been tried on at the last election.

Clapperton seconded the nomination, and assured his friends that, now the offence had been acknowledged and atoned for by the castigation of the offenders, they would try to forget it and feel to the other side as if it had not occurred.

Clapperton, of course, was cheered by his side; and yet his chief admirers did not feel as proud of him as they would have liked. His tone was patronising, and Fellsgarth could not stand being patronised, even by its captain.

Just as the meeting was settling down for the important business of the vote, a sensational incident took place.

The door swung open, and in strode Rollitt, with Fisher minor, panting and pale, at his heels.

The new-comer, heedless of the astonishment caused by his appearance, strode negligently up to the front where the other prefects were, while his escort modestly slipped into the arms of his admiring friends.

For a moment the meeting looked on with amused bewilderment. Then it suddenly dawned on everybody that this meant a new voter; and terrific shouts of jubilation went up from the Classics; during which Fisher minor had his back thumped almost in two.

For once in his life he was a hero! How he wished his young sisters could have seen him then!

"Never mind," shouted Percy across the room, "he's bound to vote the wrong side, or forget to vote at all."

"Order! Those who vote for Brinkman, hold up your hands."

It was far too serious to humbug now. Even D'Arcy was grave as he surveyed the force of the enemy.

Two tellers had been appointed from either side, so that the votes were counted four times, and the total was not allowed till all were agreed on the result.

"Brinkman has one hundred and twenty-eight votes."

Loud and long were the cheers which greeted this announcement. The knowing ones felt that it practically meant victory for the Moderns, for it was one more vote than Fisher major had won with last time.

"Now, hands up for Fisher major."

Amid dead silence the Classic hands went up. Anxious eyes were cast in Rollitt's direction. But he, strange to say, was all there, and held up his hand with the rest.

Fisher major himself at the last moment kept his own hand down. He had decided that, if Brinkman voted for himself, he would do the same. Brinkman had voted. But, when it came to following his example, the candidate's pride went on strike, and, whether it lost the election or not, he declined to vote, Three of the tellers evidently agreed, but the other had to count again before he made the figure right. Then the written paper was handed up to Yorke, "Brinkman 128, Fisher major, 129—Fisher is elected."

Chapter Nine
Carried Nem. Con

It must not be supposed that in the midst of the excitement of School politics the intellectual side of the Fellsgarth juniors, life was being quite neglected.

On the contrary, they complained that so far from being neglected it was rather overdone.

The Classic juniors, for instance, suffered many things at the hands of the cheerful Mr Stratton, who really worked hard to instil into their opening minds some rudiments of those studies from which their side took its name. He took pains to explain not only when a thing was wrong, but why; and, unlike some of his calling, he devoted his chief attention to his most backward boys. This was his great offence in the eyes of D'Arcy and Wally and some of their fraternity, because under the arrangement they came in for the special attention alluded to.

"That kid," said Wally, one day, *sotto voce*, as class was proceeding, "has no more idea of teaching than my hat. We don't get a chance to *do* things ourselves, with him always messing about and looking over. It's rude to look over. I mean to mark my exercise *private* in future."

"The thing is," said D'Arcy, "if he'd anything original to say it wouldn't matter so. But he's always talking the same old rot about roots. What's the use of a root, I should like to know, if you can't bury it? Eh, kid?"

Fisher minor, to whom the question was addressed, did not know, and remarked that they didn't teach Latin here the same way as when he learned from a governess at home.

He regretted this admission almost as soon as he had made it. For Wally and D'Arcy immediately got paper and began to draw fancy portraits of Fisher minor learning Latin under the old *régime*. The point of these illustrations was not so much in the figures as in the conversation. The figures were more or less unlike the originals; at least, Fisher minor declared that the three isosceles triangles piled by Wally one on the top of the other were not a bit like his governess; while the plum-pudding on two sticks, with a little pudding above for a head which emitted four huge tears, the size of an orange, from either eye, he regarded as a simple libel on himself. In one sense the likenesses were speaking—that is, a gibbous balloon proceeded from the mouth of each figure, wherein the following dialogue was indicated. "*Governess.*—'Naughty little Tommy-wommy, didn't know his Latin. Tommy must have a smack when he goes bye-bye.' *Tommy.*— 'Booh, hoo, how bow, yow, wow, oh my! I'll tell my ma!'"

"Bring up that paper, Wheatfield," said Mr Stratton.

Wally made a wild grab at Ashby's exercise, and was proceeding to take it up when the master stopped him.

"Not that; the other, Wheatfield. Bring it immediately."

Whereupon Wally with shame had to rejoice Ashby's heart by restoring his *exercise*, and take up in its place the fancy portrait.

Mr Stratton gazed attentively and critically at this work of art.

"Not at all well done, Wheatfield," said he. "Sit down at my table here and draw me thirty copies of it before you leave this room. Next boy, go on."

Wally confessed, in later life, that of all the impositions he had had in the course of his chequered career, none had been more abominable and wearisome than this. Oh, how he got to detest that governess and her ward, and how sickening their talk became before the task was half over!

He sat in that room nearly three hours by the clock, groaning over this task, and when at last he went in search of Mr Stratton with the original and thirty copies in his hand, he felt as limp and flabby, bodily and mentally, as he had ever done in his life.

Mr Stratton, who was having tea in his own room, examined each picture in turn, and rejected two as not fair copies of the original.

"Do these two again—here," said he.

Wally meekly obeyed. He had not a kick left in him.

"That's better," said the young master when they were done. "Now sit down and have some tea."

It was a solemn meal. Mr Stratton went quietly on with his meal, looking up now and then to see that his guest was supplied with bread and butter and cake and biscuits. Wally was equally silent. He felt sore against the master, but he liked his cake—and the tea was "tip-top."

The ceremony came to an end about the same time as the cake, and then Mr Stratton said, pointing to the papers—

"You can put them in the fire now, Wheatfield."

Wally obeyed with grim satisfaction.

"Thanks. You can go now. You must come another day and bring your friends. Good-bye," and he shook hands.

"I wonder if the chap's all there," said Wally to himself as he limped over to his quarters. "He forgot to jaw me. Wonder if I ought to have reminded him? Wonder who he gets his cake from? I wouldn't care for many more impots like that. It was pretty civil of him asking me to tea, when you come to think of it. Not sure I sha'n't back him up a bit this half, and make the chaps do so too. Wonder if he meant all four of us to come to tea? One cake wouldn't go round. Besides, there's no saying how that young cad Fisher minor would behave."

This little episode was not without its effect on all the occupants of Wally's study. For that young gentleman had not the slightest intention of turning over a new leaf by himself. No, bother it; if he was going to "back up" Stratton, the other fellows would have to back up too.

His one grief was that the stock of impositions stored up by the industry of the two new boys would not be likely to be wanted now, which would be wicked waste. D'Arcy had already occasionally drawn on them, and one day nearly spoiled the whole arrangement by taking up to Mr Wakefield fifty lines of Virgil precisely five minutes after they had been awarded. Fortunately, however, his hands were exceedingly grimy at the time, so that Mr Wakefield sent him back for ablutions before he would communicate with him. And in the interval he fortunately discovered his error, and instead of taking up the imposition with his clean hands, he delighted the master with a knotty inquiry as to one of the active tenses of the Latin verb "To be."

However, there was no saying when the impositions might not come in useful, and meanwhile Ashby and Fisher minor were taken off the job and ordered to sit up hard with their work for Stratton.

"You know," said Wally, propounding his scheme of moral reform in a little preliminary speech, "you kids are not sent up here to waste your time. No more's D'Arcy."

"How do you know what I was sent up here for?" said D'Arcy. "It wasn't to hear your jaw."

"Shut up. I've just been having tea with Stratton, and we were talking about you chaps, him and I—I mean he and *me*."

"You didn't get on to English grammar, did you, while you were about it?" asked Ashby.

"No. Look here, you chaps, no larks. It would be rather a spree if we put our back into it this term, wouldn't it?—beastly sell, you know, for the others; and rather civil to Stratton too, for asking us to tea."

This last argument was more impressive than the first; and the company said they supposed they might.

"All right—of course we may have to shut off a lark or two, but unless we stick— Hullo, I say, look at those Modern chaps down there punting a football on our side of the path! Cheek! Why, it's Cash and my young brother. I say, let's go and drive them off, you fellows."

So the four descended, and a brisk scrimmage ensued, which resulted in the complete rout of the invaders and the capture of their football.

With which tremendous prize the victorious army returned to quarters and continued their discussion on moral reform.

"Yes, as I was saying, we shall have to stick to it a bit. But young Stratton'll make it worth our while, I fancy."

This hidden allusion to the tea and cake completed the speaker's argument, and the party forthwith sat down with one ink-pot among them for preparation.

As it happened, the preparation for the day was an English Essay on "Your favourite Animal," with special attention to the spelling and the stops.

It was always a sore point with the Classic juniors to be set an English lesson. They could understand being taught Latin, but they considered they ought to be exempt from writing and spelling their own language. It wasn't Classics, and they didn't like it, and they oughtn't to be let in for it. However, it was no use growling; and as the subject (apart from the spelling and points) was a congenial one, it seemed a fair opening for the commencement of their reformed career.

"Look here," said Wally, "don't let's all have the same beast. I'm going to have a dog."

"Oh, I wanted a dog," said Fisher minor.

"Can't; he's bagged. Have a cat?"

"No, I don't like cats—can't I write about a dog too?"

"That would be rot. Haven't you got the whole of Noah's Ark to pick from—lions, tigers, ants, hippopotamuses, cobra de capellos?"

"How much?" asked D'Arcy. "Are they good to eat?"

"Uncommon good. Will you take cobra de capellos?"

"Ah right," said D'Arcy; "I don't mind."

"I shall take pigs," said Ashby.

"There you are," said Wally; "there's lots left. You have cows, kid—"

"No—if you won't let me have the dog—"

"Dog in the Wheatfield. Joke!—laugh, you chaps," interjected D'Arcy.

"I shall have rabbits," said Fisher minor.

"Good old rabbits! Did you ever keep any? What were their names?" said Wally.

"Don't you know?" said Ashby, solemnly. "One was called 'How' and the other 'Now,' weren't they, Fisher minor?"

Whereupon there was mirth at the expense of Fisher minor.

Silence having been procured, D'Arcy began to write.

"'Cobbrer de Capillars is my favrite—' What is it? Bird, beast, or fish, Wally?"

"Shut up; bird, of course."

"'Bird,'" continued the essayist. "'It was in Nore's arck and is good eating'—that's all I know about it. Tell us something more, Wally, there's a good chap."

"Oh, bother. Don't go disturbing, it spoils everything."

"'The cobberer oart not to be disterbd for it spoyls everything—it spoyls your close and—' wire in, Wally, what else does it do? You might tell a chap."

"What I'll do to you, you cad, and that's pull your nose if you don't shut up!" retorted Wally, who was busy over his own theme.

"'—and puis yore knows if yore a cad, and don't shut up.' There, bother it, that ought to do—twelve lines. Good enough for him."

"Stuck in the stops?" asked Ashby.

"No; by the way—glad you reminded me—I suppose about every four words, eh?"

"Something about that," said Ashby.

So D'Arcy sprinkled a few stops judiciously through his copy, and having done so began to upbraid his partners for their slowness.

Some time was lost in suppressing him, but he was eventually disposed of under the bath, which was turned upside down to accommodate him and sat upon by the other three, who were thus able to continue their work in peace.

Ashby was done first. He had a congenial subject and wrote *con amore*.

"I shall now say something about the pig which is my favourite annimal—The pig is a quadruped—Sometimes he is male in which case he is called a hog. Sometimes he is female in which case he is called a sow. Pigs were rings in their noses and are fond of apple-peal. Their young are called litter and are very untidy in their habbits. Pig's cheek is nice to eat and pork in season is a treat." (The writer was very proud of this little outbreak of poetry.)

"It is preferrablest roast with sage and apple sauce. I hope I have now described the pig and told you why he is my favourite."

Fisher minor, on the uncongenial topic of the rabbit, found composition difficult and punctuation impossible.

"I like rabbits next best to dogs which Wally has taken mine were black and white one was one and the other the other the white one died first of snuffles he had lobears the other had the same pequliarity and was swoped for 2 white mice who eskaped the first-night owing to the size of the bars there is a kind of rabbit called welsh rabbit that my father is fond of he says it goes best on toast but I give mine oats and bran it is a mistake for boys to keep rabbits because first they give them too much and burst them and then they give them too little and starve them which is not wright and makes the rabbit skinny to eat if a boy feeds rabbits well he can get his mother to give him half-a-crown a peace to make pies of them which is very agreeable so I therefore on this account consider rabbits favourites."

Before this conclusion had been reached, Wally, with a complacent smile, had laid down his pen, flattering himself he had made a real good thing of the dog. He scorned commonplace language, and, mindful of the eloquent periods of certain newspapers of his acquaintance, had "let out" considerably on his favourite theme, which, if the spelling and punctuation had been as good as the language, would have been a fine performance.

"The dog is the sublymest, gift of beficient nature to the zografical Speeches, He has been the confidenshul playmate of; man since before the creation, he is compounded of the most plezing trays and Generaly ansers to the endeering name of carlo? if you put his noes at the extremity of a rat-Hole he: will continue their ad libbitums till he has his man; In Barberous lands there is an exorable law ordayning muscles but It can be invaded by a little despeshun and sang frore, as one side of the streat is not unfrequentedly Outside the rools so that if you take him that side the politician cannot Run him in which is the wulgar for lagging him for not (waring Mussles I have) ockasionaly done bobys this Way myself so that I am convinzed of my voracity, the lesson we learn from this is that dogs should be treeted kindly and not Injected to unkind tretemant there? was Ice a dog with the pattrynamie of dognes who lived in a tub but; tubs are not helthy kenels because, they Roal when you dont stick brix under, which teechus to be kind 'to our' fello animals and pleze Our masters—I will. Only include by adding that dogs like cake? which Shoes how like they are to boys who have kind masters that they strive to pleas in ewery way in Their incapacity as the righter of this esay strives ever to endevor."

"That ought to fetch him," said the delighted author, as he dotted his last "i," and released D'Arcy from under the bath. "Now I vote we stow it, and—"

Here there was a loud knock at the door and a senior's voice calling, "Open the door, you youngsters."

The intruder was Dangle, at sight of whom the backs of our four heroes went up.

"What do you youngsters mean by bagging one of our balls!" said the Modern senior. "Give it me directly."

"It doesn't belong to you," said Wally; "it's my young brother's."

"Do you hear?—give it to me," said Dangle. "He can fetch it if he wants it. You're not our prefect," retorted Wally.

None of the four were more astounded than Wally himself at the audacity of this speech. It must have been due to the exhilarating effect of his tea and essay combined.

Dangle was evidently unprepared for defiance of this sort and became threatening.

"If you don't give me that ball at once, I'll give the lot of you the best hiding you ever had in your lives."

"Try it. We're not going to give up the ball. There! If Percy wants it, let him come for it. Back up, you chaps."

In a tussle between one big boy and four small ones, the odds are usually in favour of the former, but Dangle on the present occasion did not find his task quite as easy as he expected. The juniors defended themselves with great tenacity, and although the senior's blows came home pretty hard, he could only deal with them one at a time. It got to be a little humiliating to discover that he would have to fight hard to gain his end, and his temper evaporated rapidly.

Seizing his opportunity, when Fisher minor, who had been fighting perhaps the least steadily of the four—yet doggedly enough—was within reach, he struck out at him wildly, determined to get him disposed of first. It was a cruel blow even for a fellow in Dangle's plight. The small boy recoiled half-stunned, and uttered a yell which for an instant startled the bully.

Before Dangle had time to recover, the three survivors were upon him tooth and nail; at the same moment the door opened again, and Rollitt, of all persons, stood in the room.

He took in the situation at a glance—the big boy white with rage, his three assailants with heads down and lips tight, pounding away, and Fisher minor leaning against the wall with his handkerchief to his face.

"Stop!" said he in a voice which suspended hostilities at once. Then turning to Dangle he said—

"Get out."

Dangle glared defiantly, and remained where he was, whereupon Rollitt, without another word, lifted him in his arms like a child, and slinging him across his shoulders marched forth.

Wakefield's boys were just trooping up the staircase from the fields, and at this strange apparition stood still and made a lane for it to pass. Dangle's struggles were futile. The giant, if he was aware of them, heeded them no more than the kicking of a kitten, and proceeded deliberately down the stairs, past everybody, juniors, middle-boys, prefects and all, and walked with his burden out at the door. There every one expected the scene would end.

But no. He walked on sedately across the Green. Indifferent as to who saw him or what they said, until he came to the door of Forder's house, where he entered. Up the stairs he stumped amid gaping juniors and menacing middle, boys until he reached his captive's study; where without ceremony he deposited him, and, not vouchsafing a word, turned on his heel.

Strangely enough, no one had the presence of mind to challenge him or demand reparation for the insult to their house. He neither dawdled nor hurried.

At the door a bodyguard of Classics had assembled to meet him and escort him back. But he had no need of their services. He made his way through them as coolly as if he was coming from class; and utterly indifferent to the rising clamour and shouts behind him—for the Moderns had by this time recovered breath enough to use their tongues—reached Wakefield's, where without a word to any one he proceeded to his own study and shut himself in to continue the scientific experiments which had only been interrupted a few minutes before by the sudden cry of distress from the one boy in Fellsgarth to whom he owed the least obligation.

Chapter Ten
How Percy got back his Football

It was not to be expected that in the present state of party feeling at Fellsgarth the incident recorded in the last chapter would be confined to a personal quarrel between Dangle and Rollitt.

If it be true that it takes two to make a quarrel, there was not much to be feared in the latter respect. For Rollitt was apparently unaware that he had done anything calling for general remark, and went his ways with his customary indifference.

When Dangle, egged on by the indignation of his friends, had gone across to find him and demand satisfaction, Rollitt had told him to call again to-morrow, as he was busy.

Dangle therefore called again.

"I've come to ask if you mean to apologise for what you did the other day? If you don't—"

"Get out!" said Rollitt, going on with his work.

"—If you don't," continued Dangle, "you'll have to take the consequences."

"Get out!"

"If you funk it, Rollitt, you'd better say so."

"Get out," said Rollitt, rising slowly to his feet.

Dangle reported, when he got back to his house, that argument had been hopeless. Yet he meant to take it out of his adversary some other way.

But if the principals in the quarrel were inactive, their adherents on either side took care to keep up the feud.

The Modern juniors especially, who felt very sore at the indignity put upon their house, took up the cudgels very fiercely. Secretly they admitted that Dangle had cut rather a poor figure, and that they could have made a much better job over the impounded football than he had by his interference.

But that had nothing to do with the conduct of the enemy, whom they took every opportunity of defying and deriding.

"There go the sneaks," shouted Lickford, as the four Classic juniors paraded arm in arm across the Green. "Who got licked by our chap and had to squeal for a prefect to come and help them? Oh my—waterspouts!"

"Ya—*how now*—*oh no, not me!*" Percy shouted for the special benefit of Fisher minor.

"Look at them! They daren't come our side. Cowards!—daren't come on to our side of the path," chimed in Cash.

"Look at their short legs," called Ramshaw; "only useful for cutting away when they see a Modern."

"Who got licked on the hands for cheating at Elections, and blubbed like anything!" put in Cottle.

The four heroes walked on, hearing every word and trying to appear as if they did not. They spoke to one another with forced voices and mechanical smiles, and did their best not to be self-conscious in the matter of their legs.

But as the defiance grew bolder in proportion as they walked further, Wally said—

"I say, this is a drop too much. We can't stand this, eh?"

"No; the cads!" chimed in the other three.

"Tell you what," said Wally, "it wouldn't be a bad joke to have a punt-about with their football right under their noses, would it?"

"How if they bag it?"

"Bother!—we must chance that."

"I say," said Ashby, "if we could bag their boots first!"

"Can't do that; but we might wait till they're in their class after breakfast in the morning. They go in half an hour before us. I know, they all sit near the window, and are squinting out at everybody that passes. Won't they squirm?"

Next morning therefore at early school, as Percy and Company sat huddled at their desks in the Modern class-room, biting their pens, groaning over their sums, and gazing dismally from the window all at the same time, they had the unspeakable anguish of beholding Wally, D'Arcy, Ashby, and Fisher minor, with *their* ball, having a ding-dong game of punt-about on the sacred Modern grass, under their very eyes.

How these four enjoyed themselves and kicked about the ball, nodding and kissing their hands all the while at the mortified enemy, who sat like caged beasts glaring at them through their bars, and gnawing their fingers in impotent fury!

Sometimes, to add a little relish to the sport, they invited a passing prefect of their own house to give the ball a punt, and once a neat drop-kick from D'Arcy left a muddy splotch on the face of the sundial above border's door.

This was too much; and when, a few minutes later, they caught sight of the marauders waving to them and calling attention by pantomimic gesture to the fact that they were carrying off the ball once more to their own quarters, Percy could contain himself no longer.

"Beasts!" he ejaculated.

"Wheatfield," said Mr Forder, who was in charge of the class, "write me out fifty lines of the *Paradise Lost* and a letter of apology in Latin for using bad language in class."

Percy was conducted home by his friends that morning in a critical state. He felt it necessary to kick somebody, and therefore kicked them; and they, entirely misunderstanding his motives, kicked back. Consequently, a good deal of time was occupied in arranging matters all round on a comfortable footing; by the end of which time the fraternity, though marred in visage, felt generally easier in its mind.

It was no use appealing to the Modern prefects. They had made a mess of it so far, and weren't to be trusted. Nor did the course of lodging a complaint with Yorke commend itself to the company. It might be mistaken for telling tales. How would it do to—

Here entered Robert, the school porter, with a letter addressed "Wheatfield minor, Mr Forder's," in a scholarly hand.

"Wheatfield minor," snarled Percy; "that's not me, Bob. What do you take me for! Here, take it over to Wakefield's, and look about for the dirtiest, ugliest, beastliest kid you can see. That's Wheatfield minor."

"You'll be sore to know him by his likeness to Percy," added Cash, by way of encouragement.

"But Wakefield's ain't Forder's," observed the sage Robert. "Look what the envelope says."

True; it must be meant for Percy after all.

"You go and tell him it's like his howling cheek to call me minor, whoever it is; and when I catch him I'll welt him. Do you hear?"

"Very good, sir, I'll tell him," said the porter with a grin.

Meanwhile Percy had opened the letter and caught sight of the signature.

He uttered a whistle of amazement.

"Hullo!" he cried, "it's from Stratton! Whatever—Oh, I say, Bob, it doesn't matter about that message; do you hear!"

"Won't be no trouble, sir," said the porter.

"If I want to give it I'll do it myself," said Percy.

"Whatever's it about?" said his friends.

"Dear Wheatfield minor,"—(cheek!) read Percy, "Mrs Stratton and I will be glad to see you and three or four of your friends to tea this evening at six. I will arrange with Mr Forder to give you exeats from preparation."

"Humph!" grunted Percy—"rather civil—I hear he gives rather good grub. I vote we go."

"May as well. It gets us off preparation too," said Cash.

"Who said *you* were in it?" replied Percy. "Catch me taking you unless you behave. I've a good mind to take Clapperton and Brinkman and Dangle and Fullerton."

This threat reduced the clan to obedience at once, and Percy sat down presently, and wrote in his most admired style—

"Wheatfield major," (the "major" was heavily underlined) "is much obliged to Mr Stratton for his invitation to him to tea in his room, and he will be glad to bring the following of his friends, if he has no objection, with him; viz. Lickford, Ramshaw, Cash, and Cottle. With kind regards from P.W.;" and sent the note over by the hand of the youngest of the Modern juniors.

This diversion served for a time to heal the mental ravages of the morning, and to occupy the attention of the company most of the afternoon.

"Case of Sunday-go-to-meeting, isn't it?" said lickford.

"Rather. Mind you tog up well, you chaps; I'm not going to take four louts out to tea with me, I promise you."

Whereupon ensued great searchings of hearts and wardrobes, to see what could be done in the way of appropriate decoration. The invitation came at an awkward time, for it was Friday afternoon, and Mrs Wisdom rarely sent home the washing before Saturday. Consequently it was a work of some difficulty to muster five clean collars among the party, still less as many shirt-fronts.

Lickford spent at least an hour over his last Sunday's shirt with ink-eraser, trying to get it to look tidy; while Cottle, more ingenious, neatly gummed pieces of white paper over the dirty spots on his.

A great discussion took place as to chokers. Percy, who had one, threatened to leave behind any one not similarly adorned. It was only by adroit cajolery, and persuading him that he, as personal conductor of the party, had a right to be sweller than the rest, that he could be induced to waive the point.

The same argument had to be urged with regard to boots, as none of the others had patent leathers, which Percy insisted was the first thing any one looked to see if you had on at a party. It was urged that as most of the time would be spent with the feet under the table, this, though sound in law, was not in the present case of such vital importance in equity. Objection waived once more.

Finally, when all was ready, Percy held a full-dress parade of his forces, and looked each of them up and down as minutely and critically as an officer of the Guards inspecting his company. He objected to Cash wearing white gloves, as he had none himself, and he nearly cashiered Cottle for having a coloured handkerchief, because he himself had a brand-new white one. At length, however, all these little details were arranged, and as the school clock began to chime the hour the order to march was given, and the company proceeded at the double to Mr Stratton's house.

Mr Stratton was more or less of a favourite with both sides at Fellsgarth. He had a small house, in which were representatives of both factions, but most of them of the quieter sort, who, being obliged to live together under one roof, did not see so much to quarrel about out of doors. Mr Stratton, too, took the juniors' divisions of each school, and so kept fairly well in touch with both. Add to this, that he was a good all round athlete, that he had a serene and cheerful temper, and, what is of scarcely less importance, a charming young wife, and you have several very good reasons why he was one of the most popular masters at Fellsgarth. The juniors, on the whole, appreciated him. When he was down on them they forgave him on account of his youth, and when he complained that he could not get them to understand his precepts, they asked one another whose fault was that. Occasionally he condoned all his offences by an act of hospitality, and for once in a way betrayed that he recognised the merits of a select few of his pupils by asking them to tea.

This was evidently the ease now, and as our five young Moderns trotted across the Green, they wished their enemies in Wakefield's could only have looked out and witnessed their triumph.

Little they dreamed that at that moment Wally, Ashby, D'Arcy, and Fisher minor, resplendent in shirts and collars fresh from the wash, with their eight hands encased in white kid and their eight feet in patent leather, were standing about in Mr Stratton's drawing-room, wondering who on earth it was whose non-arrival was preventing the ringing of the tea-bell.

When presently Percy and his party were ushered in, and discovered who were their fellow-guests, it did some credit to their breeding that they remembered to go up and shake hands with Mr and Mrs Stratton, and did not immediately fly at the enemy's throat. The enemy, however, were equally taken aback, and were fully entitled to half the credit for the self-control with which the discovery was received.

"There's no need to introduce you to one another, I'm sure," said Mr Stratton. "By the way, Wheatfield—you I mean," pointing to Percy, "I must apologise for calling you minor. It was very kind of you to put me right."

Wally glared up at this, and would have liked to put the matter right there and then, but Mrs Stratton said—

"It isn't fair to number twins at all, is it?"

"Unless," suggested D'Arcy, blushing to find himself talking, "unless you reckon them half each."

This only mended matters to the extent of raising a laugh at the expense of the twins, who felt mutually uncomfortable.

The tea-bell, however, relieved the tension, "Come," said the hostess. "You must take one another in. No, that won't do, all Mr Wakefield's boys together. Two of you come this side—that's right; and Cottle and Ramshaw, you go over there. Now, you're beautifully sorted. Edward, dear, you mustn't talk till you've handed round the tea-cake to our guests. Lickford, do you take cream and sugar? And you too, twins? Oh really, dear, you don't call those slices, do you? Do let Ashby cut up the cake; I'm sure he knows better than you what a slice is; don't you, Ashby?"

Apparently Ashby did; and the party, thus genially thrown together and set to work, soon began, to experience the balmy influences of a convivial high tea.

Very little was spoken at first except by Mr Stratton, who gave a brief account of a University cricket match in which he had once played—a narrative which served as a most soothing refrain to the silent exercise in which his listeners were engaged. Presently a few questions were put in by the boys, followed by a few observations which gradually, by the adroit piloting of the host, loyally backed up by his wife, developed into a discussion on the use and abuse of "third man up" in modern cricket. After this knotty point was disposed of the talk grew more general, and Wally became aware that his brother was handing him the apricot jam.

The act, simple in itself, meant a great deal to Wally. He liked apricot jam, and had not been able to get at it all the evening. As he now helped himself he admitted to himself that Percy was not quite such a lout as he had occasionally thought him.

"Thanks awfully, Percy. Did you like that toffee I gave you the other day?"

"Rather. It was spiffing," said Percy. "I say, I don't mind writing home this week if you like."

"Oh, don't you grind; I will."

"Really I don't mind."

"No more do I. I say, can you reach the butter?"

"Rather. Better rinse this dish up here between us. There's another down there."

Similar scenes of reconciliation were taking place elsewhere. Cottle was asking Ashby his riddle; D'Arcy was laying down the law in the admiring hearing of Ramshaw and Lickford as to the cooking of sprats on the shovel; while Fisher minor was telling the sympathetic Mrs Stratton all about the people at home. Mr Stratton was wise enough not to disturb this state of affairs by talk of his own. When, however, the meal began to flag, and his guests one by one abandoned the attack, he proposed an adjournment to the drawing-room.

"I want the advice of you youngsters," said he presently, "about something I dare say you all know something about. I mean the old School shop."

The party looked guilty. Didn't they know the tuck-shop?

"It seems to me," said Mr Stratton, "it's rather in a bad way just now; don't you think so? Robert hasn't time to look after it, and wants to give it up. He says it doesn't pay; and really some of his things aren't particularly nice. I went and had a jam tart there this morning. It was like shoe-leather; and the jam was almost invisible."

Wally laughed. He knew those tarts well.

"I think it would be a pity if it was given up; don't you? We all want a little grub now and then; besides, it's an old School institution."

"Robert charges three-halfpence a-piece for those tarts," said D'Arcy.

"Yes—think of that. I've no doubt you could get them for half the price at Penchurch. What I was thinking was, why shouldn't some of us carry on the shop ourselves?"

The boys opened their eyes. The idea of carrying on a tuck-shop on their own account opened a vista of such endless possibilities, that they were quite startled.

"It ought to be easy enough if we manage properly," said Mr Stratton. "Suppose, now, we who are here were to form a committee and decide to run the shop, how should we begin?"

"It depends on what Robert left behind," said Percy.

"Oh, we wouldn't take over any of his stuff. No, the first thing would be to reckon up how much we should want to start with, and either club together or get some one to advance it. How many tarts do you suppose are sold a day?"

"Hundreds," said Ashby.

"Well, according to Robert, about eighty. But say one hundred. That at a penny each would be about 8 shillings for tarts. Then the ginger-beer. Would twenty bottles do? That would be 3 shillings 4 pence, supposing they cost 2 pence each. That's 11 shillings 4 pence. What next? Apples? Suppose we put them down at 2 shillings 6 pence—13 shillings 10 pence. Sweets? Well, say 2 shillings 6 pence more—16 shillings 4 pence. Nuts 1 shilling—17 shillings 4 pence. It mounts up, you see. We ought at least to have 25 or 30 shillings to start with. Well, I happen to know somebody who would lend that amount to the shareholders for a little time if we should want it. Now suppose we've got our money. We ought to send to some of the best shops and market people in the town to see what we could get our things for. As it happens, Mrs Stratton when she was in Penchurch this morning did inquire, and this is her report. The tarts that we should sell for a penny we could get for three farthings each, so that on a hundred tarts we should make a profit of 2 shillings 1 penny. And the confectioner would send his cart up every day with fresh tarts of different kinds of jam, and take back yesterday's stale ones at half-price. That would be a great improvement, wouldn't it?"

"Rather," said everybody.

"Then the ginger-beer. Would you believe it, if we undertake to take not less than twelve bottles a day daring the half we can get them for a penny each, and might sell them for three-halfpence. That would make a great increase in the demand, I fancy, and every bottle we can sell, we make a dear halfpenny profit. The same with the sweets. You can get most sorts for 9 or 10 pence a pound, and if we sell at a penny an ounce, you see we get 7 or 8 pence profit. I should vote for only getting the best kind of sweets, and making rather less profit than that. At any rate, you see, if we are careful, we ought pretty soon to be able to pay back what we owe, and after providing for the expense of a person to mind the shop and do the selling, put by a little week by week, which will go to the School clubs or anything else the fellows decide. What do you think of the plan?"

They all thought it would be magnificent.

"I see no reason why you youngsters should not manage it splendidly by yourselves at soon as you get once started. You'll have to draw up strict rules, of course, for managing the shop, and make up the accounts; and look out sharp that you aren't selling anything at a loss. Remember, the cheaper you can sell (provided you get a fair profit), the more customers you'll have. And the better your stuff is, the more it will be liked. Mrs Stratton says she will act as banker, and take care of the money at the end of each day and pay out what you want for stores. Don't say anything about it out of doors at present; talk it over among yourselves daring the week, and if you think it will work, tell me, and we'll have a regular business meeting to settle preliminaries. Now suppose we have a game of crambo?"

When the party broke up, Moderns and Classics strolled affectionately across the Green arm in arm, deep in confabulation as to the projected shop.

When they reached the door of Wakefield's, Wally said, "By the way, have any of you chaps lost a football? There's one kicking about in our room. Hang outside and I'll chuck it to you out of the window."

Which he did. And the ball proved to be the very one the Moderns had lost a week ago! How curious!

Chapter Eleven
Fellsgarth versus Rendlesham

How it came that Rollitt played, after all, in the Rendlesham match, no one could properly understand.

His name was not down on the original list. Yorke *had* given up asking him to play, as he always either excused himself, or, what was worse, promised to come and failed at the last moment.

After the defeat of the Moderns at the second election, the question of the selection of the fifteen had been allowed to drop; and those who were keen on victory hoped no further difficulty would arise. Two days before the match, however, Brinkman was unlucky enough to hurt his foot, and to his great mortification was forbidden by the doctor to play. The news of his accident caused general consternation, as he was known to be a good forward and a useful man in a scrimmage. Clapperton increased the difficulty by coming over to say that as Brinkman was laid up, he had arranged for Corder to play instead.

Corder, as it happened, was a Modern senior, a small fellow, and reputed an indifferent player.

"He wouldn't do at all," said Yorke, decisively.

"Why not? Surely we've got a right to find a substitute for our own man," said Clapperton, testily.

"What do you mean by your own man? Who cares twopence whose man he is, as long as he plays up? The fifteen are Fellsgarth men, and no more yours than they are mine."

"If they were as much mine as yours no one would complain."

"You mean to say that if you were captain of the fifteen you'd put Corder in the team for a first-class match?"

"Why not? There are plenty worse than he."

"There are so many better, that he is out of the question."

"That means only five of our men are to play against ten of yours."

"You're talking rot, Clapperton, and you know it. If I'm captain, I'll choose my own team. If you don't like it, or if the best fifteen men in the school aren't in it, you are welcome to complain. I hope you will."

"It strikes me pretty forcibly our fellows won't fancy being snubbed like this. It would be a bad job if they showed as much on the day of the match."

"It would be a bad job—for them," said the captain.

When Yorke repeated this disagreeable conversation to his friends later on, they pulled long faces.

"I suppose he means they don't intend to play up," said Dalton.

"If that's so," said Fisher major, "why not cut them all out and make up the fifteen of fellows you can depend on?"

"That wouldn't do," said Yorke. "I expect when the time comes they'll play up all right. After all, Clapperton and Fullerton are two of our best men."

"But what about the vacant place?"

"I've four or five names all better than Corder," said the captain, "but none of them as good as Brinkman."

The company generally, it is to be feared, did not lament as honestly as Yorke did, the accident to their rival. They did not profess to rejoice, of course; still they bore the blow with equanimity.

Next morning, to the astonishment of everybody, the notice board contained an abrupt announcement in the captain's hand, that in consequence of Brinkman's inability to play, Rollitt would take his place in the fifteen.

Yorke himself could not account for this sudden act of patriotism. Rollitt, he said, had looked into his room last night at bedtime and said—

"I'll play on Saturday," and vanished.

Fisher minor was perhaps, of all persons, better able to explain the mystery than any one else. He had overheard in Ranger's study a general lamentation about the prospects for Saturday, and a wish expressed by his brother that Rollitt were not so unsociable and undependable. Everybody agreed it was utterly useless to ask him to play, and that they would have to get a second-rate man to fill the empty place, and so most probably lose the match.

Fisher minor heard all this, and when presently, on his way to his own den, he passed Rollitt's door, a tremendous resolution seized him to take upon himself the duty of ambassador extraordinary for the School. Rollitt appeared to owe him no grudge for throwing stones the other day, and had already come to his relief handsomely at the time of the second election and in the affair with Dangle. On the whole, Fisher minor thought he might venture.

Rollitt was reading hard by the light of one small candle when he entered.

"Please, Rollitt," said the boy, "would you ever mind playing for the School on Saturday?"

Rollitt looked up in such evident alarm that Fisher major put his hand on the latch of the door, and made ready to bolt.

"I'll see—get out," said Rollitt.

And Fisher minor did get out.

It was really too absurd to suppose that Rollitt was going to play in the fifteen to oblige Fisher minor. So at least thought that young gentleman, and remained discreetly silent about his interview, hoping devoutly no one would hear of it.

The joy of the Classics was almost equal to the fury of the Moderns. The latter could not deny that Rollitt was a host in himself, and worth a dozen Corders. Yet it galled them to see him quietly put in the vacant place, and to hear the jubilation on every hand.

For Rollitt was the fellow who had publicly insulted the Moderns in the person of Dangle; and not only that, but—poor and shabby as he was—had shown himself utterly indifferent to their indignation and contemptuous of their threats.

"Why," Dangle said, "the fellow's a pauper! he can't even pay for his clubs! His father's a common fellow, I'm told."

"Yes, and I heard," said Brinkman, "his fees up here are paid for him. Why, we might just as well have Bob in the fifteen."

"A jolly sight better. Bob knows how to be civil."

"It is a crime to be poor," said Fullerton. "I hope I shall never commit it."

"Well," said Clapperton, ignoring this bit of sarcasm, "if he was well enough off to buy a cake of soap once a term, it wouldn't be so bad. I believe when he wants a wash he goes down to Mrs Wisdom and borrows a bit of hers."

"By the way, that reminds me," said Dangle; "did you fellows ever hear about Mrs Wisdom's boat? The lout had it out the other day in the rapids, and let it go over the falls, and it got smashed up."

"What!" exclaimed everybody.

"Do you mean," said Brinkman, "poor Widow Wisdom has lost her boat owing to that cad? Why, she'll be ruined? However is she to get a new one?"

"That's the extraordinary thing," said Dangle. "It was she told me about it. She says that Rollitt went straight away to the lake and bought her a boat that was for sale there; and she's got it now down in the lower reach; and it's a better one than the other."

"What!" exclaimed Clapperton, incredulously; "Rollitt bought a new boat! Bosh!"

"It was a second-hand one for sale cheap. But it cost five pounds. She showed me the receipt."

"Stuff and nonsense. She was gammoning you," said Clapperton.

"All right," said Dangle, snappishly; "you're not obliged to believe it unless you like."

And there the conversation ended.

The day of the great match came at last. The Rendlesham men, who had to come from a distance, were not due till one o'clock, and, as may be imagined, the interval was peculiarly trying to some of the inhabitants of Fellsgarth. The farce of morning school was an ordeal alike to masters and boys. If gazing up at the clouds could bring down the rain, a deluge should have fallen before 10 a.m. As the hour approached the impatience rose to fever heat. It was the first match of the season. For the last three years the two teams had met in deadly combat, and each time the match had ended in a draw, with not one goal kicked on either side. Victory or defeat to-day would be a crisis in the history of Fellsgarth. Woe betide the man who missed a point or blundered a kick!

Percy and his friends put on flannels in honour of the occasion and sallied out an hour before the time to look at the ground and inspect the new goal and flag posts which Fisher major, as the first act of his treasurership, had ordered for the School.

It disgusted them somewhat to find that Wally and his friends—also in flannels—were on the spot before them, and, having surveyed the new acquisitions, had calmly bagged the four front central seats in the pavilion reserved by courtesy for the head-master and his ladies.

Since the tea at Mr Stratton's, the juniors had abated somewhat of their immemorial feud, although the relations were still occasionally subject to tension.

"Hullo, you kids," cried Wally, as his brother approached, "how do you do? Pretty well this morning? That's right—so are we. Have a seat? Plenty of room in the second row."

Considering that no one had yet put in an appearance, this was strictly correct. Yet it did not please the Modern juniors.

"You'll get jolly well turned out when Ringwood comes," said Percy. "Come on, you chaps," added he to his own friends. "What's the use of sitting on a bench like schoolboys an hour before the time? Let's have a trot."

"Mind you don't dirty your white bags," cried D'Arcy.

"No, we might be mistaken for Classic kids if we did," shouted Cottle. "Ha, ha!"

Whereupon, and not before time, the friends parted for a while.

When Percy and Co. returned, they found the pavilion was filling up, and, greatly to their delight, the front row was empty. The enemy had been cleared out; and serve them right.

"Come on, you chaps," said Lickford; "don't let's get stuck in there. Come over to the oak tree, and get up there. It's the best view in the field."

Alas! when they got to the oak tree, four friendly voices hailed them from among the leaves.

"How are you, Modern kids? There's a ripping view up here. Have an acorn? Mind your eye. Sorry we're full up. Plenty of room up the poplar tree."

The Moderns scorned to reply, and walked back sulkily to the pavilion, not without parting greetings from their friends up the oak tree, and squatted themselves on the steps.

The place was filling up now. Mrs Stratton was there with some visitors. All the little Wakefields were there, of course—"minor, minimus, and minimissima," as they were called—uttering war-whoops in honour of their house. And there was a knot of Rendlesham fellows talking among themselves and generally taking stock of the Fellsgarth form. Mr Stratton, in civilian dress, as became the umpire, was the first representative of the School to show up on the grass. A distant cheer from the top of the oak tree hailed his arrival, and louder cheers still from the steps of the pavilion indicated that the popular master was not the private property of any faction in Fellsgarth.

To Fisher minor it was amazing how Mr Stratton could talk and laugh as pleasantly as he did with the umpire for the other side. He felt sure *he* could not have done it himself.

Suddenly it occurred to Fisher minor, by what connection of ideas he could not tell, what an awful thing it would be if Rollitt were to forget about the match. The horror of the idea, which had all the weight of a presentiment, sent the colour from his cheeks, and without a word to anybody he slid down the tree and began to run with all his might towards the school.

"What's the row—collywobbles!" asked D'Arcy.

But no one was in a position to answer. A fusillade of acorns from the tree, and derisive compliments of "Well run!" "Bravo, Short-legs!" from the pavilion steps, greeted the runner as he passed that warm corner. He didn't care. Even the captain and his own brother, whom he met going down to the field of battle, did not divert him. He rushed panting up the stairs and into Rollitt's study.

Rollitt was sitting at the table taking observations of a crumb of bread through a microscope.

"Rollitt," gasped the boy, "the match! It's just beginning, and you promised to play. Do come, or we shall be licked!"

Rollitt took a further look at the crumb and then got up.

"I forgot," said he; "come on, Fisher minor."

"Aren't you going to put on flannels?" asked the boy.

"Why!" said Rollitt roughly, stalking out.

Fisher minor wondered if the reason was that he had none. But he was too full of his mission to trouble about that, and, keeping his prize well in sight, for fear he should go astray, had the satisfaction of seeing him arrive on the field of battle just as the opposing forces were taking their places, and just as the Classic seniors were inwardly calling themselves fools for having depended for a moment on a hopeless fellow of this sort.

The Classic juniors felt a good deal compromised by the champion's shabby cloth trousers and flannel shirt, but they cheered lustily all the same, while the Moderns, having expressed their indignation to one another, relieved their feelings by laughing.

But a moment after, everybody forgot everything but the match.

The Rendlesham men looked very trim and dangerous in their black and white uniform; and when presently their captain led off with a magnificent place-kick which flew almost into the School lines, Classics and

Moderns forgot their differences and squirmed with a common foreboding. Fullerton promptly returned the ball into *medias res*, and the usual inaugural scrimmage ensued. To the knowing ones, who judged from little things, it seemed that the present match was likely to be as even as any of its predecessors. The forwards were about equally weighted, and the quarter and half-backs who hovered outside seemed equally alert and light-footed.

Presently the ball squeezed out on the School side and gave Ranger the first chance of a run. He used it well, and with Fisher major and Yorke on his flanks got well past the Rendlesham forwards amid loud cheers from the oak tree. But the enemy's quarter-back pinned him in a moment; yet not before he had passed the ball neatly to Fisher on his left. Fisher struggled on a few yards further with the captain and Dangle backing up, but had to relinquish the ball to the former before he could reach the half-backs. Yorke, always wary and cool-headed, had measured the forces against him, and as soon as he had the ball, ran back a step or two, to break the ugly rush of two of the enemy who were nearest, and then with a sweep distanced them, and charging through their half-backs made a dash for the goal. For a moment friend and foe held their breath. He looked like doing it. But in his *détour* he had given time for Blackstone, the Rendlesham fast runner, to get under way and sweep down to meet him just as he reeled out of the clutches of the half-backs. Next moment Yorke was down, and Dangle was not there to pick up the ball.

This rush served pretty well to exhibit the strong and weak points of either side. It was evident, for instance, that both Ranger and Yorke were men to be marked by the other side, and that Dangle, on the contrary, was playing slack.

A series of scrimmages followed, in the midst of which the ball gravitated back to the centre of the field. Runs were attempted on either side; once or twice the ball went out into touch, and once or twice a drop-kick sent it flying over the forwards' heads. But it came back inevitably, so that after twenty minutes' hard play it lay in almost the identical spot from which it had first been kicked off.

The onlookers began to feel a little depressed. It was not to be a walk-over for the School, at any rate. Indeed, it seemed doubtful whether from the last and toughest of these scrimmages the ball would ever emerge again to the light of day.

Suddenly, however; it become evident that the *status quo* was about to give way, and that the fortunes of either side were going to take a new turn. No one in the game, still less outside, could at first tell what had happened. Then it occurred to Yorke and one or two others that Rollitt, who had hitherto been playing listlessly and sleepily, was waking up. His head, high above his fellows, was seen violently agitated in the middle of the scrimmage, and presently it struggled forward till it came to where the ball lay. A moment later, the Rendlesham side of the scrimmage showed signs of breaking, and a moment after that Rollitt, quickly picking up the ball, burst through both friend and foe.

"Back up, Dangle! back up, Ranger!" shouted Yorke.

"Look out behind!" cried the Rendlesham captain.

Rollitt carried that ball pretty much as he had carried Dangle a day or two before, almost contemptuously, indifferent as to who opposed him or who got in his way. The only difference was that whereas he then walked, now he ran. And when Rollitt chose to run, as Fellsgarth knew, even Ranger, the swift-footed, was not in it.

The enemy's forwards were shaken off, and their quarter-backs distanced. The half-backs closed on him with a simultaneous charge that made him reel. But he kept his feet better than they, and staggered on with one of them hanging to his arm.

"Look out in goal!" shouted the Rendlesham men.

"Back up, you fellows!" cried Yorke.

In his struggle with the man on his arm, Rollitt lost pace enough to enable Blackstone to overtake and make a wild dash, not at the man, but the ball. The onslaught was partly successful, for the ball fell. Dangle, who was close behind, made an attempt to pick it up, but before he could do so, Rollitt, like a hound momentarily checked, dashed back to recover it himself, knocking over, as he did so, both Dangle and Blackstone.

He had it again, and once more was off, this time with only the enemy's back to intercept him. The back did his best, and sacrificed himself nobly for his side, but he was no match for the Fellsgarth giant, who simply rode over him, and followed by a mighty roar of cheering from the onlookers, carried the ball behind the goals, touching it down with almost fastidious precision exactly half-way between the poles.

A minute later and Yorke, with one of his beautifully neat "places," had sent the ball spinning over the bar, as unmistakable a goal as the School had ever kicked.

The cheers which followed this exploit were completely lost on Rollitt, who, having completed his run, dawdled back to his fellow-forwards, and had not even the curiosity to watch the issue of the captain's kick.

As the sides changed ends, Dangle, with a black face, came up to him.

"You knocked me over on purpose then, you cad, I could see it!" snarled he.

"Get out!" said Rollitt, shouldering the speaker aside.

This was too much for Dangle. Full of rage, he went to Yorke.

"I don't mean to stand this, Yorke. Rollitt—"

"Shut up!" said the captain. "Spread out, you fellows, and be ready. Go to your place, Dangle."

Dangle sullenly obeyed.

"I'll let you see if I'm to be insulted and made a fool of before all the school," growled he. "Catch me bothering myself any more."

As if to give him an opportunity of enforcing his protest, the kick-off of the losing side fell close at his feet. He picked it up, and for a moment the sporting instinct prompted him to make a rush. But he caught sight of Yorke and Rollitt both looking his way, and the bad blood in him prevailed. He deliberately sent the ball with a little side-kick into Blackstone's hands, who, running forward a step, sent it, with a mighty drop, right over the School line. It almost grazed the goal post as it passed, and it was all Fullerton could do to save the touch-down before the whole advance guard of the enemy were upon him.

The whole thing had been so wilfully done that there was no mistaking its meaning.

"Hold the ball!" cried Yorke, as the side ranged out for the kick-off. "Dangle, get off the field."

"What do you mean?" said Dangle, very white.

"What I say. You'll either do that or be kicked off."

Here Clapperton interposed.

"Don't go, Dangle; he's no right to turn you off or talk to you like that before the field because of an accident. If you go, I'll go too."

"Go, both of you, then," said Yorke.

The two Modern boys looked for a moment as though they doubted their own ears. What could Yorke mean, in the middle of a critical match like this?

He evidently meant what he said.

"Are you going or not?" said he.

It was a choice of evils. To play now would be to surrender. To stay where they were would render them liable to a kicking in the presence of all Fellsgarth. They sullenly turned on their heels and walked behind the goals. Most of the spectators supposed it was a case of sprained ankle or some such damage received in the cause of the School. But the acute little birds who sat in the oak tree were not to be deceived, and took good care to point the moral of the incident for the public benefit.

"Whiroo! Cads! Kicked out! Serve 'em right! Good riddance! Play up, you chaps!"

The chaps needed no encouragement. With two men short it was next to impossible to add to their present advantage. But they contrived to stand their ground and save the School goal. And when at last the welcome "No side" was called, the cheers which greeted them proclaimed that the School had won that day one of the biggest victories on its record.

Chapter Twelve
The Moderns on Strike

In the festivities with which the glorious victory of the School against Rendlesham was celebrated Yorke took no part.

The captain was very decidedly down in the mouth. This was the end of his endeavour to administer rule with a perfectly even hand, and give no ground for a whisper of anything like unfair play to the opposition! This was what his popularity and authority were valued at! For the first time in her annals, Fellsgarth fellows had mutinied on the field of battle and to their captain's face.

Had it been Dangle only, it would have mattered less. His feud with Rollitt was notorious, and would account for any ebullition of bad temper. But when Clapperton not only patronised the mutiny but joined in it, things were come to a crisis which it required all Yorke's courage and coolness to cope with.

It might have solaced him if he could have heard a discussion which was taking place in the rebels' quarters.

"It served them precious well right," said Clapperton, trying to justify what, to say the least of it, wanted some excuse. "We'd stood it long enough."

"It's bad enough," said Dangle, "to have the fifteen packed with Classic fellows; but when they take to attacking us before the whole field, it's time something was done. I'm as certain as possible that Rollitt deliberately knocked me over that time."

"It was rather warm measures, though," said Brinkman, "to walk off the field. We might have got licked."

"I'm not at all sure if it wouldn't have been a very good thing if we had," said Clapperton. "At any rate, it will be a lesson to them what it might come to."

"Nothing like scuttling a ship in mid-ocean if you want to be attended to. The only awkward thing is, you are apt to go down with it," said Fullerton.

"Do shut up, and don't try to be funny," said Clapperton. "Of course no one wants to wreck the clubs. We shall play up hard next time, and then they'll see it's worth their while to be civil to us."

"Yes," said Brinkman, "it won't do to let them say we aren't the friends of the School."

"There's not the least fear of any one thinking that now," gibed Fullerton.

"Well," said Dangle, "as we are to play the return with Rendlesham this day week, we shall have a chance of letting them see what we can do. Only if that cad Rollitt plays, it won't be easy to be civil."

These patriotic young gentlemen were a good deal disconcerted next morning to find that they had been reckoning without their host. The captain had posted up the fifteen to play next week. The list contained the names of Fullerton, Brinkman, and two others on the Modern side, but omitted those of Clapperton and Dangle.

In their wildest dreams the malcontents had never reckoned on the captain taking such a step as this. They knew that they were necessary to the efficiency of any team, and that without them, especially against Rendlesham, it would be almost a farce to go into the field at all.

At first they were disposed to laugh and sneer; then to bluster. Then it dawned on them gradually that for once in their lives they had made a mistake. They had not even the credit of refusing to play, but had been ignominiously kicked out.

A council of war was held, in which mutual recriminations, assisted by Fullerton's candid reflections on the situation, occupied a considerable share of the time.

The result of their deliberations was that Clapperton and Dangle went over in no very amiable frame of mind to the captain.

Yorke, as it happened, was having an uneasy conference with his own side at the time. Delighted as the Classics were at the blow which had been struck at the mutineers, the prospect of almost certain defeat next Saturday made them anxious for compromise.

"If I were you," said Fisher major, "I'd give them a chance of explaining and apologising."

"There can be no apology," said Yorke.

"You are quite right in theory," said Denton; "but wouldn't it be rather a crow for them to see that we are licked without them?"

"We mustn't be licked," said the captain. "We held our own without them yesterday."

"Yes; but we were on our own ground, and had a goal to the good before they struck."

"I think old Yorke is quite right," said Ranger. "We may be licked, and if we are they'll crow. On the other hand, if we let them play now they'll crow worse. I think we'd better be beaten by Rendlesham than by traitors."

"Shan't you let them play at all this half?" said Fisher.

"That depends on themselves," said Yorke.

"Hullo! here they come," said Ranger.

The two Moderns were a little disconcerted to find themselves confronted with the body of Classic seniors.

"Oh, you're engaged," said Clapperton; "we'll come again."

"No, we were talking about the team; I suppose that's what you've come about."

"Yes," said Clapperton; "we want to know what it means!"

"Really I don't see how it could have been put plainer. It means that the fifteen men named are going to play on Saturday."

"Look here, Yorke," said Clapperton, "if you think I've come over here to beg you to put Dangle and me into the team, you're mistaken—"

"I don't think it. You know it's impossible."

"All I can say is, it's sheer spite and nothing else. Dangle was deliberately knocked over by that cad Rollitt—"

"Who is not present, and may therefore be called names with safety," said Ranger.

"Shut up, Ranger, there's a good fellow," said the captain.

"And Dangle had a right to object," continued Clapperton.

"He had no right to play into the hands of the other side," said Yorke.

"How do you know I did?" said Dangle.

"Do you mean to say you didn't?" said Yorke.

"I didn't come here to be catechised by you. Are you going to put Clapperton and me in the fifteen or not? That's what we came to know."

"No—certainly not," said the captain; "and as that's all, you may as well go."

"Very well," sneered Clapperton, who was in a high temper, "you'll be sorry for it. Come on, Dangle."

"There's only one thing to be done now," said he, when they had got back to their own side; "we must none of us play. That will bring them to reason."

Brinkman approved of the idea.

"There's more sense in that," said he, "than you two sticking out. That will reduce the team to a Classic fifteen, and if they get licked it won't matter."

"There's no possible chance of their making up a fifteen without us?" asked Dangle.

"None at all. They haven't the men," said Clapperton, brightening up. "The fact is, we have them at our mercy; and if they want us to play again they'll have to ask us properly."

"Meanwhile Fellsgarth will get on splendidly," said Fullerton.

"Shut up. Don't you see it will be all the better for everybody in the long run?"

"I can't say I do at present. It may come by and by—"

"We must see that everybody backs up in this," said Brinkman. "One traitor would spoil everything."

"That's what Yorke said on Saturday, wasn't it?" asked Fullerton innocently, "At least, he said two traitors. Yorke will not see that what's right for one fellow is naughty for another."

"Look here, Fullerton," said Clapperton, who was sensitive enough to feel the sting of all this, "you don't suppose we're doing this for fun, do you? Will you promise not to play on Saturday, even if you are asked?"

"What if I don't?" said Fullerton.

"You won't find it particularly comfortable on this side of the School, that's all," said Brinkman.

Fullerton meditated and turned the matter over.

"I think on the whole," said he, mimicking Clapperton, "that as this is for the highest good of the School, and as everybody is to be all the better in the long run, and as we're all going to be noble and sacrifice ourselves together, you may put me down as not playing on Saturday. *Dulce et decorum est pro patriâ*—I beg pardon, I'm not on the Classic side yet."

The other players named on the list consented more or less reluctantly to follow the same example. After morning school, therefore, when the fellows looked at the notice board, they saw, to their bewilderment, the names of the four Modern fellows struck out and the following note appended to the captain's list—

"Notice.

"The following players protest against the exclusion of two names from the above list, and decline to play on Saturday, viz., Brinkman, Fullerton, Ramshaw major, and Smith."

Underneath this, a juvenile hand had carefully inscribed in bold characters—

"Jolly good riddance of bad rubbish." Signed, "Wheatfield, W., D'Arcy, Ashby, Fisher minor."

Fisher minor, who signed this latter manifesto by proxy had hastened to carry the news of it to his brother.

"The cads!" said the junior. "We are sure to be beaten; I shall never dare to get Rollitt twice running."

"What do you mean?" asked the elder brother, turning round.

"Oh, don't tell," said Fisher minor, "I didn't mean to say anything; you see, I thought he wouldn't fly out, so I asked him last time."

"You! What do you know of Rollitt? Why should he play to oblige you?"

Fisher minor, wishing he had not mentioned Rollitt's name, related, somewhat apologetically, the story of the adventure on the Shayle.

"Why," said the elder brother, "you saved his life, young 'un. No wonder he's civil to you!"

"Oh, please don't tell him I told you."

"All right; but what about the boat? It must have been smashed to bits. What did Mrs Wisdom say?"

"Oh, Rollitt was very honourable and bought her another. She told me so—and I've seen the new boat."

"Rollitt bought it! Why, he's as poor as a church mouse. How could he get the money, I'd like to know?"

"He got it the very next day," said Fisher minor. "I suppose he had some; but promise you won't say anything."

"What's the use of making a secret of it? I won't say anything unless you like. But I must go to Yorke."

The captain was quite prepared for the action of the Moderns.

"They've struck," said he. "Now the question is, shall we play on Saturday, or scratch the match?"

The unanimous verdict was in favour of playing, whatever the result.

"Of course we are never sure of Rollitt until we've got him," said he, "so we may have to play without him."

"Would Stratton play for us?" asked some one.

"No, don't let's go outside and ask masters. We're in for a licking; but we'll make the best fight we can."

So yet another notice appeared on the board before nightfall.

"The School team on Saturday will consist of the following." (Here followed the names, all, of course, on the Classical side.)

"A meeting of the clubs is summoned for October 3, at four p.m., in Hall."

Of these two announcements the first amused, the second perplexed the good young men of the Modern side. The new fifteen consisted half of raw outsiders who had never played in a first-class match before, and were utterly unknown to fame on the football field. But the summons for October 3 was puzzling. Did it mean a general row, or was the captain going to resign, or was an attempt to be made to expel the mutineers?

Clapperton did not like it. He had expected Yorke would have come to terms before now, and it disconcerted him to see that, on the contrary, the captain seemed determined to carry the thing through.

The only thing, of course, was for the Moderns to abstain in a body from the meeting. But could they depend on their forces to obey their leaders? It was all very well to compel four players to refuse to act; but to constrain 120 boys to do the same was a less easy task.

It seemed to Clapperton that he would do best to strike the iron while hot; and for that purpose he made a descent next morning into the quarters of his fag. If he could secure the juniors, it would be something.

He found Percy there alone, diligently working. That young gentleman had in fact been reminded in pretty forcible terms by Mr Forder that he had not yet handed in his Latin letter of apology ordered a week ago. Percy had hoped if he forgot it long enough Mr Forder would forget it too, and it had startled and grieved him very much to-day to receive notice that unless he brought his *poena* in an hour he would be sent up to the doctor.

Consequently, while his comrades were out enjoying themselves, he was here in a shocking bad temper, with a Latin Dictionary in front of him, trying to express his contrition for having used bad language in class a week ago.

He had got a little way. Latin prose for a Modern junior is a trifle thorny; but Percy had a rough and ready way with him which, if it did not emulate Cicero, at least made his meaning tolerably clear.

"Care Magistere Fordere, Ego sum excessivé tristis ut ego usebam malam linguam in classem alteram diem. Ego apologizo, et ego non facerebo illud iterum. Ego spero ut vos voluntas prodonnere," (it took him some time to arrive at this classical term for "you will forgive") "me hanc tempus."

This was all very well, but it only took up about six lines out of ten, and he was in despair how to continue. His ideas, his temper, and his Latin had all evaporated. When Clapperton entered, he did not even look up.

"Cut, whoever you are, and hang yourself," said he.

"Hullo, Percy! What's the row with you?"

"Don't talk to me," said Percy. "It's that beast Forder."

"Where are the others? I want to talk to you youngsters."

"How do I know where every ass in the place is? What do you want?"

The tone in which the inquiry was made was not encouraging.

"It's about the meeting next week. We don't mean to attend it."

"Don't you? Our lot does. We're going. Rather."

"It's a dodge of the other side. They're going to get the clubs into their own hands, and we've decided none of our fellows shall go. Then they can't do anything."

"Can't they? You don't know my young brother Wally as well as I do. He'll do something, bless you; but I rather fancy they won't have it all to themselves. *We'll* put a spoke in their wheels."

"Look here, young Wheatfield," said Clapperton, put out by the obtuseness of his fag, "the long and short of it is you're not to go. You know what's happened. Our side has been snubbed and cut out of the games by those fellows; and now they want to get us to come to their precious meeting to help them collar the clubs."

"That's just why I and my chaps are going to turn up," said Percy. "We'll let them know!"

"Do you hear what I say? You're not to go, you or any of them. If you can't understand the reason, I dare say you'll understand a thrashing. You'll get it unless you stand out like the rest of us."

"I say, what's the Latin for 'wrong,' Clapperton?"

"Do you hear what I say?"

"Yes, yes—is it 'malus,' or 'unrectus,' or what?"

"Are you going to do what I tell you?"

"How can I say what the chaps'll do?"

"You must tell them; you're fags' captain. They must do what you tell them."

"I'd jolly well like to catch them not," said Percy, tossing his head: "I'd teach 'em. I say, do you think 'unrectus' will do?"

"Remember, you'll get it pretty hot if you disobey in this, I promise you."

"Perhaps 'malus' is better form," suggested the junior.

Clapperton left in despair.

"What a fearful ass I was," said Percy when he had gone, "not to make him write my impot! Just like me. Catch our lot not going to that meeting! We aint going to skulk. Whew! there goes the quarter to! I shall never get done this brutal thing."

"Id est malus non facere quad magister dicit. Vos voluntas laetus audire ut Fellsgarthus liquebat Rendleshamus ad pedemballum super Saturdaium durare," (Saturday last). "Nos obtenebanus unum goalum ad nil quod non erat malum. Ego debeo nunc concludere. Ego sum vestrum fideliter Perceius Granum agrum." (Percy flattered himself he knew the correct Latin for his own name.)

He had a rush to get this work of art over to Mr Forder in time, and was considerably mortified to observe that the master did not seem at all gratified by the performance. Just like Forder! the more you laid yourself out to please him, the worse he was.

"Leave it, sir. I'll speak to you to-morrow."

"That means a licking," said Percy to himself. "I can see it in his eye. All serene. That's his way of showing his gratitude."

And he went back in a very bad temper to his own room, where his comrades had arrived to greet him.

"Why ever can't you chaps be in the way when you're wanted?" prowled Percy. "There was Clapperton in here just now talking rot about the meeting next week. What do you think? He says we're not to go to it."

"Why not?"

Percy in his lucid manner tried to explain.

"All gammon," said Lickford. "If we're to be stopped going to Hall, we shall be stopped grub next."

This was an argument that went home.

"If Clapperton had made it worth our while, you know," said Cottle, "it might have been different. I don't care much about the meeting; but if I stop away for him, I'll get something for it."

This mercenary view of the subject was new to Percy, but he frankly accepted it.

"I tell you what," said he; "here, give us a pen; we'll just draw up a few conditions. If he accepts them we'll stay away; if he don't, he may hang himself before we sit out."

After much deliberation, the following charter of six points was drawn up and laid on Clapperton's table.

"On the following conditions the undersigned will stop out of Hall on October 3,—namely, to wit, viz., i.e.:—

"1. No more fagging.

"2. Don't go to bed till 9:30.

"3. A study a-piece.

"4. The prefects shall be abolished. Any prefect reporting to Forder to be kicked.

"5. Except between 9:30 p.m. and 7:30 a.m. we do as we like.

"6. That the four following Classic cads get their noses pulled; namely Wheatfield, W., D'Arcy, Ashby, and Fisher minor.

"If these are agreed to, we won't go to the meeting."

(Signed by) Wheatfield, P., M.P.
Cottle, Major-General.
Lickford, D.D.
Ramshaw minor, F.S.A.
Cash, LL.D., etcetera, etcetera.

Chapter Thirteen
Corder to the Front

The morning of the return match with Rendlesham was damp and muggy, and so assorted well with the spirits of Fellsgarth generally.

The juniors of course were cheerful—everything came in the day's work for them—but among the seniors on either side gloom prevailed. Even Ranger, the lighthearted, was snappish, as his fag discovered; and Denton, the amiable, hoped he would not, for his temper's sake, meet too many Moderns between morning and evening. The captain, though he kept up his usual show of serenity, was evidently worried. But he had no notion of giving in. No! If the School was to be thrashed let them take their thrashing like men, and not whine about like the "other boys."

"After all," said he to Ranger, "we may not get glory, but we needn't lose it. Only, for goodness' sake, let us keep our rows to ourselves, and not talk about them out of doors."

"Right you are!" said his friend. "I wish I had your temper. The cads! And after the way you've treated them, too. Why, some of us thought you went out of your way to favour them."

The captain grunted, and began to throw his flannels into his bag.

"What about Rollitt?" he asked.

"No go. He's gone off for a day's fishing."

The captain whistled dismally. "Then we must play a man short. There's no one else worth putting in. It's like marching to one's execution," he said; "I wish it was all over. But it's only just beginning."

The Moderns were gloomy too. They had taken their course, and they must stand by it now. When they came to reflect, it was not a particularly glorious one, nor did it seem to promise much by way of compensation. They were done out of football for the rest of the term; they were reduced to a faction in Fellsgarth, and what was worse, they were secretly doubtful whether they were quite as much in the right as they tried to persuade themselves.

They had taken their course, however, and must go on.

"I suppose none of our side will go on the omnibus," said Brinkman.

"Why not?" said Clapperton. "It will do them good to have spectators. I shall go; not that I care about it, but just to assert my rights."

"Hurrah for self-sacrifice!" said Fullerton. "If your principles will allow you to take chicken and tongue sandwiches with you, I'll go too."

"It's ten to one they'll try to prevent our going," said Dangle; "I hope they'll try."

When the two coaches drove up to carry the fifteen and the prefects and other privileged boys to the scene of conflict, a good deal of surprise was evinced at the appearance of Clapperton, Brinkman, Dangle, and Fullerton, in ordinary costume, and without bags, ready to accompany the party.

Contrary to their expectations and hopes, no protest was made, and, as far as the Classic seniors were concerned, no notice was vouchsafed them. This was annoying, particularly as the juniors present took care to call attention to their presence.

"Look at 'em," cried Wally; "don't they look clever?"

"Kicked out of the team—serve 'em right!" shouted Ashby.

"Who's kicked out?" retorted the Modern fags. "It would take better chaps than you to kick them out."

"Don't you wish you could kick them in? They know better," retorted Percy and Co.

Amid such embarrassing comments, the four Modern heroes mounted to their places.

The cheers of their adherents hardly made up for the chilly welcome of their travelling companions. Yorke, seeing Clapperton looking for a place, politely moved up to make room, and then turned his back and talked to Ranger. The other three were similarly cut off, Dangle finding himself in between Fisher major and Denton, who talked across him. Brinkman, on another coach, was tucked in among some rowdy Classic middle-boys who were discussing the "strike" very vigorously among themselves. As for Fullerton, he was lucky enough to get the seat beside the driver, where, at any rate, he could count on one sympathetic soul into whose ears to pour his occasional words of wisdom.

Just as the first coach was starting, a shout was heard from across the Green, and Corder, the Modern boy whose services were declined on the previous occasion, equipped in an ulster and with his bag in his hand, appeared signalling for the *cortège* to wait.

"Well! what is it?" demanded Dangle.

"Is Yorke there? Yorke, can I play to-day?"

"No, you can't," said Dangle in a menacing undertone. "None of us are playing; you know that."

"I don't see why I mayn't play if I have the chance," said Corder. "I awfully want to play in the fifteen."

"We're a man short," said Yorke. "You can play, Corder."

"If you dare to come and play," said Dangle, still in a whisper, "you'll find it so precious hot for yourself afterwards that you'll be sorry for it."

"Yorke says I may play," persisted Corder; "I don't see why I shouldn't."

"Cad! traitor! blackleg!" yelled Percy and Co., as they saw their man mount the coach.

"Ha, ha! got *one* man among you who isn't a coward and a sneak, and—and a howling kid!" retorted Wally. "Gee up!" Whereat the whips cracked and the happy party drove off.

Corder was one of those obtuse youths who can never take in more than one idea at a time. His present idea was football. He had come up this term with a consuming ambition to get into the fifteen, and had played hard and desperately to secure his end. Last week, when Brinkman was obliged to retire, he thought his chance was come, and great was his mortification when he found that his nomination was not accepted by the captain. Still he didn't despair. When he saw the vacancies caused in the team by the defection of the Moderns, his hopes rose again; but once more they were dashed by the captain's announcement of a fifteen made up wholly of Classics.

To-day he had not had the heart to come out and see the coaches start, and was moping in his own room, when some one brought in word that Rollitt was not going to play after all, and that the team was setting out a man short.

Whereupon Corder dashed into his ulster, flung his flannels into his bag, and tore out of his house just in time to secure for himself the long-coveted honour, and find himself in the glorious position of "playing for the School."

How was such a fellow likely to trouble his head about strikes, and protests, and organised desertion?

Fortunately for the comfort of his journey, he had to pack himself away on the floor between the feet of Ridgway and another of the team, who, if they kicked him at all, only did it by accident or by way of encouragement, and not as Dangle or Brinkman might have done, in spite.

The rain was coming down pretty steadily by the time the party got to their destination, and the gloom on the brows of the four Modern prefects deepened as they looked up and speculated on the delights of standing for an hour on the wet grass watching their rivals play.

"Dangle," said Clapperton, "we must stop that cad Corder's playing at all cost. It will upset everything. Come and talk to him."

But Corder, perhaps with an inkling of what was in store for him, had entrenched himself behind a number of other players, and in close proximity to Ranger, who had evidently told himself off to see that the last recruit of the fifteen was not tampered with.

The signals of the two seniors were studiously not observed, and when Dangle, getting desperate, said—

"Corder, half a minute; Clapperton wants you." Ranger interposed with—

"Come on, you fellows, it's time we got into our flannels," and effectually checkmated the manoeuvre.

"If he doesn't get paid out for this," growled Clapperton, "I'm precious mistaken."

"Yes; and the other fellows must see that he is. If this sort of thing spreads, we may as well cave in at once."

The Rendlesham fellows hovered about under shelter till the last moment, grumbling at the weather, the grass, and the dock. At length the Fellsgarth boys put in an appearance; sides were solemnly tossed for, and the order to "spread out" was given.

"Hullo!" said one of the Rendlesham men as he passed Clapperton and Dangle, "why aren't you playing? Afraid of the cold?"

"No, we scratched because—"

"Have you got that big man down who was so hot in the scrimmages? I forget his name. *He's* not one of the delicate ones, I fancy."

"No more are we; we're not playing because—"

"Hullo! they're waiting," said the player, and went off, leaving the explanation still unfinished.

One of the last to run out was Corder.

"You young cad," growled Clapperton as he passed; "take my advice and don't play, unless—"

"Come on, Corder—waiting," shouted Yorke.

Corder obeyed like lightning.

The match began disastrously for Fellsgarth. Within five minutes of the kick-off, a run up by one of the Rendlesham quarter-backs carried the ball right into the School lines, and a touch-down resulted. On a fine day like last Saturday a goal would have been certain, but on the wet grass, the try did not come off. But five minutes later, a drop-kick from the middle of the field by the Rendlesham captain secured a magnificent goal for the home team.

Clapperton sneered.

"What I expected," said he. "They'll be lucky if they don't lose a dozen."

Yorke, on the contrary, was cheering up. Bad as these opening ten minutes had been, he fancied his team was not going to do so badly after all. The new players were working like mad in the scrimmage. Ranger was as quick on his feet in the wet as in the dry; and Corder at half-back had been surprisingly steady.

Before kicking off again he made one or two changes. He moved Ridgway, who was a heavy weight, up into the forwards. Corder, greatly to his delight, was entrusted with the goal, and Fisher major moved up to half-back. The forwards were ordered on no account to break loose, but if necessary to keep the ball among them till time was called.

Then, with his well-known "On you go!" he lacked off.

The ball was almost immediately locked up in a tight, fierce scrimmage. The boys took the captain's advice with a vengeance, and held the ball among their feet doggedly, neither letting it through on their side, nor forcing it out on the side of the enemy.

At length, however, it could be seen filtering out sideways, just where the captain was hovering outside the scrimmage.

"Let it come!" he whispered. "Look out, Ranger!"

Next moment the ball was under his arm, and before any one realised that the scrimmage was up, he was off with it and among the enemy's half-backs. The half-backs knew Yorke of old, and closed upon him before he could double or get round them.

"Pass!" shouted Ranger.

It was beautifully done, while Yorke was falling and Ranger brushing past. The enemy's half-backs were not in it with the fleet Fellsgarth runner, nor was their back; and to their own utter amazement, three minutes later the School placed to their credit an easy goal.

Then did Clapperton and Dangle and Brinkman gnash their teeth till they ached, and Fullerton, standing near, had his gibe.

"It was worth coming here in the rain to see that, wasn't it?"

The match was not yet over. The Rendlesham men, startled into attention by this unexpected rebuff, took care that such a misadventure should not happen again, and making all the use they could of their superior weight, bore down the scrimmages and forced the ball into the open. Once they carried it through with a splendid rush, and their captain picking it up under the very feet of the boys, ran it forward a few yards, and took a drop-kick which missed by only a few inches.

A little later came Corder's chance. He had lived all the term for this moment. If he was taken back to Fellsgarth on a shutter he would not care, so long as he did himself credit now.

He had a clear field to start with, and was well out of touch before the advance guard of the enemy bore down on him. Then it was a sight to see him wriggle and dodge, and twist and turn in and out among them, threading them like a needle through a string of beads, and slipping through their hands like an eel.

"Well played indeed, Corder!" cried Yorke.

Oh, what music was in the sound! What would he not dare now!

On he went, now diving under an arm, now staggering round a leg; now jumping like a kangaroo against an opponent. The very sight of his evolutions seemed to demoralise the Rendlesham men. They floundered and slid on the slippery grass, and made wild grabs without ever reaching him. It was really too ridiculous to be eluded by a raw hand like this—and yet he eluded them.

Half-way down the field he ran with a roar of applause at his back, and only a handful of the enemy left ahead. How splendid if he could only pass them, and make his record with a run from one goal to the other!

Alas! a swoop from behind greeted the proud thought; two hands clawed at his shoulders, and from his shoulders slipped to his waist, and from his waist slid down to his ankles, where for a moment they held, and sent the runner tripping over on his nose in the mud, with the ball spinning away a yard ahead.

It was all up. No! Fisher was on the spot, and at Fisher's heels Ridgway. The Rendlesham backs flung themselves in the way, but only to divert, not to stop their career. When Corder picked himself up and rubbed the mud out of his eyes, the first thing he saw was Ridgway sitting behind the enemy's line with the ball comfortably resting on his knee! It was another for the School—perhaps a goal.

Alas! on that ground the long side-kick was too much even for Yorke. It shot wide, and Rendlesham breathed again.

But the long and short of it was that the match was a tie; a goal and a try to each side; and that to Corder belonged the credit of a big hand in the lesser point.

"Awfully well run, Corder," said the captain, as, time having been called, the two walked off the field together. "You must play for us again."

After that, who should say life was not worth living?

The very weather seemed to change for Corder. The sun came out, flowers sprang up at his feet, birds started singing in the trees overhead. What a letter he would have to write home to-morrow! The captain's pat on the back sent a glow all through him. Who wouldn't be a Fellsgarth chap after all?

It scarcely damped his joy to perceive that neither Clapperton, Dangle, nor Brinkman shared in the general congratulations, but looked more black and threatening than ever as he passed. Pooh! what did he care for that!

How he enjoyed the glorious Rendlesham high tea, and the drive home in the rain with everybody talking and laughing and rejoicing, singing songs and shouting war-cries! He was quite sorry when it came to an end, and he had to dismount and go over alone to his own house.

He could hear the shouts and huzzas of the Classics across the Green as Wakefield's turned out in a body to welcome their men. No one at Forder's turned out to welcome him. The four prefects themselves had not even waited for him.

For the first time that day Corder felt himself wishing he had a little sympathy in his jubilation. It was dull, when everybody over on the other side was shouting himself hoarse, to hear not a "cheep" of congratulation from his own fellows.

However, it didn't matter much. He went to his room and changed, and hoped his messmate Wilson would not be long in coming for supper and a gossip.

Wilson came presently, but his face was glum and his manner frigid.

"Oh, here you are, old chap; I'm peckish. Did you hear about the match, we—"

"Shut up," said Wilson; "you're a cad. I don't want to talk to you."

Corder put down his knife and fork, and looked up in amazement. This from Wilson! He knew Clapperton was sore about it, but Wilson—

He went on eating while thinking it out, and Wilson ate too in silence, and then rose to go.

"Are you not going to prepare to-night?"

"Yes, in Dangle's room."

And Corder was left alone.

This was too bad of Wilson—to-night of all nights. He would go and look up Selby. Selby, he knew, would be interested in the day's news, for had they not practised drop-kicks together for an hour a day all this term?

Selby was in, but not at all glad to see him.

"Are you busy, old man?" asked Corder.

"I don't want you here," said Selby.

"Why, what's the row?"

"Row? You're a sneak, that's the row. Cut!"

Surely Selby must be out of sorts to talk like that. Corder stood in the door for a moment, on the off-chance that his friend might be joking. But no; Selby turned his back and began to read a book.

This was getting monotonous. Corder returned to his study to think it out a little more. His fag, Cash, was there looking for a paper.

"Hullo, youngster! that you? We didn't get beaten after all, to-day, I suppose you heard."

Cash's reply was laconic, to say the least of it. He turned round and put out his tongue.

"None of your cheek, I say," said Corder, "or I'll—"

"How *dare* you speak to me!" said the junior; "you're a cad—I'm not going to fag for a cad."

And he vanished.

Corder went to bed that night sorely perplexed. And his perplexity was not relieved when he rose next morning and found a paper on his table with the following genial notice:—

"Any boy in Forder's found speaking to Corder the sneak will be cut by the house. By Order."

Chapter Fourteen
The Shop Opens

Robert—no one knew his surname—was a regular institution at Fellsgarth. Pluralist and jack-of-all-trades as he was, he seemed unable to make much of a hand at anything he took up. He was School porter, owner of the School shop, keeper of the club properties, and occasional School policeman; and he discharged none of his functions well. The masters did not regard him with much confidence, the boys, for the most part, did not care for him, the other men about the place disliked him. And yet, as part and parcel of Fellsgarth, every one put up with him.

As has already been hinted, his management of the School shop had been a conspicuous failure—both for himself and the young innocents who squandered their substance on his tarts. He complained that he could make no profit; and as his method for recouping himself was to supply the worst possible article at the highest possible price, his young customers neglected him and aggravated his loss.

It was rumoured that another more questionable method of replenishing his exchequer was by laying odds on the School games, which (as in the case of the second Rendlesham match) did not always turn out in the way he expected. This, however, was only rumour, and was not to be reckoned among Bob's known transgressions, which were general stupidity, surliness, unsteadiness, and an inveterate distaste for veracity.

Such being his reputation, it astonished no one on the Monday following the events recorded in the last chapter to see the shutters of the shop at the Watch-tower Gate up, and a rudely scrawled announcement, "This shop is closed."

But what did cause astonishment was a subsequent announcement inscribed in print letters:—

"This establishment will reopen on Wednesday under entirely new management. Superior grub at greatly reduced prices. No more shoe-leather or flat swipes! Best tarts 1 penny each; ditto ginger-beer 1½ pence a bottle. Fresh fruit and pastry daily. Rally round the old shop!

"By Order."

Speculation ran high as to who the enterprising new tradesman could be. Some said it was Mrs Wisdom. Others said one of the Penchurch shops was going to run it as a branch. Others suggested that some of the seniors had a hand in it. But the truth never once leaked out.

Our nine juniors played an artful part in that day's business. They mingled with the crowd in front of the notice, and freely bandied about wild conjectures as to who the new manager or managers could be, at the same time hinting broadly that *they* intended to patronise the new concern.

"Tell you what," said D'Arcy, "perhaps it's the doctor wants to turn an honest penny. Don't blame him either."

"Perhaps it's Rollitt," suggested Cash, amid laughter. "What a game! He'll go selling tarts by the pint and ginger-beer by the ounce. Whew! think of Rollitt's ginger-beer."

"I asked Bob if he knew who it was," said Wally, "and he said, 'No, he wished he did; he'd get something out of him for good-will.'"

"What's that?" asked Ashby. "If he'd said bad temper, there might have been some of that going about."

"Anyhow," said Wally, "I rather fancy the thing myself. The things can't be worse than they have been, and if they're fresh every day, they're bound to be better, and the tarts are a halfpenny less, and so's the ginger-pop."

"Hooroo!" said Cottle; "you can get half as much again for the same money. I wish they'd open to-day."

After which, one by one they tailed off, leaving a general impression behind them that whoever else was in the secret, these nine young innocent lambs were not.

Matters had not advanced to this stage without considerable deliberation. Several committee meetings had been held, some of which, under Mr Stratton's presidency, had been of a practical nature, others, without his controlling presence, had ended in dust. On the whole, however, the young merchant adventurers had exhibited a reasonable grasp of their responsibilities and an aptitude for dealing with the necessary details.

One point discussed was whether the shop should be open all day, or only at certain times. Mr Stratton was in favour of the latter. He urged that during the off hours between eleven and twelve, and in the afternoon between four and six, would be ample.

The committee argued, from personal experience, that there were other hours of the day when a fellow felt in the humour for a "blow out." To this Mr Stratton replied, "Let him 'blow out' by all means, but not on the company's premises. He could do his shopping during shop hours, and 'blow out' with his purchases at any hour of the day or night the School rules permitted. They couldn't undertake to provide a banqueting hall for their customers."

"But," urged the committee, "if you have a shopman, why not get your money's worth out of him?"

"Why waste our money on a shopman at all?" propounded Mr Stratton to his astounded fellow-directors. "Why not take turns behind the counter ourselves; say one of the Wheatfields and Cash one week, and Cottle and Ashby the next, and so on? The hours proposed were not school hours; and though the persons on duty might occasionally be done out of a game, still it would fall on all alike, and would be a little sacrifice for the common good."

"But," said Percy, whose hair was on end at this tremendous proposition, "suppose Wally—that is, I mean, wouldn't it be necessary to count the tarts before each chap went on duty and see how many there were at the end?"

"It might with you and your lot," retorted Wally, very red in the face. "It'd be best to have a weighing machine handy and charge you 8 pence a pound for every pound extra you weighed at the end of the day!"

"We'll neither count nor weigh," said Mr Stratton; "we'll trust to every fellow's honour. Why, if we couldn't do that, do you suppose the shop would keep open a week?"

This impressed the meeting vastly, and the discussion was changed to the question of profits.

The boys were in favour of screwing all they could out of their customers. They didn't see why, if Bob sold bad tarts for three-halfpence, they shouldn't sell good ones at least for the same price.

"It's giving it to 'em both ends," said they.

"Why not?" said the master. "We want the fellows to get the benefit. We don't want all the profit. As it is, we shall make a farthing on every tart we sell. We ought to sell four times as many as Bob did, oughtn't we?"

"Quite that," said they.

"Very well; see how that works out."

And Mr Stratton took his chalk and worked out this sum on the blackboard:—

12 bad tarts at 1½ pence = 1 shilling, 6 pence, cost 9 pence, profit 9 pence.

48 good tarts at 1 penny = 4 shillings, cost 3 shillings, profit 1 shilling.

"You see," said he, "if we can only increase the demand, we shall easily make Bob's profit, and more. Having good tarts will increase it in one way, and selling cheap will increase it another. It's worth trying, anyhow."

And so the deliberations went on, and the boys' minds gradually took on the new idea.

The thirty shillings, Mr Stratton reported, had been advanced, and Mrs Stratton was appointed a subcommittee to lay it out. A method of accounts was arranged. The first day's stock was to be charged at the selling price to the shopman for the day. At the end of the day he was to hand over to the treasurer the money he had taken and what was left of the stock, which two items together ought to make up the sum of his responsibility. It was felt that in a very few days the committee would ascertain pretty nearly what quantity of each article was consumed, and would be able to order accordingly. Any deficiency was to be set down to bad management, and no other reason; and any shopman deficient three days running was to forfeit his right to officiate again during that term.

Lots were solemnly drawn for the distinction of opening the shop, and the choice fell on D'Arcy, and Lickford, who for the next day or two went about shaking in their shoes. As the day drew nearer, the venture seemed a tremendous one, and Mr Stratton had to use all his powers of encouragement to keep his colleagues from not taking fright at the last moment.

"It will all go swimmingly, you'll see," said he. "I will hold myself in readiness to come down and back you up if there's the least hitch, but I shall be greatly disappointed if you need me."

The last act of the committee before commencing proceedings was to draw up a manifesto, which was copied out and duly affixed to the notice boards and the shop-shutters on the morning of the opening.

Under the distinguished patronage of Mr and Mrs Stratton.

The Fellsgarth Shop will be opened this day from 11 to 12,
And 4 To 8,
and daily (sundays excepted) till further notice.
The following prime goods, at the cheap prices affixed.
(Here followed a list of the stores.)
Ready money. No tick. Change given.
no more stomach-ache!!
Real jam!
Ripe fruit!

Fresh pastry!
All the season's novelties. Nothing stale.
Boys of Fellsgarth—
Come in your thousands!
No risk to man or boy.
No favour.
Masters and fags treated alike.
All the profits for the clubs.
Treasurer, Mrs Stratton.
Managing directors, Nine gentlemen, Carefully Selected.
President, Mr Stratton.
Plenty for all. No questions asked.
All are welcome.
Come early and stay late.

By Order.

This soul-stirring manifesto, which had the hearty approval both of the president and treasurer (who carefully revised the spelling), threw some satisfactory light on the mystery. Who were the "carefully selected gentlemen" was still obscure, although it was generally held that Fellsgarth only contained nine individuals answering to that particular description. What was more important was that Mr and Mrs Stratton were at the back of the venture. If so, it was not a swindle, and the grub was pretty sure to be right. The new price list, moreover, was very satisfactory, and on the whole the hours were approved of.

When the eleven o'clock bell sounded, on the Wednesday morning, a general movement was made for the Watch-Tower Gate, where, firmly entrenched behind a clean counter piled up with the good things a schoolboy holds dear, demurely stood D'Arcy and Lickford, looking very anxious and scared.

At judiciously selected points among the crowd their friends looked on sympathetically.

After the laughter which had greeted the discovery had died away, an awkward pause ensued. No one exactly liked to start. The seniors present felt their dignity would be compromised. The middle-boys did not like to do what the seniors were too shy to do. The juniors were afraid some one might laugh if they led off. Consequently for a minute or two every one stared at the two shopmen, who cast down their eyes, and blushed and simpered.

At length, however, the ice was broken in a very pretty way. For Mrs Stratton on her way out of the school looked in, and taking in the situation, advanced to the counter and said—

"A bottle of ginger-beer, if you please, Lickford."

Lickford, who, to use his own polite phrase, was "bossing the drinks and fruit" for the day, nearly tumbled down with the shock of this sudden challenge, and made a wild grab at the nearest bottle within reach. The eyes of Fellsgarth were upon him; he lost his head entirely, and made herculean efforts to draw the cork without loosing the wire. His contortions were terrible.

When he could not hold the bottle firm enough between his knees, he tried gripping it between his feet. Then in a hot whisper he besought D'Arcy to hang on to the end, and for a time the bottle was invisible under the two. Then he took another, amid the enthusiastic cheers of the spectators, and was proceeding to release the corkscrew from the refractory vessel, when Mrs Stratton said in her pleasant way—

"I see you keep the new kind of bottles that have the corks wired down. They are much better than the old, and it's very little trouble undoing the wire."

This saved Lickford. In a moment the wire was removed, and the cork burst out triumphantly, even before it was pulled, showering a grateful froth of fizz into the waistcoat of the operator.

"It's beautifully well up. Thank you, Lickford, how much?" said Mrs Stratton.

"They're a shilling a dozen. I mean three-halfpence each," said D'Arcy. "We can give you change."

"Here's twopence. I'll take a halfpenny apple. That will make it right, won't it?"

And amid loud cheers she departed.

The ice thus broken, a rush took place, as Ridgway, who was poetical, said—

"Fellows may step in where angels didn't fear to tread."

Then did D'Arcy and Lickford pant and perspire, and wish they had never been born. Hands reached in from all sides, and helped themselves to cakes and tarts, and coppers showered in on them from nobody could tell where.

They found themselves handing change out into space, and sowing sweets broadcast among the crowd.

The other directors meanwhile, as in duty bound, nobly rallied round them, and added to their embarrassment.

"Walk up, walk up!" shouted Wally. "Try our brandy-balls, eight a penny. Eight brandy-balls for Dalton; you chaps, look sharp. Change for a sov. for Clapperton; beg pardon, sixpence (didn't know he kept such small coins). Hullo, hullo! stand by for my young brother Percy! He's just a-going to begin. Fifteen jam tarts, half a pound of peppermints, half a dozen ginger-beer. Bite his money hard, D'Arcy; see there are no bad 'uns. I know the chap!"

"Bah! I hope they've got better toffee here than that muck you make," said Percy.

"Come, wake up!" cried Cash. "I've been waiting five minutes for my cake."

"Can't have 'em; we've run out," said D'Arcy.

"Well, you must be a green one only to get such a few," said a middle-boy, who had also built his hopes on the same delicacy.

"Very sorry," said Percy to the company generally. "You must excuse these chaps—raw hands—they don't know how to manage at present. Give 'em time. They'll do better; won't you, Lickford? Takes some time to get a notion into Lickford's head, but when it gets there, my word, it sticks. Get in a double lot of cakes to-morrow, do you hear, or I shall give you the sack."

Despite these pleasant recriminations the business went on merrily. The "tuck" was pronounced a great advance on anything Robert had provided, and rumours of its excellence penetrated into quarters which had never contributed customers to the old shop.

In the afternoon the crowd was less, but the business more steady. Mr Stratton dropped in for a slice of cake, and Mrs Wakefield and the three little Wakefields came to patronise the undertaking. One or two fellows, too, sent their fags to secure "extras" for tea, and one or two left orders for another day. Inquiries were made, moreover, for certain articles, such as lemons, tea-cakes, etcetera, which the shopmen took a note of as worth laying in a stock of. And the lack of demand for a few of the things they had, suggested to the same astute young merchants that they might be dispensed with in future.

Of course, a few boys tried to interfere with the regulations by demanding "tick," and wanting to make bargains. But they were promptly met by a *non possumus* from the directors present, and finally brought to reason by being referred to Mr Stratton.

The day passed without the necessity of any appeal to the president. An anxious consultation was, however, held in his room after closing time. Naturally, owing to the exceptional rush, the accounts were a little out, but as they happened to be on the right side this was a matter for congratulation rather than distress. Nearly two pounds had been taken, and the stock left on hand was valued at five shillings, so that actually it was possible to repay half of the thirty shillings lent, after the very first day. Mr Stratton, however, advised that only ten shillings should be repaid this time, and the other five shillings put into a reserve fund, in case of need.

"Of course, you can't expect to do as big a business as this every day," said he. "It will settle down to a regular jog-trot in a few days, and then we shall be able to judge much better how we stand. I shall be very well satisfied if we make about five shillings clear a day."

"I think you boys have started very well," began the treasurer, but her husband held up his finger admonishingly.

"I should have been very disappointed with them if they had not," said he. "It's easy enough to start, the thing will be to keep it up."

"Remember," he added, "it will be better not to brag out of doors about our profits or that sort of thing. It will be time enough to talk about that when we are able to hand over a good lump sum to the clubs. Now it's time you went to preparation. Good night all."

"I tell you what," said Lickford to his fellow-shopman as they walked across the Green, "we shall have to be pretty smart to-morrow if we're to get to the club meeting."

"Why," said D'Arcy, "I thought none of you Modern cads were going to show up?"

"We heard you'd all funked it," said Wally.

"I don't blame them," said Ashby; "they've not much to be proud of, those Modern chaps."

"Never mind," said Fisher minor, "Fellsgarth can get on well enough without them."

The party came to a halt and regarded one another seriously, and Percy said—

"Whoever told you we weren't going to turn up, told crams. We're coming. We'll see you don't have it all to yourselves, rather!"

"My eye, won't you get licked for it! Nice to belong to a house where you mayn't sneeze unless your senior lets you."

"Go on! Shut up! See if you can't canvass a bit. That's what you're best at—that, and getting it hot on the hands for cheating." Whereupon the troops separated.

The taunts of the Classics made their rivals wince, despite their affected contempt. To-morrow was the day of the meeting; and between now and then they must decide whether or not they would obey their own seniors and stay away, or revolt and take the consequences. The unanimous opinion was in favour of revolt, unless Clapperton made it uncommonly worth their while to obey.

They were not destined to remain long in doubt, for the senior invaded their quarters that very evening.

"Just remember, you youngsters," said he, "no one is going to the meeting to-morrow from our side."

"Oh?"

"Any fellow who goes will get it hot, I promise him."

"Ah! What about our conditions? What have you done about them?"

"Put them in the coal-scuttle; and I've a good mind to put all five of you there too, for your impudence."

"Ah!"

The captain turned on his heel, with a final warning.

"That settles it, you chaps," said Percy, when he had gone. "We go."

"Rather," replied everybody.

Chapter Fifteen
Something Wrong in the Accounts

Fisher major sat in his study after morning class, next morning, the picture of boredom and perplexity. Lists of names, receipt-books, cash-box, bills, and account-books were littered on the table before him. Between these and a cobweb on the ceiling his troubled looks travelled, as he gnawed the end of his pen, and passed his fingers aimlessly through his hair.

There was something wrong; and what it was he could not for the life of him make out. To any one familiar with Fisher major's business—or, rather, unbusiness—habits, there was nothing wonderful in that. He was happy-go-lucky in all his dealings. He could receive a subscription one day, and only remember, in a panic, to enter it a week after. His money he kept all over the place; some in his desk, some in the cash-box, some in the drawer of his inkstand. He had a vague idea that he had a special reason for dividing it thus—that one lot may have belonged to the School clubs, another to the House clubs, and another to something else. But which was which it passed his wit to remember.

He had had his doubts of the business all along. His friends had urged him to take the office, and with their help he had persuaded himself its duties were simple and easily discharged. He had determined he would do the thing thoroughly well. He had bought these account-books out of his own private purse, and spent an evening in beautifully ruling them in red ink, with one column for the date, one for the name, and three for pounds, shillings, and pence. He had procured two letter-files, labelled respectively "Club" and "House," into which to put his receipts. And he had provided himself with a dozen elastic bands and an equal number of paper-fasteners. What more could a treasurer desire?

Alas! the beautiful account-books got mixed up with one another, the letter-files remained empty, and the elastic bands somehow did duty as football garters. The Club accounts were scrawled, for the most part, in pencil on the backs of envelopes, awaiting a grand transcription into the books; and the receipts, pending a similar fortunate time, where huddled away in the drawer with Greek verses and letters from the people at home.

Things had now come to a pass. The captain had yesterday suggested that, in view of the meeting to-day, it would be well to have the accounts made up, so as to be able, if called upon, to state exactly how they stood financially.

"All serene," said Fisher; "I'll let you have the lot in ten minutes."

It was now considerably more than ten hours since the rash undertaking had been given, and the accounts were considerably more confused than they had been when Fisher sat down to square them.

The Club and House accounts were hopelessly mixed. Some fellows appeared to have paid several times over to both funds, and others not once to either. Worse than that, Fisher could not find his memorandum of what he had paid out in small disbursements since term began. Still worse, when he did come in desperation to lump both funds together, and deduct the total amount he had spent, he found himself between £4 and £5 out of pocket!

That was the serious discovery which, on this particular morning, was preying on his spirits and making him look a picture of bewilderment.

"I'm bothered if I can make it out," said he to himself. "Everybody's marked down as paid—I remember noticing that weeks ago. At that rate I ought to have £25 for the Clubs, and £9 12 shillings for the House. Yes, that's right—I had that; there's a note of it; three lots—£15 7 shillings 6 pence on September 1, £7 2 shillings 6 pence on September 13, and £12 2 shillings on another day—that makes the total. There you are. Why on earth did I put them away in separate lots? Then I paid £5 for the new goals, and something else—what was it? Oh, that was for the House balls—oh, but we are lumping the two together. What was it? I know, 17 shillings 6 pence—that's £5 17 shillings 6 pence; and something else, I know, came to a pound—£6 17 shillings 6 pence. Take that from £34 12 shillings, leaves £27 14 shillings 6 pence—and I've only got £22 18 shillings 6 pence! Where, in the name of wonder, has the rest gone?"

And once more the dismal operation of adding up, counting, and subtracting began anew, with the same, or almost the same, result—there was a mistake of something like £4 10 shillings, whichever way you looked at it.

Dalton, who came in presently, could throw no further light on the problem. He added up the columns, counted the money, subtracted the payments and arrived at the same result.

Had the difference been smaller, it might have been accounted for by a few subscriptions omitted or a few payments not entered. But £4 10 shillings was too big a sum to leak away by accident; and, with the exception of the new goals, Fisher major was confident nothing had been spent approaching the figure.

Dalton then proposed a fresh hunt through the study, in case the missing sum might be hidden for safety in some corner. So the room was turned upside down; the bed-clothes were shaken out, pockets searched, books turned over, tea-pots peered into; but all to no purpose.

The captain looked in while the search was proceeding.

"Have you got the— Hullo, what's up?"

"Why," said Fisher major, "there's a discrepancy. We ought to have £27 14 shillings 6 pence, and there's about £4 10 shillings short."

"Do you mean that's missing in the Club accounts?"

"Well, either in that or the House clubs, or in both lumped together. I say, I wish you'd add that up, there's a good fellow. The addition may be wrong."

But no; the captain made it the same as Dalton.

Ranger and Ridgway dropped in while the audit was in progress, and were promptly pounced upon to add the columns too. Evidently the mistake was not there. They made the total precisely the same.

"It must be in the payments, then," said Fisher. So the whole party sat down, and scrutinised the hapless treasurer's bills and vouchers, and, after allowing him the benefit of every imaginable doubt, still brought the deficit out at the same uncompromising figure.

"Let's have another look round," suggested Fisher. So once more the study was turned topsy-turvy, and every nook and cranny searched. But no money was there, nor any sign of it.

The captain looked grave.

"It's precious awkward," said he.

"It's sure to turn up," said Fisher. "I'll go over the whole thing again, and have the room searched."

"Meanwhile," said Ranger, "it's to be hoped no questions are asked by the fellows opposite."

"Not much chance; I hear they are none of them going to turn up," said Dalton.

"That's their look-out," responded the captain.

Much to their disgust, Ashby and Fisher minor were summoned from the vicinity of the shop that morning to assist the treasurer in his hopeless search. They did not mind turning a study upside down on their own account, but they strongly objected to have to do it for any one else.

Fisher major did not at first vouchsafe much information with regard to the missing object.

"Look round everywhere," said he, "and see if you see anything."

Ashby looked, and said he saw a lot of things.

"I mean money, of course," said the treasurer.

Whereupon the two simultaneously made a grab at the loose cash on the table, declaring they had found it first go off.

"No—not that. It's some that's missing."

"How much?" asked Ashby.

"Never mind—a pound or two."

"Are you sure it's about in the room?"

"That's what I want you to look and see, you young donkey!"

"Two pounds," said Ashby; "was it all in silver?"

"No—it was three or four pounds—about £4 10. I don't know what it was in."

"Four pound ten—that's a lot," said the young brother. "I thought you said you were hard up?"

"So I did. It's not my money, but the club's. What's that to do with it? I want you to see if you can find it while I'm down in class."

Whereupon they set to work. They emptied the contents of every drawer in a glorious heap on the floor. They shook out his socks, and turned the pockets of all his coats inside out. They pulled his bed about the room, and shook out all his sheets. They raked out his fire, and prised up a loose board in the floor. They emptied his basins into his bath, and investigated the works of his eight-day clock. But high or low they could find no money.

Fisher's study did not get over that morning's quest in a hurry. When the owner returned, he wished devoutly he had never been ass enough to confide the task to a couple of raw Goths like these. Whatever chance there may have been before of discovering any mislaid article, it was now hopelessly and irredeemably gone.

He dismissed the two youngsters with a kick, which they felt to be very ungrateful after all the trouble they had taken. Limp in spirits and grimy in personal appearance, they crawled away to the shop to console themselves with ginger-beer and a cheese-cake.

"Hullo," said Lickford, as they arrived, "what have you been up to? Sweeping the chimneys? I heard they wanted it on your side. What'll you have? We've been doing prime. Where have you been?"

"We've been hunting about in my senior's study for some club money that's lost; about four pou—"

"Shut up!" said Ashby, nudging his companion. "What do you want to blab all over the place about it for?"

"How much?—four pounds?" said a voice near; and looking round, to their horror they saw Dangle.

"All right," said Ashby, trying to save the situation, "it's bound to turn up. He stuck it in a specially safe place, and can't remember where. Look sharp with the ginger-beer, young Lickford."

"Money down first," said Lickford. "Catch me trusting any of you Classic chaps with tick! You've got no tin generally, to begin with, and then you go and lose it."

"That's better than stealing it," retorted Ashby.

"The thing is," said Dangle, breaking in on these pleasant recriminations, "it wouldn't matter if it was Fisher's own money that was lost. But it belongs to all of us."

"I tell you he's found it by now," said Ashby. Then, turning to Fisher minor, he whispered, "you howling young ass, you've done it! Now there'll be a regular row, and your brother will have you to thank for it!"

"Don't blame him," said Dangle. "It's quite right of him to tell the truth."

With which highly moral pronouncement the Modern senior strolled away.

Lickford was too much engrossed by a sudden influx of customers to improve the occasion; and Fisher minor, who never enjoyed ginger-beer less in his life, was allowed to depart in peace to meditate on the evil of his ways, and the possible hot water he had been preparing for his brother.

He had sense enough to reflect that he had better make a clean breast of it to his brother at once.

To his surprise, the latter took the news that Dangle had heard of the deficiency in the accounts more quietly than he had expected.

"I do wish you'd hold your tongue out of doors about things that don't concern you," said he.

"Will Dangle get you into a row?" asked Fisher minor.

"Dangle? I'm not responsible to him more than to any one else. The money's lost; and unless I can find it or make out where the mistake comes in, I shall have to stump up—that's all."

"But, I say, you haven't got money enough," said the boy.

"I know that, you young duffer."

"Whatever will you do?"

Fisher major laughed.

"I shan't steal it, if that's any comfort to you; and I shan't cook the accounts."

"I say, I wonder if Rollitt could lend it you. He must have some money, for he paid for Widow Wisdom's new boat, you know."

"I heard of that. I wish I saw my way to paying my debts as well as he did."

"I say, shall I ask him?"

"Certainly not. The best thing you can do is to shut up."

Fisher minor felt very grateful to his brother for not thrashing him, and went in to afternoon school meekly, though out of spirits.

"Well," said D'Arcy, as he took his place, "what's the latest? Who are you going to get into a mess now! Has Yorke been swindling anybody lately, or Ranger been getting tight! You're bound to have some story about somebody."

"I didn't mean— It's not wicked to lose money," pleaded Fisher minor. "I never thought—"

"That's just it," said Wally. "You couldn't if you tried. Dangle will make a nice thing out of it, thanks to you. Classic treasurer been and collared Modern boys' money—that sort of thing—and they'll kick him out and stick in one of their own lot, and call it triumph of honesty. Oh, you beauty; you *can* do things nicely when you try?"

"I wish I'd never come up here at all," moaned Fisher minor.

"Humph. That would have been a bad go for Fellsgarth," said D'Arcy. "Shut up—Forder's looking. If we're lagged we shan't get in to the meeting."

The dreaded misadventure did not occur; and punctually at the hour our four young gentlemen trooped into Hall. Everything was very quiet there. The place was only half full. The Classics had turned up in force, but the mutineering house was so far unrepresented. Presently, however, five juvenile figures might be seen marching arm in arm across the Green, keeping a sharp look-out on every side.

Before they arrived in Hall, a solitary figure wearing the Modern colours had made his way up to the seniors' end. It was Corder, looking very limp and haggard, and with a savage flash of the eyes which told how ill "Coventry" was agreeing with his spirits. The cheers, with which he was greeted, due quite as much to his pluck in coming to-day as to his exploit at the match last Saturday, appeared to disconcert rather than please him, and he took a corner seat as far as possible from the Classic seniors present. When, however, Percy and Co. entered the Hall, a much livelier demonstration ensued. Cheers and compliments and pats on the back showered fast on the youthful "blacklegs," and tended greatly to exaggerate in their own eyes the importance of their action.

"We shall get jolly well welted for it, you fellows," said Percy, with all the swagger of a popular martyr. "Never mind; we aren't going to be done out of Hall for anybody."

"At any rate, they won't hurt *you* for it," cried Wally, disparaging. "Kids like you won't hurt."

"We've come to see you cads don't get it all your own way," said Cash. "That's what we've come for!"

"Ho, ho! Hope you've brought your lunch. You'll be kept here a day or two, if you're going to wait for that!"

When Yorke and the other prefects arrived on the scene there were, of course, loud cheers; but as the opposition was not there to make any counter-demonstration, it was not quite as noisy as on former occasions.

Percy did, indeed, attempt to get up a little opposition at this stage by calling for "three cheers for the Moderns"; but as he was left to give them by himself—even his own adherents declining to be drawn into cheers for Clapperton—the display fell rather flat.

The captain's speech was short and to the point. Of course they knew why the meeting was called. There had been mutiny at Fellsgarth. Fellows had deliberately set themselves against his authority as captain, which was a minor thing, and against the success of Fellsgarth in sports, which was a low and shabby thing. (Cheers.) He wasn't going to mention names; but he meant to say this, that they had much better dissolve the club right away—

(No, no)—than not all pull together. Last Saturday, as every one knew, they had been left utterly in the lurch; and but for good luck, and the good play of some of the fifteen—amongst whom, he was glad to say, was one fellow who had had the pluck to act on his own judgment of what was due to the School—(loud and prolonged cheers, in the midst of which Corder perked up, and looked pleased)—they had held their own with a very scratch team. They couldn't expect to do as much again—(Why not?)—and it *was not* fair to the School to play matches without all their best men in the team. The proposal he had to make was that unless the fellows now standing out chose to return to their allegiance to the School within a week, all future matches for the term should be scratched, and the club dissolved.

The captain's proposal caused considerable consternation. Ridgway rose, and said he considered the motion dealt far too leniently with the mutineers. He would say, drum them out of the club, and reorganise without them.

Denton asked if it would not be more honest and straightforward to summon them to the next match, and if they didn't turn up give them the thrashing they deserved?

Fisher major said he supported the captain's proposal. It was nonsense their playing with scratch teams, and letting it be supposed that was the best the School could do. Some of the fellows on strike were no doubt good players, and that made it all the more discreditable of them to try to damage the School record by crippling the team. They no doubt hoped that they would be begged to rejoin on their—own terms. Rather than that, he was in favour of disbanding the club, and letting the fellows devote their energy to running and jumping, and other sports, where each fellow could distinguish himself independently of what any others chose to do. (Hear, hear.)

Ranger also supported Yorke's motion. Very likely the mutineers would crow, and say the club couldn't get on without them. No more they could, in a sense. But he, for one, was not going to ask them to come back, and would sooner break up the club, and let them have the satisfaction of knowing they had injured Fellsgarth.

Amid loud cheers Corder followed. He was sorry, he said, there was to be no more football, but supposed there was nothing else they could do. He was glad to see some Moderns present, even though they were only juniors. (Laughter.) It showed that there were some fellows on the Modern side that stuck by the School. He fancied these youngsters could take care of themselves. He was glad to hear a human voice again. (Laughter.) It might be fun to some present, but he could assure them it was none to him. No one had spoken to him for four days. He was cut by his house, and had to thank even some of the juniors present for assisting to make his life in Forder's miserable. He didn't care much, so far. They might make him cave in, in the long run. (No! Stick out!) Let the fellow who cried "Stick out," come and try it. His only offence had been that he had played for the School. To do anything for the School was now considered a crime on the Modern side. (Shame.) Anyhow, he should vote for the captain's motion; and though he wasn't particularly sweet on the Classics as a body, he was beginning to think they weren't quite as bad as his own side.

Percy hereupon rose, amid derisive cheers. He didn't know why the names of him and his lot had been brought in; but he just wanted to say that they were here to-day because they had a right to come, and weren't going to be kept out by anybody—not if they knew it. (Rather not!) He and his lot thought there wasn't much to choose between anybody, especially the juniors of the Classic side, who thought they were jolly clever, but were about the biggest stuck-uppest louts he— (Order. Kick him out.) He hoped the meeting would rally round the School shop, where every one was treated alike, and got the best grub for the money of any school going. They were going to get some Ribston— (Order. Time.) All right. They shouldn't hear what he was going to say now. (Loud cheers.)

Yorke said they all seemed to be pretty much of the same mind; and he would put his motion to the vote.

This accordingly was done, and carried without a dissentient voice.

Chapter Sixteen
A Beleaguered Garrison

The decision arrived at by the club meeting speedily came to the ears of the recalcitrant Moderns, and by no means pleased them. They had expected at least that some one would propose that they should be met half-way, and appealed to, for the sake of the School, to abandon their attitude. That would have given them an opportunity of figuring in an heroic light before Fellsgarth, and showing how, for the general good, they could afford even to overlook the slight which had been put upon them.

But now, so far from that, they figured as the party who had wrecked the School clubs for the sake of a petty pique, and in their absence had been quietly deposed along with every one else from office and privilege, and left looking uncommonly foolish and uncommonly ridiculous.

Yorke himself hardly realised, when he made his downright motion, that he was dealing the hardest blow possible at the mutiny. A mutiny is all very well as long as there is some one to mutiny against. But now, even this luxury was denied them.

Naturally the wrath of Clapperton and his friends fell on the traitors in their own camp whose presence at the meeting had made it impossible to discredit it as entirely one-sided in its composition.

That Corder would go, every one was prepared for. He had laid up for himself yet one more rod in pickle, and should punctually taste its quality.

But the mutiny of the juniors was a surprise. No one imagined that their threats at revolt were anything more than the ordinary bluster in which these young braves notoriously dealt. Had they sinned in ignorance it would have mattered less. But they had gone to the meeting in deliberate defiance of their captain's order, and in the face of his warning as to what the consequences of disobedience would be.

The discipline of the house was at an end if a flagrant act of insubordination like this was to be allowed to pass unnoticed. Besides, if allowed to spread, other fellows would go over to the enemy, and the "moral" effect of the strike would be at an end.

A peremptory summons was therefore dispatched to Percy and his friends to appear before the prefects of their house that same evening.

"That all?" inquired Percy of the middle-boy who brought the message. "We hear you. You needn't stop."

"I'll tell him you'll come?" said the messenger.

"I don't mind what you tell him. Cut out of our room, that's all. We aren't particular, me and my chaps; but we draw the line at louts."

"He says if you don't come—"

"What's to prevent him saying anything he likes? Look here, young Gamble," (Gamble was at least two years the senior of any boy present), "if you don't cut your sticks, they'll be cut for you. So there."

Gamble gave a general invitation to the party to come and try to tamper with his sticks, and departed with a final caution as to the desirability of obeying their captain.

"Lick," said Percy, when he had gone, "how much grub have we got in the room?"

"What are you talking about? You aren't hungry surely, after that go-in at the shop?"

"Have we got enough for two days?"

The party opened their eyes, and began to suspect the drift of the inquiry.

"No; but Maynard owes us a loaf, and Spanker some butter, and those kids in Reynolds' study half a tongue."

"All right; go out and get it all in, sharp. Scrape up all you can."

"What, are we going to have a blockade?"

"Rather. You don't suppose we're going to cave in to Clapperton, do you?"

"But we shan't want enough for two days, shall we?"

"Shan't we, that's all! To-morrow's exeat day, and no school. Next day's Sunday, and next day exeat doesn't end till twelve. We may have to stick out three days."

"Whew! we *shall* want a lot of grub," said Cash.

"You young pig; that's all you think about. You'll have to go on jolly short rations, I can promise you. Do you know what we're going to do?"

No one had an idea what they were going to do.

"Do you know those four Classic kids," said Percy, "my younger brother and his lot? They've not been quite such cads lately as they used to be, have they?"

"They've been a bit more civil," said Cottle. "I suppose that's because of the shop."

"What about them?" asked Ramshaw.

"Why, I fancy if we asked them, they might come over and back us up. Of course they'd have to bring their own grub; and we'd kick them out if they weren't civil. What do you say?"

"Rather a lark," said Lickford.

"All serene. I'll go and see about it. Keep it dark, whatever you do, and mind you scrape up all the grub that's owing us. There's no time to lose, I say; Clapperton expects us in half an hour. Wire in!"

By the end of half an hour the larder had been fairly well replenished. Lickford and Cash had gone round on a general raid; recovering by force, where persuasion failed, their outstanding loans, and in other cases borrowing additional supplies in the same genial manner. Among other booty, they secured a tin of pressed beef from Spanker, who had to be clouted on the head before he would "lend it," and some sardines from another boy, who was thankful to find any one to take them off his hands at any price.

Cottle and Ramshaw, acting on sealed orders from their leader, had been round borrowing a screw-driver and screws, a few yards of rope, and other material of war, among which was a squirt belonging to Reynolds, who had been pleased to "swap" it for a couple of Greek stamps which Cottle had to dispose of.

Many were the fears lest not only should Percy fail to secure the services of the Classic juniors, but should himself be too late to take part in the siege. However, much to their relief, this was not so; as presently he came over arm in arm with Wally (who carried a parcel under his arm), followed at a respectful distance by D'Arcy, Ashby, and Fisher minor, the bulkiness of whose pockets gave promise of a further addition to the sinews of war.

By general consent the visitors slipped in, not in a body, but casually one by one, and so escaped special observation. As soon as they were all assembled, Percy gave the order to screw up, and pile on the barricades.

Wally, who was disposed to be patronising, snuffed up somewhat at his brother's calm assumption of the command.

"Why didn't you say you wanted screws?" said he; "we've got one or two long ones. That's not the way to stick it in, young Lickford; make the hole more sideways. Here, I'll do it for you."

"I'll tell you what," said D'Arcy, "you chaps had better begin to move up the bed against the door, in case they come before we're fast in. Fire away. Stick it close up, and young Lickford can stand on to it to put in the screw."

"Come on, Cash; stick these parcels out of the way," said Ashby, handing out the provender; "they'll be better in the cupboard. Mind how you put them in."

"You've got a knife, Cottle," said Fisher minor. "Cut these bits of wood into wedges to go under the door. They'll make it pretty secure."

In this manner the Classic auxiliaries coolly took charge of the arrangements before ever their hosts had time to realise that they had been relegated to a back seat.

However, just now there was no time for arguing questions of precedence and authority. The enemy might be upon them at any moment, and they had a lot to do before their outworks could be said to be in a proper state of defence.

The screws in the door were driven hard home into the wainscot; the wedges underneath were tightly fixed. The bed, with bedding complete, was drawn against the entry. A second line of defence was thrown up of chairs, chest of drawers, book-case, and wash-stand. Beyond that were stacked against the wall cricket bats, stumps, boxing-gloves, and other dangerous-looking implements, for use in a last emergency. At Percy's suggestion, and under Wally's direction, an additional loophole was bored in the panel of the door (in flagrant forgetfulness of the rights of School property), through which, as well as through the ventilating holes above, the enemy might be reconnoitred and operated on.

These preliminaries being complete, and Fisher minor having been perched on the table (which was on the bed), with his eye to the loophole, the company, to pass the time, resolved itself into a committee on the School shop, and waited anxiously for the attack.

Percy was specially anxious, for he had enlisted his four recruits on the distinct understanding there would be a row, and all the blame would fall on his head if by any ill-luck the evening passed off quietly.

Already the Classic juniors were beginning to get impatient, and hinting that they saw no fun in the proceeding so far, when Fisher minor scrambled down from his perch and cried:

"Sh!—here comes somebody."

"About time," said Wally, taking possession of the squirt.

As he spoke, the footsteps halted at the door, and the handle turned.

"Lie low, you chaps," whispered Percy. "Don't let them know you're here to begin with. Hullo! who's that?"

"Let me in!" cried Gamble, outside.

"Can't; we're busy," replied Lickford.

"We've got a committee meeting, and you'd better cut," cried Percy.

"Do you hear?" replied the ambassador; "let me in."

"There's plenty of room in your own study, ain't there? Why don't you go there? We don't want you here."

"Cut your sticks, and learn your rotten Modern lessons," shouted Wally, who began to be tired of being a listener.

Luckily, Cottle knocked over one of the chairs at this juncture, which served to conceal the voice of the speaker from the ears outside.

"All right," said Gamble; "you'll catch it. Clapperton sent me to tell you if you don't come to his room directly, he'll come and fetch you himself. There!"

"Good evening," cried Ramshaw. "Our love to them all at home."

D'Arcy, meanwhile, had mounted the bed, and by means of a pea-shooter materially assisted in the departure of the discomfited envoy.

"Now we're getting livery," said Wally, proceeding to load his squirt out of the jug. "Better light the candle, one of you, and have some light on the subject."

A terrible discovery ensued. Neither candle nor matches could be found! In a quarter of an hour daylight would depart, and after that—well, the prospect was not brilliant, at any rate. However, there was no time to do anything but recriminate, which the company industriously did until the sentinel again gave the signal to stand by.

"Look here," said Percy, "we'd better keep him jawing as long as he'll stand it, and not let fly till he begins to get violent—eh?"

"All serene," said Wally; "that won't be long."

"No; and he'll bring the whole kit of prefects with him. What a high old time there'll be!" chuckled D'Arcy.

"There's one lucky thing," said Cash. "Forder and his dame have gone out for the evening; so we shan't hurt *their* feelings."

"Look out—it's Clapperton," whispered the sentinel.

Clapperton tried the door, and on finding it fast, gave it a kick.

"Hello! who's there?"

"Open the door; let me in!"

"Who is it? that young cad Gamble again?" cried Percy, with a wink; the company generally.

"No. Do you hear? Let me in!"

"Say what your name is. How do we know you aren't a Classic cad? Oh! ow!"

This last interjection was in answer to a fraternal kick from behind.

"You know who I am," replied Clapperton. "Let me in!"

"Very sorry, Corder, we can't let you in. Clapperton says we're to cut you, because you played a jolly sight too well last week."

"It's not Corder, it's me—Clapperton."

"Go on! no larks, whoever you are. Clapperton's got something better to do than go to tea-parties in fags' rooms. Go and tell that to the Clap— Oh! ow! I mean, try it on next door!"

"I tell you what," said Clapperton, whose temper, none of the best, was rapidly evaporating, "if you young cads don't open the door instantly, I'll break it open."

"If you do, we'll tell Clapperton. He'll welt you for it. *He* won't let you spoil our new paint, not if he knows it. Good old Clappy?"

A thundering kick was the only reply, which shook the plaster of the walls, and nearly sent Fisher minor headlong with terror off his perch.

This was getting serious. But in Percy's judgment the time was not even yet ripe for extreme measures. The assailant might be given a little rope yet.

He took it, and worked himself into a childish passion against the refractory door, encouraged by the friendly gibes of the besieged. "Go it!"

"Two to one on his boots!"

"Keep your temper!"

"Come in!" "Stick to it!" "One more and you'll do it!" and so on.

It was hardly likely that the spectacle of the captain of the house in a towering rage, toying to kick his way into a fag's room, would long be allowed to continue unheeded by the rest of the inhabitants of Forder's, and in a very short time new voices without apprised the beleaguered garrison that the enemy was sitting down in force.

Brinkman's voice could be heard demanding admission, and presently Dangle's; while a *posse* of mercenary middle-boys relieved Clapperton of the kicking. The stout old door held out bravely and defied all their efforts.

Presently a pause was made, and Dangle's voice outside was heard demanding a parley.

"Young Wheatfield," he said, "it will be wiser for you to open the door at once. If you don't it will be broken open, and you needn't expect to get off easy then. Take my advice, and don't be a fool."

"Thanks awfully," said Percy. "I and my chaps are just going to sit down to tea. Wish you could join us, whoever you are. We've got as much right to have tea in our study as you have in yours. That's right! Kick away! Never mind the varnish! Somebody tapping at the study door."

"It's no good wasting time over young asses like them," Brinkman was heard to say.

"I don't mean to go now," said Clapperton. "They shall have such a hiding, all of them, as they won't forget in a hurry."

"It's funny how when we seniors strike against the School it's so noble, and when these juniors strike against us it's so inexcusable," said Fullerton. "Strikes always did puzzle me."

"If, instead of talking rubbish, you'd go and fetch Robert with a crowbar to smash open the door," said Clapperton, "you'd be more use."

It was getting quite dark in the room by this time, but Wally could be heard refilling his squirt at the jug, "I mean to start now," said he.

Percy came beside him.

"All serene," said he; "but why use water when there's ink?"

"My eye! I never thought of that. Rather! I say, old man, while I remember it, I'll write home this week. Don't you fag, good old Percy."

"Oh no, it's my turn."

"Oh, let me. Is that the ink-pot? Hold it tight while I get a good go at it."

"Suppose we tickle them up with the pea-shooter first," suggested Lickford. "Mind how you go over the chairs, Cash," added he, as that hero in the dark got entangled in the second line of fortifications.

"All serene—wire away! Young Ashby, you'd better mix up some soap and coal-dust in the water for use when the ink's done."

By this time the attack without had redoubled, and Cash, mounting up to the loophole, began to operate on the besiegers with his pea-shooter. He had to guess where to shoot, for though the gas was alight in the passage, he was unable for anatomical reasons to look and shoot through the same hole at the same time. However, he had the satisfaction of feeling sure his fire was taking effect, by the aggravated exclamations of the besiegers, who vowed terrific vengeance for this fresh insult. In due time the marksman fell short of ammunition and was carefully helped down from his post in the dark, while Wally and Percy, gingerly carrying the squirt, ascended in his place.

"Hand up the basin," said Wally, "and get another lot of water ready."

"I say," said Fisher minor, who was always being seized by heroic impulses, "if you could let me down out of the window by the rope, I'd be able to get a candle."

"Good old 'How now!' awfully good notion," said Wally. "You chaps see to that, while my young brother and I work the squirt. Don't tell anybody what's up, young Fisher, and get back as soon as you can."

So, while the squirt was carefully being levelled in the face of the enemy, Fisher minor, with the end of the rope round his waist, was swinging precariously in mid-air out of the window, heartily repenting, until his feet touched *terra firma*, of his rash and desperate undertaking.

Before he was safe, the great attack had been delivered through the loophole. The kickers had receded from the door a pace or two in order to get up impetus for a combined onslaught, and Clapperton with a poker in his hand was advancing to annihilate the lock, when Percy, who was reconnoitring from the ventilating holes, gave the signal to have at them.

Whereupon Wally let fly with all his might, and converted half of the enemy, their captain included, into Ethiopians.

The effect was instantaneous. The four-footed kick did not come off. Clapperton's poker fell with a clatter on the floor, and a howl went up which electrified both besiegers and besieged.

"Look alive now!" said Wally. "Let 'em have the water! Keep it up!"

For five minutes an almost uninterrupted flow of coloured water poured through the loophole and kept the enemy at bay. But even a jugful will not last for ever, and presently the squirt gave a dismal groan on the bottom of the basin.

Almost at the same moment an ominous crack proclaimed that the good old door was giving way by degrees under the now renewed attack of the besiegers.

"They'll have it, after all," said Percy.

"Tell you what! Suppose we slip out by the window, and you chaps come and have supper in our room. Rather a lark, eh? It's getting a bit slow here. Nice sell for them too. Besides, they can't get at you over on our side."

This hospitable invitation fitted in with the humour of the company generally, particularly as every moment the door gave a more doubtful sound than before.

In three minutes the whole party was on the grass below, where Fisher minor, returning breathless, with a candle and matches, encountered them.

"Come on, you chaps," said Wally. "I'd give sixpence to see how they look when they find we've gone—ha! ha!"

They salved their honour with a keen sense of the humour of the situation, and followed their host across the Green in the dark, not at all sorry to have a harbour of refuge in sight, though very loth to admit that this rearward movement was a retreat.

At the door of Wakefield's, to their consternation, they met Ranger.

"What on earth are all you youngsters up to at this hour?"

"It's all right," said Wally. "The shop committee, you know. We're going to talk things over in my room. Come on, you Modern kids. We'll make an exception for you this once, and let you into Wakefield's; won't we, Ranger? But it mustn't occur again."

Yet another peril awaited them before they were safe in port. This time it was Mr Stratton on the stairs.

"Ah, here you are—all of you," said he. "I came to look for you. I want to hear how the shop is doing."

"Very well, thank you, sir. I say, Mr Stratton," said Wally, with a presence of mind which moved the admiration of his friends, "would you mind coming to a committee meeting in my and my chaps' room! We can show you the things we want ordered next week, if you don't mind."

"Certainly; I'll come. I'm delighted to find you're sticking so well to the business."

And so it happened that when at last Percy's door succumbed, and the besiegers rushed in, vowing vengeance and slaughter, to find the room empty, the nine innocents were sitting prettily round the table in Wally's room with Mr Stratton in the chair, deciding that until November was out it would be premature to order oranges for the Fellsgarth shop.

Chapter Seventeen
Hawk's Pike

Victory has its drawbacks, like everything else. The brilliant retreat of the Modern juniors and their auxiliaries under the enemy's fire was all very well as a strategic movement. But when it came to deciding what to do next, the difficulties of the situation became painfully apparent.

Mr Stratton stayed half an hour chatting over the shop affairs, and then rose to go.

"Good night, boys. It's time for Mr Forder's boys to be back in their house."

This unpleasant reminder had a very damping effect on the conviviality of the party generally. As soon as the master had gone, Wally said —

"It strikes me you Modern kids are in a bit of a mess."

"I'm afraid your bedroom will be a little untidy," said Fisher minor.

"The best thing you can do is to climb back by the window," suggested D'Arcy.

"I don't fancy you'll want a warming-pan to-night," said Ashby.

This was all very nice and helpful. The heroes looked at one another dismally.

"We must lump it," said Percy. "They can't do anything very bad."

"Can't they?" said Cottle. "Were you ever licked by Brinkman?"

"No," said the others.

"All right—I have been—that's all." This sounded alarming. D'Arcy said —

"Why don't you come over to our side, and out that lot! We could have no end of larks if you were Classics, instead of little Modern beasts."

"Our side's as good as yours," snapped Lickford. "All serene; you'd better go and join them," said Wally.

This did not advance the argument much further. Of course it was out of the question to go and tell tales to the Classic prefects, or even to their own master. Nor was the suggestion of sleeping that night on the Classic side hailed with enthusiasm by either party.

On the whole D'Arcy's suggestion of getting back by the window seemed the most hopeful. When once back they would go straight to bed, where they would be safe for a while. Then, if they could manage to rise at the supernatural hour of six, they might succeed in evading the penalties of rebellion for another day. For to-morrow being exeat day, they would be free to roam where they liked. And they had a very good idea that wherever it was, they would give Forder's house a very wide berth.

"Tell you what!" exclaimed Wally, slapping his brother on the back so hard as to cause him to yell loud enough to bring every prefect of Fellsgarth on to the spot. "Tell you what, old chappies; of course we will! Why ever didn't we think of it before—eh?"

"Think of what?"

"Why, we'll go up Hawk's Pike, of course."

"Of course we will," said everybody.

What mattered it to *them* that Hawk's Pike had defied the ordinary tourist for generations? *They* weren't ordinary tourists, or anything like.

"You come over for us at six," said Wally. "Bring the grub we left in your room. It'll be a regular sell for all those chaps. We'll make a day of it."

It seemed a magnificent solution of the problem; and on the strength of it the five truants departed, not without misgivings, for their quarters.

The rope was still dangling from their window, and Cash, whose father was in the Navy, was selected by general consent as the member of the party best qualified to make the first ascent. He modestly tried to induce some one else to assume the honour, but he was outvoted, and, devoutly hoping to find the coast clear of the enemy, he addressed himself to the venture.

It was not particularly arduous for a decent climber, and in a couple of minutes his companions saw him swing himself on to the ledge, and disappear into the room.

In a moment he put out his head.

"All clear," said he. "The door's smashed in, and all the things kicked about anyhow; but there's no one about."

That was the main thing. The company speedily followed, materially assisted in their clamber by sundry knots tied in the rope by the ingenious Cash, and by his energetic hauling from above.

The programme was carried out without a hitch. Without waiting for the bed-bell they one and all presented themselves to the dormitory dame, and requested permission to turn in, pleading severe fatigue (which was by no means imaginary) as the reason for this unwonted haste. So smartly was the retirement effected, that no one was aware of their return to their house until half an hour later. When the dormitory filled up, their five noses were discernible peeping from out the sheets.

Whatever chastisement the prefects may have had in store for them evidently could not be administered at present. For a disturbance in the dormitory was a capital offence in Mr Forder's eyes, and, as the master's room was adjacent, and he was known to have returned and to be within earshot, the only thing possible was secretly to promise the rebels a warm time of it as soon as they woke next morning.

But Revenge sleeps sounder than Caution. As five struck in the clock tower, Ramshaw, who had had it on his mind he might oversleep himself, and, in consequence, had been up looking at his watch every ten minutes during the night, slipped finally out of bed, and roused each of his partners. He expected no gratitude for his good offices, and was not disappointed. The sleepers growled and grunted at his well-meant efforts, pulled the clothes over their heads, called him unfriendly names, threatened him with untold vengeance, and scouted all idea of danger by delay, till he was almost tired of trying. But by the end of three-quarters of an hour, with the aid of a moist sponge and other persuasives, he got them to their feet well awake to a sense of the undertaking before them.

They still grumbled—at the cold, and the darkness, and the fatigue, and blamed Ramshaw for all three. They heartily despised themselves for their promise to the Classic boys last night, and still more for the row with their own prefects, which was the cause for all this inconvenience. But as they gradually slipped on their clothes, and the warm bed receded more into the background, they cheered up and recovered their courage.

There was no difficulty in getting out. The dormitory door stood open. Brinkman, who was the prefect on duty, lay snoring loud and long in the end bed. Mr Forder's bedroom was on the safe side of a brick wall. Carrying their boots in their hands they slunk off to their study, where they made a hasty selection from the miscellaneous provisions stored over-night, and then, one by one, solemnly slid down the rope.

Once on the grass, in the chill, dark air, depression fell upon them a second time. Their thoughts returned to the snug beds they had left. Even Brinkman and Clapperton could not take it out of them more than this white frost and nipping air. However, the bell began to toll six; and the thought of their companions in discomfort spurred them on to energy. They crawled across the Green to Wakefield's.

Four ghostly figures were visible in the feeble dawn, hovering under the wall.

"Got the grub?"

It was the cheery voice of Wally Wheatfield, at sound of which the pilgrims took comfort, and were glad they had turned out after all.

The first thing was to get clear of Fellsgarth, which was easily accomplished, as no one was about. Even had they been observed, beyond the general wonder of seeing nine juniors taking a morning walk at 6 a.m., there was nothing to interfere with their liberty. As soon as they got into Shargle Woods a brief council of war was held.

"It's a jolly stiff climb," said Wally.

"I've got a compass," said Ashby, as if that disposed of the difficulty. Ashby had an ulster, which just then seemed to some of his comrades a still more enviable possession.

"How many miles?" asked Lickford.

"Miles? Who ever reckoned mountains by miles? It's three hours to the top."

"That'll be nine o'clock," wisely observed Cash.

"Who knows the way up?" Percy asked.

"Way up? Can't you see it?" said Wally. "When you get to the bottom, you go straight up."

"All very well for you. I can't walk up a perpendicular cliff. I dare say I could come straight down if I tried," submitted Percy.

"Oh, there are lots of paths. It's as easy as pot," said Wally. "Suppose we have a bit of grub now. It'll be less to carry, you know."

Whereupon an attack was made on the provisions, with the result that considerably less was left to carry up.

The meal ended, a start was made in earnest, and the party trailed down the valley towards the lake at an easy jog-trot, and came to the conclusion that ascending a pike was ridiculously simple work.

By the time they reached the lake, and began to strike up the winding lane that led round to the rearward slopes of the great mountain, an hour had passed.

"Nearly half-way there," said Fisher minor, hoping some one would corroborate the statement.

"Oh, we don't count that bit we've come anything," said Wally. "We're just starting up now."

"Oh," said Fisher, again hoping to be confirmed. "Then it's only two hours' climb?"

"That's all you know about it. Wisdom used to say he could do it in three hours from the lake-side. But he was a wonner to go. Come along; wire in, you chaps."

"Where did Wisdom get killed?" asked Percy, by way of a little genial conversation.

"I heard over the other side, down the cliffs above the lake. He got caught in a mist and lost his way."

"How do you know this is the right way up?" asked Cottle.

"Because it's as plain as the nose on your face," retorted the guide.

It was a long dreary pull up the lower slope, over the wet grass and through the bracken, and Fisher minor before he accomplished the first stage was heartily sick of Hawk's Pike. One or two of his companions, to tell the truth, were not quite as enamoured of the expedition as they tried to appear, but they kept their emotions to themselves. Wally was the only member of the party who was uniformly cheerful, and no one, not even Percy, exactly liked to incur his contempt by appearing to enjoy the clamber less than he.

"Come on, you chaps," cried the leader as he staggered to the top of the slope. "Keep it up. What a crow it will be for us, when we get to the top!"

"I suppose," gasped Fisher minor, as he threw himself on the grass, "we're half-way now?"

"Getting on," said Wally. "I dare say on the top of that next ridge we shall be able to see the top."

"What, isn't that the top?" said poor Fisher, craning his head up towards the beetling crag above them.

"Top? No, that's the knob half-way down we see from the school window. The stiff part begins after that."

Really Wally, if he had tried to be heartless, could not have succeeded better. Had he but expressed some hint at regret that the distance was so long, or vouchsafed the least semblance of a growl at the labour involved, they would have loved him. As it was, they durst do nothing but hate him, and accept his information joyously.

"That's nothing," said Lickford. "I feel quite fresh; don't you, you chaps?"

"Rather!" they chimed in plaintively.

"Better get on," said Wally, after a few minutes more. How they loathed Wally then!

The new slope was worse than the first; for the grass was more boggy, and big stones here and there jarred their tender feet. Besides, it grieved them to see Wally zigzagging steadily on ahead, utterly regardless of their distress behind. Yet no one exactly liked to stop. Had any one had the courage to do so, they would have gone down like a row of ninepins.

Let no one charge these boys with chicken-heartedness. On the contrary, they worked up that slope like heroes; all the more so that they were ready to drop, and durst not for very shame. There is no hero like the coward who compels himself to be brave. Many a man in history has become famous for an exploit that cost him far less than this climb cost the Fellsgarth juniors. Therefore let this record at least award the the credit they deserve.—It was some satisfaction, when the knob was reached, and they looked up at the black towering crags above, to see that even Wally seemed staggered for a moment.

"We may as well have a rest and some grub before we tackle that lot," said he. "What do you say?"

The motion was carried unanimously.

"It's eleven o'clock," said Cash. "We've been five hours already."

"Thank goodness we've broken the back of it," said Fisher minor.

"I don't know so much about that," said Percy.

"We shan't get up that as easily as we've done so far, I fancy."

"Rather not," said Wally, cheerfully, with his mouth full of sandwich. "I believe it's not so bad after we get past those rocks though, on to the top."

"What," cried Fisher, "isn't *that* the top then?"

"Bless you, no. We have to go down a bit when we get there, and cross a bog, and then the real pike begins."

The information was received with dead silence, and the party sat grimly munching their lunch with upturned eyes.

"Which way do we go?" asked Cottle presently.

"I suppose up by the stream. It's bound to lead up to the bog."

The stream in question was a torrent which fell in a series of leaps through a narrow gorge in the rocks.

Fisher minor looked very blue.

"I wish I'd got my strong boots," said he.

The dismal tone in which he uttered the words startled the others.

"I say, young Fisher," said D'Arcy, "you're not done yet, are you!"

Fisher minor had not the pluck to say "Yes."

"I'll be game after this rest. I got a little blown up that last bit, that's all."

"It doesn't look awfully far now," said Ashby.

"It's further than it looks. Come on; let's be jogging," said Wally.

The new ascent, which consisted chiefly in clambering from stone to stone up the rocky ravine, was less exhausting than the tramp up the bog, and as Wally was no better at this sort of climbing than any of the rest, he did not dishearten them by getting hopelessly ahead, but kept with the party. Occasionally they had to help one another up a specially stiff ledge, and this mutual accommodation was an additional source of comfort to the weak goers. Progress was very slow. Cash, having hauled himself up on to a little platform of moss, looked at his watch and was alarmed to find it was past one. The huge ravine, at the far head of which they could see the open sky, seemed a tremendous distance yet. And after that, according to Wally, was to come the bog and the cliffs beyond, on which Wisdom lost his life.

Yet none of these things was quite so bad as the rolling up of some fleecy clouds behind them, which effaced the view below, and seemed to be crawling up the mountain in pursuit of them.

Cash pointed this out to Wally, who grunted.

"We shall miss the view from the top," said he.

"If we ever get there," said Cash.

On they scrambled again, casting every now and then a longing look upward at the grim ravine head, and now and then an anxious glance behind at the fast overhauling clouds.

"We're bound to get out of it up there," sang out Wally.

But almost as he spoke the light mist swept past him, blotting out everything but the boulder he stood on and a rift of the dashing water at his feet.

The clouds had befriended Fisher minor. They did what he durst not do; ordered the party to halt.

"Where are you?" shouted Wally from the invisible. "Here; where are you?"

"Stay there; and I'll come to you."

Slowly the party foregathered, and stood huddled in the blinding mist on a flat rock.

"It's blowing over," said Wally. "We'd better make back for the hill-side, and get out of this ravine till it clears up."

It was no easy task scrambling back, down that difficult way, over boulders already made slippery by the moist mist, and not able to see four yards ahead. The clouds poured up to meet them in column upon column, growing denser and wetter every minute. At last, how they scarcely knew, they came down to where the rush of the water ceased and the stones gave place to wet grass.

"We must be somewhere near where we sat down last," said Ashby. "Whew! it's cold."

"The thing is," said Percy, "aren't we too much out to the left? There's no sign of a path that I can see."

"This looks like one," said a voice ahead, which they recognised as Wally's. "Come along—this way."

They followed as well as they could, and groped about for the path. Then they shouted.

Wally replied out of the mist.

"Stay there a bit—it's not a path. I'll yell when I've got it."

They waited, and for five minutes listened anxiously for the signal. Then they thought they heard it away to the right, and floundered off in pursuit. But after a little they discovered that they were going uphill.

"Hadn't we better go back to where we were," said Cash, "or we may miss him?"

It occurred to most of the party that they had missed him already. Still, they decided to go back.

Presently they distinctly heard what sounded like a voice below them.

"That must be he. Yell!"

They shouted, and again there seemed to come a faint response.

"All right," said Percy. "Stay where you are, and I'll go and fetch him up."

And he vanished into the mist.

"What's the time?" said Ashby, as the party stood dismally waiting.

"Half-past four. It's a good job it doesn't get dark till six."

"Only an hour and a half," said Cottle; "I wish those chaps would come."

But though they strained their ears and eyes, no sign of the missing ones came; nothing but the swish of the rain and the whistle of the wind through the grass.

"We'd better go on," said D'Arcy presently; "they'll probably get down some other way. Look sharp, or it will be dark."

So they started at a fast walk down the boggy slope.

"Keep close," said D'Arcy after a time. "Are you all there?"

Everybody answered for himself, but not for his neighbour.

"You there, young Fisher minor?"

"Yes," replied Fisher's voice from the rear.

He seemed so near that they started on again.

But after another five minutes, Ashby, who was last but one, shouted again.

"Where are you, Fisher minor?"

There was no answer.

"Wait a bit, you fellows. Fisher minor's behind."

But no answer came from that direction either.

"Here's a go," said Ashby to himself. "That kid Fisher's gone lame, and he'll be lost if I don't wait for him."

So he dismally turned back, shouting and whistling as he went.

The clouds all round grew duller and heavier in the fading light, and the wind-blown rain struck keenly on the wanderer's cheek.

"That kid," said Ashby to himself, as he sturdily tramped through the marsh, "ought not to have come. He's not up to it."

But despite all his shouting and whistling and cooeying, not a sound came out of the mist but the wind and the driving of the rain.

Still Ashby could not bring himself to leave the "kid" in the lurch. Even if he did not find him it would be better to—

"Ah! what was that?"

He clapped his hands to his mouth and shouted against the wind with all his might.

His voice was flung back in his face; but with it there came the feeble sound of a "coo-ey" somewhere near.

Ashby sprang to it like a drowning man to a straw. If it was only a lost sheep it would be some company. For ten minutes he beat round, shouting all the time, and once or twice fancying he heard an answer.

Then suddenly he came upon a great boulder, against which leaned Fisher minor, whimpering and shivering.

"Here you are!" said Ashby, joyously. "Thank God for it! I gave you up for lost. The others are gone on. Come on. Hang on my arm, old hoss."

"I can't; I'm too fagged to go on. I'm awfully sleepy, Ashby. You go on; I'll come presently."

Ashby's reply was prompt and vigorous. He took his fellow-junior by the arm and began to march him down the slope as fast, almost faster than his weary legs would carry him.

And as they started, the last of the light died out of the mist, and left them in blank darkness.

Chapter Eighteen
Rollitt makes a Record for Fellsgarth

The Modern seniors had slept on soundly that morning, secure of their prey. The military operations of the preceding evening, although they resulted in the night of the besieged, had not tended to the glory of the besiegers. Indeed, when the door had at last been broken in and it was discovered that the birds had flown, a titter had gone round at the expense of Messrs Clapperton, Dangle, and Brinkman, which had been particularly riling to those gentlemen.

When in the morning the birds were found to have flown once more, the position of the seniors became positively painful. Fullerton, as usual, did not salve the wound.

"I should say—not that it matters much to me—that that scores another to the rebels," said he. "How very naughty of them not to stay and be whopped, to be sure!"

"The young cads!" growled Clapperton, who had the grace to be perfectly aware that he had been made ridiculous. "I don't envy them when I get hold of them."

"No more do I," said Fullerton, "with their door off its hinges. It will be very draughty."

"Do shut up. Why don't you go and join the enemy at once, if you're so fond of them?" said Dangle.

"Well," said Clapperton, "they will keep; but we must have it out with Corder now. It's no use simply cutting him; he'll have to be taught that he can't defy the house for nothing. Go and tell him to come, Brinkman."

But Corder's back was against the wall, literally and metaphorically.

To Brinkman's demand (almost the first voice he had heard speaking to him for a week) he returned a curt refusal.

"Well, I'll make you come," said Brinkman. Whereupon Corder retreated behind his table and invited the interloper to begin.

To dodge round and round a study table after a nimble boy is not a very dignified operation for a prefect, particularly when the object of his chase is a prefect too; and Brinkman presently abandoned the quest and went off, breathing threatenings and slaughter, for reinforcements.

So did Corder. Less sensitive than his junior fellow-martyrs, he marched straight across to Yorke's study. The captain was away, but in the adjoining room he found Fisher major and Denton, poring over their endless accounts.

"You two," said Corder, "you're prefects. You're wanted over on the other side to stop bullying."

"Who's being bullied?"

"I am. I've been cut dead for a week. I'm sick of it. Now they're going to lick me. I'd take my chance against them one at a time, but I can't tackle three of them."

"Is it for playing in the match?"

"Yes, that and going to the meeting. Nothing else. I'd go to twenty a day, if I had the chance, to spite them."

"Who are bullying you?"

"Clapperton, Brinkman, and Dangle, of course."

"I tell you what," said Denton, "we couldn't go over. We've no authority. But there's nothing to prevent you staying here and letting them fetch you. Then we can interfere."

"All serene," said Corder; "I hope they will come. I say, I wish you'd let me wait here and hear you fellows talk. I've not had a word spoken to me for a week. I can tell you it's no joke. I laughed at it at first, and thought it would be nice rather than otherwise. But after two days, you chaps, it gets to be decidedly slow; you begin to wonder if it isn't worth caving in. But that would be *such* a howling come down, when all you've done is to do what you had a right to do—or rather what you're bound to do—play up for the School."

"And jolly well you played too," said Usher.

"It was a lucky turn. You know I was so awfully glad to be in the fifteen, and felt I could do anything. Of course the lucky thing was my getting past their forwards, and then—" And then Corder bunched into a delighted account of the never-to-be-forgotten match, during which the cloud passed away from his face, the light came back to his eyes, and the spirit into his voice.

"What business have they to stop me," said he, "or bully me for it?"

"None. And Yorke, when he hears of it, will report it to the doctor."

"No, don't let him do that. What's the use? If I can stay here it's all right."

An hour later, about the time that the young mountaineers were beginning to look out for their second wind on the lower slope, Dangle came across in a vicious temper.

He had not come to look for Corder, the sight of whom in the sanctuary of a Classic study took him aback.

"That's where you're sneaking, is it?" said he. "I'm not surprised."

"Not much need to sneak from *you*. It's three against one I object to," said Corder. "But if you like to fetch Clapperton and Brinkman over here, we can have it out comfortably now."

"You must think yourself uncommonly important if you suppose we're going to trouble about an ass like you," said Dangle. "I never once thought of you."

"What have you come for, then?" said Fisher. "Hadn't you better wait till you're invited before you come where you're not wanted?"

"I've come on club business, and I've a perfect right to come. You fellows, I hear, have taken it into your heads to dissolve the club."

"What of that? Why didn't you come and vote against it if you didn't like it?"

"Thank you. It wasn't quite good enough. What I want to know is, what is the treasurer going to do with the money? I suppose that's hardly going to be treated as a perquisite for him?"

Fisher major looked troubled. He had dreaded this awkward question for days. For the lost money was still missing.

"You know it's nothing of the kind."

"What are you going to do with it, then?"

"That's for the club to decide. If you'd come to the meeting you could have proposed something."

"It's funny how sore you are about that precious hole-and-corner meeting of yours. How much is there on hand?"

"You'll know presently."

"I dare say—as soon as you've hit on a dodge for getting over that little deficiency of four or five pounds—eh?"

Fisher major looked up in astonishment. How had the fellow heard about that?

Dangle laughed.

"You thought it was a snug little secret of your own, didn't you? You're mistaken. And you're mistaken if you think we aren't going to get at the bottom of it."

Fisher major rose to his feet.

"Look here, Dangle," said he; "do you mean to insinuate that *I've* taken the club money!"

"I never said so."

"Or that I was going to cook the accounts so that it should not be known?"

"I didn't mean *you* were."

"Whom did you mean? Me?" said Denton.

"No; I didn't say anybody," said Dangle, beginning to feel himself in a fix. "All I meant was, we want to know what's become of the money?"

"You don't want to know more than I do," said Fisher major. "I'd have handed over the money days ago, if I could only have found it."

"Do you suspect any one?" said Dangle.

"Suspect? No. No one comes here that would be likely to take it."

"You leave it about, though. I've noticed that myself. Who's your fag?"

"As honest a man as you, every bit, and that's saying a good deal for *you*," retorted Fisher major, hotly.

"Keep your temper. Who's study is that next yours?"

"That's Yorke's."

"No: on the other side."

"That's Rollitt's. I suppose you're going to insinuate—"

"Stop a bit," said Dangle, suddenly, turning to close the door before he proceeded. "When did you first miss the money?"

"You're uncommonly interested in the accounts," said Fisher; "if you want to know so much, it was ten days ago."

"I'm interested because I've an idea. When did you get in the subscriptions?"

"They were all in a week before the first Rendlesham match, the match where you—"

Fisher major stopped.

Dangle took no notice of the broken taunt, and said—

"Look here, Fisher. There's no love lost between you and me, and it doesn't affect me."

"Or me."

"For all that, I don't care to see you or the clubs robbed without giving you a friendly hint."

"You're very kind. Who is the culprit? The doctor?"

"No; *Rollitt*. Stay," said he, waving down the interruption, "I shouldn't be fool enough to say it unless I was pretty sure. Tell me this, Fisher; when you go out and leave money about do you lock your door?"

"No. We don't have to do that this side."

"Did you ever see Rollitt in here?"

"No."

"Do you know that on the first half-holiday this term Rollitt nearly came to grief on the river?"

"What on earth has that to do with it?"

"Everything. You heard of it? Your young brother was with him, of course. And you heard that he lost Widow Wisdom's boat over the falls."

"Yes," said Fisher, suddenly beginning to see the drift of the cross-examination.

"And you heard that the very next day he bought her a new one for five pounds?"

"Yes, I did; but whatever right have you to connect that with the missing money?"

"Wait a bit. You were away all that afternoon, weren't you!"

"Yes."

"I wasn't. I happened to come over to look for you, and found you were out. The only fellow I met in the house was Rollitt. He'd just got back, and I met him at the door of this room. There, you can make what you like of it. Even a Classic knows what twice two makes."

And he turned on his heel and left the room.

"There's goes a thoroughbred cad for you," said Denton.

"I don't know how we came to let him go without a kicking," said Fisher.

"Shall I call to him to come back?" asked Corder.

"Of course," said Fisher major, "it *is* a curious coincidence about Rollitt. But I never thought of connecting the two things together before."

"No. It's utter guesswork on Dangle's part."

"If it comes to that," said Corder, "if Dangle was over here that afternoon, why shouldn't he have collared it as well as Rollitt?"

"He has any amount of money. He's not hard up, like Rollitt."

"All I can say is," said Denton, "I wish that cad had kept his suspicions to himself."

The object of these suspicions, meanwhile, blissfully unconscious of the interest with which he was being remembered at Fellsgarth, was utilising his holiday in the prosecution of his favourite sport.

This time he did not fish from a boat, nor did he affect the upper stream. He tried the lower reach; and not very successfully. For he had never been able to replace the tackle lost on the eventful afternoon when Widow Wisdom's boat had gone over the falls. He had his fly-book still, and had come across an old reel which, fitted to a makeshift rod with common twine, had to do duty until he could afford a regular new turnout. It was better than nothing, but the fish seemed somehow to get wind of the fact that they were not being treated with proper respect, and refused to have more to do than they could help with irregular-looking apparatus.

Rollitt put up with their unreasonableness for a long time that morning and afternoon. With infinite patience he tried one fly after another, and either bank in turn. He gave them a chance of being hooked under the falls, or right down on the flats by the lake. But it was no go. They wouldn't be tempted.

At last, as it was growing dusk, he became conscious that it had been raining fast for half an hour, and that he was wet through. He looked up and saw a grim pall of wet lying over the lake and all up the side of Hawk's Pike, of which only the lower slope was distinguishable through the mist. It was not a promising evening; and Rollitt, now he came to think of it, might as well go back to Fellsgarth as stand about here.

So he collected his tackle and turned homeward. His path from the lake brought him across the track which leads round to the back of the mountain;

and he was just turning in here when he heard what sounded like a halloo on the hill-side. It was probably only a shepherd calling his dog, but he waited to make sure.

Yes, it was a shout, but it sounded more like a sheep than a man. Rollitt shouted back. A quick response came, and presently out of the mist a shadowy form emerged running down the slope, hopping over the boulders, and making for the lane.

A minute more and Wally presented himself.

"Hullo, is that you, Rollitt? I thought I was lost. I say, have you seen the others?"

Rollitt shook his head.

"Whew! I made sure they'd come down. I say, what a go if they're lost up there, a night like this?"

Rollitt looked up at the dim mountain-side and nodded again.

"I thought I was on a path, you know, and hallooed to them. They didn't hear, so I went back for them, and—so we've missed."

"Who!" said Rollitt.

"Do you know my young brother Percy, a Modern kid? He was one, and all our lot, you know, D'Arcy and Ashby and Fisher minor and—"

"Fisher minor," said Rollitt, suddenly becoming interested; "up there?"

"Yes—he's the lame horse of the party—not up to it. What's up, I say?"

Rollitt had suddenly deposited his rod under the wall, and quitting the path was beginning to strike up the base of the hill.

"Go, and bring guides," he growled.

"You'll get lost, to a dead certainty. I say, can't I come too?" said the boy, looking very miserable.

"No. Fetch guides. Come with them. Quick."

There were no guides to be had nearer than Penchurch, four miles off, and Wally, very cold and wet and hungry and footsore, with a big load on his heart as he thought of Percy, pulled himself together with an effort and stumped off.

Rollitt strode on up the slope in the gathering night. Cold and weather mattered little to him, still less did danger. But Fisher minor mattered very much. For Percy or any of the rest he might probably have stayed where he was; but for the one boy in Fellsgarth he cared about he would cheerfully go over a precipice.

Every now and again he stood still and shouted. But in the wind and rain it was impossible to say if any one heard him or called again.

After an hour or more he found himself on the first ridge, where for a few yards the ground is level before it rises again. Here he called again, once or twice. Once there came, as he thought, a faint distant whistle, but by no manner of calling could he get it to come again. He started off in the direction from which it seemed to come, calling all the way, but never a voice came out of the darkness. For a couple of hours he doggedly haunted the place, loth to leave it while a chance remained. Then he gave it up, and started once more up the steep slope. He looked at his watch by the light of a match. It was eleven o'clock. He shuddered, but not with the cold, and went on.

Something—who could say what?—told him that he must go higher yet. Once last year, in company with Wisdom, he had been as far as the upper bog, and had wanted to go to the top. But Wisdom had dissuaded him. Now, even in the darkness the ground seemed familiar, and he tramped on up the swampy steep till presently he found himself near the sound of rushing water at the foot of the great ravine.

The stream had grown so strong since the afternoon that to shout against it was more hopeless than ever. Yet Rollitt shouted. Had a voice replied, he felt sure he could have heard it. But none did.

Up the steep ravine he went, finding the going easier than through the spongy swamps below. About half-way up, just where the juniors ten hours ago had decided to turn back, as he looked up, he saw what seemed like clear sky through a frame in the mist. Was it clearing after all? Yes. The higher he got the more the mist broke up into fleeting clouds, which swept aside every few moments and let in a dim glimmer of moonlight on the scene.

At the top of the ravine he shouted again; but all was still. Even the wind was dying down, and the rain fell with a deadened sob at his feet. Three o'clock! Wisdom had told him, the day they had been up there, that the top was only three-quarters of an hour beyond where he stood. Something still cried "Excelsior" within him, and without halting longer than to satisfy himself by another shout, he started on.

How he achieved that tremendous climb he could never say. The clouds had rolled off, and the moonlight lit up the rocks almost like day. Never once did he pull up or flag in his ascent. He even ceased to shout.

The Cock-House at Fellsgarth | 171

Presently there loomed before him, gleaming in the moonlight, the cairn. For the first time in its annals, a Fellsgarth boy had got to the top of Hawk's Pike.

But, so far from elation at the glory of the achievement, Rollitt uttered a groan of dismay when he looked round and found no one there after all. That he would find Fisher minor there he had never doubted; and now—all this had been time lost.

Without waiting to heed the glorious moonlight prospect over lake and hill, he turned almost savagely, and scrambled down the crags. It was perilous work—more perilous than the scramble up. But Rollitt did not think of danger, and therefore perhaps did not meet it. In half an hour he was down on the bog—and in an hour after, just as a faint break in the east gave warning that the night was gone, he stood bruised and panting at the foot of the gorge on the second ridge.

He was too dispirited to shout now. It had not been given to him after all to rescue his friend. He would have done better if he had never—

There was a big boulder just ahead, poised almost miraculously on its edge, on the sloping hill-side. It looked as if a moderate blast of wind would send it headlong to the bottom. But it had stood there for centuries, a shelter for sheep in winter from the snow and hail.

What made Rollitt bound now in the direction of this rock, like a man shot? Surely not to admire a natural curiosity, or to seek shelter under its wing.

No. He had found that his quest after all had not been in vain. There, curled up under the overhanging rock, lying one almost across the other for warmth, with cheek touching cheek, and Ashby's coat covering both, were Fisher minor and his chum—not dead, but sleeping soundly!

Chapter Nineteen
Corder strikes a Blow for Liberty

The absence of the juniors had excited no curiosity in either house till evening. It was a holiday, and though the rule was that even on a holiday no boy should go "out of touch," as it was called, that is, beyond a certain radius, without permission, it was not always enforced. The Modern seniors had every reason to guess the object of this prolonged absence. They had promised many things to the juniors when they caught them. It was not surprising, while things were as warm as they were, that the young rebels should give Fellsgarth a wide berth.

As to the Classic juniors, no one was surprised at anything they did, in reason.

But when "call-over" came and all nine names were returned absent (in addition to that of Rollitt and a few other habitual vagrants), fellows began to ask where they were.

"Has any one seen Wally?" asked Yorke, who had just had the unusual experience of making his own tea and cooking his own eggs.

"He's probably fooling about somewhere out of bounds with my fag," said Ranger. "He'll have to catch it, Fisher, though he is your brother."

"Let him have it," said Fisher. "I'd do the same to your young brother if I had the chance. But to change the subject, I've something to tell you fellows that's rather awkward. That money hasn't turned up yet."

"That is awkward," said Yorke. "I wish I could help you out with it, but I'm cleaned out."

"Oh, that's not it. Of course I'm responsible, and must get the governor to make it good. Dear old governor, he'll do it, but he'll pull a precious long face, and go round the house lowering the gas and telling every one he must economise, with two such expensive sons as me and my minor at school. It's not that, though. Dangle came over this morning, and wanted to know what we were going to do about the accounts, now we've dissolved the clubs; and somehow or other he's heard of the deficiency, and wants to know all about it."

"I hope you told him," said Yorke.

"Of course I did; but he told me a lot more than I could tell him. He thinks he knows what's become of it."

And Fisher proceeded to narrate Dangle's suspicions against Rollitt.

The captain's face grew very long as the story went on. Then he said—

"I hope to goodness there's nothing in it. Is it a fact about Widow Wisdom's boat?"

"Yes; my young brother was with Rollitt that day, and told me about it as a secret. But as it's out now, there's no good keeping it."

"Dangle has a spite against Rollitt. If any one else had told you this, there might have been something in it."

"And if it had been any one but Rollitt bought the boat, it would have been nothing. But he's so frightfully poor. He'd no time to write home, even if he could have got money from there, and there was no one here he could borrow of. Why, he must have gone off very first thing in the morning and bought the boat."

"And are you quite certain you had all the money collected by that Saturday?" asked Yorke.

"Yes; and what's more, I'm almost certain I counted it and made it come right. That's the last time it has come right."

The captain drummed his fingers on the table and looked very miserable.

"I wish, Fisher," said he, "I hadn't advised you to take that treasurership. If we could only be quite sure there wasn't some mistake in the accounts, it would be different. It would be a frightful thing to suspect Rollitt unless it was absolutely certain."

"You're welcome to round on me," said Fisher, looking quite as miserable as his chief. "I was a fool to take your advice. I'd much sooner make the money up myself, and not say a word about it to any one."

"You can't do that now. You may be sure Dangle won't let it drop."

"What shall you do?" asked Ranger.

"What would *you* do?" said Yorke, testily. "Isn't it bad enough to be in a fix like this without being asked hopeless questions? I'm sorry, old man, I've lost my temper; and as it's not come back I vote we say no more on the subject at present."

The evening wore on, and still the truants did not return. At ten o'clock Yorke reported their absence to Mr Wakefield, and Mr Wakefield reported it to the head-master. A similar report reached him from the matron of Mr Forders house with regard to the missing ones there; and presently, further report was made that Rollitt was not in the school.

No one could give any account of their probable whereabouts. Rollitt had been seen going out with a rod early in the day, but no one had seen any of the juniors since last night, when they had prematurely gone to bed in their own dormitory. A consultation was held, in which all sorts of conjectures were put forward, the most plausible of which was that the juniors had organised an expedition to Seastrand, a fashionable watering-place an hour distant on the railway, which both Wally and Lickford had separately been heard to express a desire to visit. It seemed probable that they had lost the last train back, and would literally "not come home till morning."

In which case warm things were promised to be ready for my gentlemen.

As to Rollitt, his vagaries were consistent with any explanation. He may have gone to Penchurch in mistake for Fellsgarth, and curled himself up in the church porch, mistaking it for his bed.

In any case the general impression was that nothing could be done till morning, and that the juniors at least were making themselves pretty comfortable, wherever they might be.

Still, Fisher major felt a vague uneasiness. Had he been quite sure his brother was in the capable company of his fellow-fags, he would have been comparatively comfortable. But the possibility of the feckless youngster wandering about benighted somewhere on his own account added a new weight to the burden which already lay on the spirit of the luckless treasurer of the School clubs.

"I've a good mind to turn out and look for my minor," said he to Denton.

"What could you do? He's all right. You couldn't do anything in the dark, and on a night like this. I'm game to turn out any hour you like in the morning, if he's not come by then. I bet you the four young scamps will all stroll in for call-over, and wonder whatever the fuss was about."

There was nothing to be done, and Fisher lay awake all night, listening to every sound, and reproaching himself over and over again (as one will do when everything goes wrong) that he had made such a mess of everything this term.

About daybreak there came a ring at the school-bell, and half the school jumped to its feet. Fisher was down on the Green among the first, in slippers and ulster.

Five shivering youngsters were standing inside the gate, with dripping garments and chattering teeth and white faces—D'Arcy, Lickford, Ramshaw, Cottle, and Cash—but no Fisher minor.

"Where's my minor?" asked the senior.

"What! hasn't he turned up?" said D'Arcy. "Haven't Wally and Percy and Ashby turned up? We got lost on Hawk's Pike. I'm awfully hungry, I say."

"No one's turned up. Do you mean to say he's out on the hill a night like this?"

"He was behind—he and Ashby. He was a lame duck, you know. The others were in front."

"Were they together?"

"Who? Young Fisher minor and Ashby? I don't think so."

"Ashby yelled to see if we knew where he was, and must have gone to look for him. We made sure they'd be back long ago, didn't we, you chaps?"

Here the doctor and several of the prefects came on the scene. The truants were ordered to the hot bath and bed at once, and a council was held as to what should be done. Fisher major did not wait to take part in it. He rushed to his room, flung on his clothes and boots, and started off, accompanied by Denton, at full speed, in the direction of the mountain.

Neither spoke a word. As they passed Widow Wisdom's, Denton darted in.

"Have your fire alight and some food ready. Some of our youngsters have been all night on the mountain. We're going to look for them."

Half-way to the lake, they were pulled up by a shout from across the stream. It was Percy Wheatfield, dead beat, sitting on a log, as white and miserable as a ghost.

"I say, have you chaps seen Wally?" he called.

"No; we're off to look. Some of them have turned up. Can you get as far as Widow Wisdom's? There's a roaring fire and some grub waiting there. We'll see after Wally."

Percy staggered to his feet. He had been wandering, he could not say where, all night. The very mention of the words "fire" and "food" revived him.

"Get up to school as soon as you can and get to bed. You can't be any use looking for the rest. There's plenty of us to do that. Good-bye."

It was half-past seven when they reached the lake and turned up the mountain path. The mist had vanished, and the late autumn sun was shining brightly on the hill-side. The distant barking of a dog above apprised them that some one was abroad already, and the hopes of the searchers rose within them as they struck up the steep slope.

Half-way up they stood and shouted; but no reply came except the far-away barking of the shepherd's dogs. "We shall be able to see a good way all round when we get on to the ridge," said Denton.

Almost as he spoke, a shout close by startled them. Looking up they perceived emerging from behind some boulders a little procession.

Fisher major's blood ran cold as he saw it. For at the head stalked a stalwart guide, who carried in his arms one small boy, while in the rear followed a form which they recognised as Rollitt's carrying on his back another. Between the two tramped a third junior, hanging on to the arm of another guide.

What terrified Fisher major more than anything was to see that the head of the boy on Rollitt's back had fallen helplessly forward on the shoulder of his porter.

With a groan the elder brother bounded to the spot. The history of years flashed through his mind as he did so. He saw the people at home and heard their voices. He seemed to be in the nursery, hectoring it, as big brothers will, among the little ones, amongst whom was a little boy with curly hair and a shrill piping voice. He called to mind the first-night of this term, and the vision of his young brother breaking down with his new-boy troubles next morning. All this and more fleeted through his mind as he bounded to where Rollitt stood.

"Hush!" said the latter, almost gruffly. "Asleep."

So he was. It had scarcely roused him when Rollitt had picked him up two hours ago from his roost under the rocking-stone. And having once been perched on his preserver's back his head fell forward again, and there it had lain ever since. How Rollitt had carried him so far, resting only now and then, and that in a way not to disturb his burden, only those who knew the huge strength of the Fellsgarth giant could understand.

"Hullo," said Wally, greeting the new-comers in a limp, sleepy way, "have you seen my young brother Percy? He was—"

"Yes—Percy's all right; so are all the rest."

"I'm all right," sang out Ashby from the front. "This chap wanted to carry me, so I let him."

"Jolly glad you were to get the lift," said Wally. "You new kids oughtn't to have come. Twenty-four hours on the hills is nothing when you get used to—"

Here Wally (who had had twenty-six hours) suddenly collapsed and tumbled over from sheer fatigue on the grass.

Fisher and Denton made a chair of their hands for him, and so the procession went on.

A cart was in waiting at the foot of the slope, filled with warm wraps and other restoratives, and in less than two hours the whole party was safe inside the walls of Fellsgarth.

Hot baths, blankets, food, and a little physic, succeeded in a very few days in restoring the invalided truants to their sorrowing class-mates. Fisher minor was the only member of the party about whom any serious uneasiness existed, and he, thanks to a wiry constitution and a rooted dislike to do what nobody else did, got off with a bad cold, which detained him in his house for a fortnight.

Rollitt, as might have been expected, vanished to his own quarters as soon as he had deposited his precious burden into Mr Wakefield's charge. No one heard of his having been to the top. To Fisher's thanks he returned a grumpy "Not at all." And the curious inquiries of others he met by shutting his door and saying "Get out" to any one who entered.

As might be expected also, the Modern seniors were baulked, after all, of their promised vengeance on the rebels. On the contrary, while the fags were making merry on chicken and toasting their toes at the roaring fire in the sanatorium, Clapperton, Brinkman, and Dangle were hauled up into the presence of the head-master, and there seriously reprimanded for the damage done to one of the doors in Mr Forder's house, and cautioned not to let such a breach of discipline happen again, under a pain of severer penalties.

"If you are unable to keep order in your own house," said the doctor cuttingly, "your duty is to report the matter to me, and I will deal with it. Remember that another time."

This incident did not tend to smooth the ruffled plumes of the discomfited heroes.

Still less did another little rebuff, which happened a few days later.

Corder had taken advantage of the general excitement attending the escapade of the juniors to return to his own quarters and attempt once more to resume the privileges of ordinary civilised life. He only partially succeeded. Two or three boys, among whom was Fullerton, who were getting sick of the present state of affairs and longing for football once more, had begun seriously to doubt what advantage was coming to themselves or any one else by the strike. Among these Corder found a temporary shelter. But the authority of the seniors still controlled the general public opinion of the house, and the life of the boycotted boy was still only half tolerable.

At the first attempt at violence, however, Corder walked across to his Classic allies, and took up his quarters in their study, where he remained all day.

At bedtime he declined to return to his own house; particularly when a summons to that effect was sent across by Clapperton, who by this time had a very good idea of the rebel's whereabouts.

"I'm not going over," said Corder.

"But you can't stay here all night," said Denton.

"What shall you do—turn me out?" asked the fugitive.

"No. But you'd better go, and if you don't like the look of things out there, you'd better speak to Forder."

"No. I'd sooner stop," said Corder, doggedly. "I'm sorry to put you fellows about after your being so kind, but I'm not going over there."

Yorke was consulted, and took upon himself the responsibility of detaining the refugee for the night.

"All right, thanks," said Corder, and turned in.

Next morning word came from Mr Forder requiring that the truant should answer for his absence.

Corder obeyed, with some misgivings, and explained briefly that he had been bullied and did not want to stand it.

Mr Forder, who had a peculiar faculty for saddling the wrong horse, was not satisfied with this explanation, and chose to suspect some other. Corder had never been a satisfactory boy. He had probably been making himself objectionable, and had been glad of an excuse to break rules. The master did not demand particulars. He gave the culprit an imposition, and ordered him to obey the rules of his house; and another time, if he had any grievance, to come with it to him instead of taking the law into his own hands.

Whereupon Corder departed in high dudgeon.

It was no use holding out now. He had better give in, and own himself beaten. It would be so much easier than resisting any longer.

For an hour of two he was permitted to go in and out unmolested. But after morning school, he was going out to solace himself with some solitary kicks at the football, when just on the steps of the house Brinkman pounced upon him.

"I've got you now, have I, you cad?" said he. "You just come back with me."

"I won't. Let go!" cried Corder, in a temporary panic, wriggling himself away and escaping a few yards.

Brinkman, however, was quickly after him, determined this time to hold him fast. Corder, though a senior, was a small boy, and had never before thought of pitting, himself against the Modern bully.

But once already this term he had come suddenly to realise that he could do better than he gave himself credit for. And now that matters seemed desperate, when there was no escape, and his fate stared him in the face, it occurred to Corder he would show fight.

He had right on his side. He had done no harm to Brinkman or anybody else. Why shouldn't he let out, and stand up for himself?

So, to Brinkman's utter amazement, he was met by a blow and a defiant challenge to "come on."

What Brinkman might have done is doubtful, but at that moment Yorke and Ranger strolled by.

"Hullo! What's this? A fight?" said the captain.

"Rather," said Corder, now thoroughly strung up to the point. "I say, Yorke, will you stop and see fair play?"

The captain hesitated a moment. Any other fight he would have felt it his duty to stop. This fight seemed to be an exception. It would probably do more good than harm.

"Yes, if you like," said he.

"I'm not going to fight a little beggar like that," said Brinkman.

"Yes, you are," said Ranger, "and I'll see fair play for you."

"I promise you I'll make it so hot for him that he'll be sorry for it."

"I don't care," said Corder. "If you don't fight you're a coward. There!"

At this point Dangle came out.

"Here, your man wants a second," said Ranger; "you'll suit him better than I."

The usual crowd collected, minus the junior faction, who complained bitterly for a year after that they had been deliberately done out of being present by the malice of the principals. One result of their absence was that the proceedings were comparatively quiet. Every one present knew what the quarrel was, and not a few, for their own sakes, hoped Corder would make a good fight of it.

Dangle sneered at the whole thing, and counselled his man audibly not to be too hard on the little fool.

His advice was not wanted. Corder, for a fellow of his make and inexperience, exhibited good form, and persistently walked his man round the ring, dodging his blows and getting in a knock for himself every now and then. Brinkman soon dropped the disdainful style in which he commenced proceedings, and became proportionately wild and unsteady.

"Now's your chance, young 'un; he's lost his temper," whispered the captain.

Whereupon Corder, hardly knowing how he managed it, danced his man once more round and round, till he was out of breath, and then slipped in with a right, left—left, right, which, though they made up hardly one good blow among them, were so well planted, and followed one another so rapidly, that Brinkman lost his balance under them, and fell sprawling on the ground.

At the same moment Mr Stratton came up, and the crowd dispersed as if by magic.

"What is this?" said the master, appealing to the captain.

"A fight, sir," said Yorke. "A necessary one."

"Between Corder and Brinkman? Come and tell me about it, Yorke."

So while Corder, amid the jubilations of his supporters, who had grown twenty-fold since the beginning of the fight, was being escorted to his quarters, and Brinkman, crestfallen and bewildered, was being left by his disgusted backers to help himself, Yorke strolled on with Mr Stratton, and gave him, as well as he could, an account of the circumstances which for weeks had been leading up to this climax.

"I think it was as well to allow it," said the master, "but there must be no more of it. You have a hard task before you to pull things together, Yorke, but it will be work well done."

"Was it the right thing to dissolve the clubs, sir?" asked Yorke.

"At the time, yes. But watch your chance of reviving them. You must have some common interest on foot, to bring the two sides together."

The captain walked back to his house in a brown study. He had half hoped Mr Stratton might offer to interpose and restore the harmony of the School. But no, the master had left it to the captain, and Yorke's courage rose within him. God helping him, he would pull Fellsgarth together before he left.

On the Green he met Fullerton. It was long since the Modern and Classic seniors had nodded as they passed, but in the curious perversity of things both did so now.

"There's been a fight, I hear?" said Fullerton.

"Yes. Brinkman and Corder. Corder had the best of it."

"I'm jolly glad. Corder's got more pluck than you'd give him credit for."

"Yes; he's had a rough time of it in your house."

"So he has, poor beggar. It's rather humiliating to wait till he has licked his man before one takes his side; but upon my word, I'm as sick of it all as he is."

"It is rather rough on fellows who aren't allowed to do what they've a right to do," said Yorke. "I say, have you anything special on after afternoon school?"

"No, why?"

"Only that I wish you'd come and have tea with me."

Fullerton laughed.

"Bribery and corruption?" said he. "Anyhow, I'll come."

Chapter Twenty
"Fama Volat"

The Modern seniors had certainly experienced a run of bad luck since the inauguration of the strike, which was to have brought their rivals down on their knees and secured for the Modern side a supremacy in Fellsgarth.

The second Rendlesham match, the defection of Corder, the mutiny of the juniors, the disbanding of the clubs, the row with the head-master, and finally, the defeat of Brinkman by his own victim, might be held to be enough to chasten their spirits, and induce them to ask themselves whether the game was worth the candle.

But, such is the infatuation of wrong-headedness, they still breathed vengeance on some one; and this time their victim was to be Rollitt.

The grudge against him had been steadily accumulating during the term. His outrage on the gentle Dangle was yet to be atoned for. His crime of playing in the fifteen was yet unappeased. His contempt of the whole crew of his enemies was not to be pardoned. Even his rescue of the lost juniors told against him, for it had helped to turn the public feeling of the School in favour of those recalcitrant young rebels. So far there had been no getting at him. He would not quarrel. He would not even recognise the existence of any one he did not care for.

But now a chance had come. The more they discussed it, the more morally certain was it that he was answerable for the disappearance of the money from the Club funds. The very reluctance of his own house to take action in the matter showed that they at least appreciated the gravity of the suspicion.

It was a trump card for the Moderns. By pushing it now, they would be doing a service to the School. They would pose as the champions of honesty. They would be mortifying the Classics, even while they pretended to assist them; and, above all, they would wipe out scores with Rollitt himself, in a way he could not well disregard.

Clapperton and Dangle were not superlatively clever boys; but, whether by chance or design, they certainly hit upon an admirable method for bringing the matter to a crisis.

Dangle took upon himself to confide his suspicions, as a dead and terrible secret, to Wilcox, a middle-boy of Forder's house, and notorious as the most prolific gossip in Fellsgarth; who, moreover, was known to have several talking acquaintances in the other houses.

Wilcox received Dangle's communication with astonishment and—oh, of course, he wouldn't breathe a word of it to any one, not for the world; it was a bad business, but it was Fisher major's business to see it put right, and so on.

That night as Wilcox and his friend Underwood were retiring to rest, the former confided to the latter, under the deadliest pledge of secrecy, that there was a scandal going on about the School accounts. He mightn't say more except that the fellow suspected was one of the last he himself should have dreamt of, although others might be less surprised.

That was not all. Next morning he sat next to Calder, a Classic boy, in Hall, and asked him if he could keep a secret. Oh yes, Calder could keep any amount of secrets. Then Wilcox told him the same story that he had confided to Underwood, only adding that the amount in question was said to be several pounds.

Calder hazarded the names of several boys; but Wilcox shrugged his shoulders at them all.

"You'd better not ask me," he said; "it will only get out and make trouble."

"Oh! but I promise I wouldn't tell a soul," said Calder.

"I can't tell you, though. But I'll tell you this. You'd never guess the fellow had had as much in his pocket all his life."

"What—do you mean Rollitt?"

"I can't tell you, I say. I'm not at liberty to mention names."

The rumour thus admirably started went on merrily.

Before nightfall it was known in half a dozen Modern studies that the Club funds had been robbed of £10 or £12 by a Classic boy, and that he was being shielded by his own seniors. On the Classic side four or five fellows whispered to one another that Rollitt had been caught in the act of stealing money out of Fisher major's rooms a day or two ago.

Presently, one enterprising gossip sent the story of Widow Wisdom's boat rolling in and out with the rumour of the stolen money. Encouraged by that, some one else hinted that there had been deficiencies last term as well as this; and in and out with the new story was started the report that last term Rollitt had set up with a fishing-tackle and book of flies worth ever so much.

A couple of days later the number of boys in the secret had multiplied fast, and Rollitt, as he walked across the Green to Hall or class, was watched and pointed out mysteriously by a score or more of curious boys.

Of course the story grew to all sorts of curious shapes. Percy (who was the first of the invalided juniors to appear in his usual haunts) had it from Rix, who had had it from Banks, who had had it from Underwood, who had had it from Wilcox, who had had it from Dangle, who had been present on the occasion, that Rollitt had met the head-master in a lane near Widow Wisdom's, and holding a pistol at his head had made him turn out all his pockets, and relieved him of fifty pounds.

Percy said he didn't believe it.

Whereupon Rix reduced the amount to thirty pounds.

Percy still could not accept the story.

Whereat Rix, anxious to meet his friend as far as possible, substituted a walking-stick for the pistol.

Still Percy's gullet could not swallow even what was left.

Whereupon Rix suggested that it was open to doubt whether it was the doctor who was robbed or Fisher major. It *might* have been the latter.

Still Percy looked sceptical.

Which called forth an explanation that Rix did not mean to say that Dangle actually witnessed the occurrence; but that he knew it for a fact all the same.

Percy shook his head still.

And Rix, feeling much injured, laid the scene of the outrage in Fisher's study, and conceded that the money might belong to the clubs, and might be only five pounds.

Percy had the temerity once more to express doubt. Whereupon Rix flatly declined to come down another penny in the amount, or alter his story one iota, with one possible exception; that the money may have been taken when Fisher major was not in his room.

Percy considered the anecdote had been boiled down sufficiently for human consumption, and grieved Rix prodigiously by saying that he knew all about it weeks ago, and what did he mean by coming and telling him his wretched second-hand stories?

However, whatever variations the rumour underwent as it passed from hand to hand, it managed to retain its three most salient points all through— namely, that Fisher major had been robbed; that the money taken belonged to the club; and that the suspected thief was Rollitt.

For a week or two Rollitt remained profoundly ignorant of the charges against him. His unapproachable attitude was the despair both of friend and enemy. Yorke, who would have given anything to let him have an opportunity of denying or explaining the charge, was at his wits' end how to get at him. Dangle, on the contrary, who was chiefly interested in the penalties in store for the thief, was equally at a loss how to bring him to bay.

He would see no one. He shut himself in his study and fastened the door. In class and Hall he was practically deaf and dumb; and in his solitary walks by the river it was as much as any one's comfort for the whole term was worth to accost him.

By one of those strange coincidences which often bring the most unlikely persons into sympathy, Yorke and Dangle each decided to write what they hesitated to say.

Yorke had endless difficulty over his letter. He could not bring himself to believe Rollitt a thief, yet he could not deny that suspicions existed. Still less could he evade his duty as captain to see things right. The latter duty he might have put off on Mr Wakefield or the doctor. But the mere reporting to them of the circumstances would fix the suspicions on Rollitt more pointedly than they were already, and certainly more pointedly than Yorke wished them to be.

"Dear Rollitt," he wrote, "I hope you will not resent my writing to tell you of a rumour which is afloat very injurious to you, and one which I feel quite sure you can dispose of at once. I would not write about it, only I am very anxious for the sake of everybody you should deny it, and so shut up others who would be glad enough if it were true. A sum of money, about £4 10 shillings, belonging to the Club funds has been lost from Fisher major's room. The rumour is that you have taken it, and those who accuse you make much of the coincidence that about the time when the money was said to be lost, you spent a similar sum in the purchase of a new boat for Widow Wisdom. If I didn't feel quite sure you would be able to deny the charge and explain anything about it that seems suspicious, I should not have cared to write this.

"Yours truly,—

"C. Yorke."

Dangle's letter was less ingenuous.

"The secretary of the Fellsgarth clubs has been requested to ask Rollitt the following questions in reference to a sum of about £4 10 shillings missing from the funds in the treasurer's hands.

"1. Is it true that Rollitt was seen at the door of Fisher major's room on Saturday afternoon, September 21, at a time when everybody else was absent from the house?

"2. Is it true that immediately afterwards Rollitt paid five pounds for a new boat for Widow Wisdom?

"3. Where did that money come from?

"4. Does Rollitt know that he is suspected by every boy in Fellsgarth of having stolen it; and that now that the clubs are dissolved the treasurer will be called upon to refund the money?

"5. What is Rollitt going to do? Does he deny it? If not, will he take the consequences?

"Signed for the Club Committee,—

"T. Dangle, Sec."

Fisher minor, the only boy to whom a missive to the School hermit might safely be entrusted, was on his way to Rollitt's study with the captain's note in his hand, when he was met on the stairs by Cash.

"What cheer, kid?" said the latter. "Where are you off to?"

"Taking a letter to Rollitt," said Fisher minor.

"That's just what I am, from Dangle. I say, you may as well give him the two. No answer. Ta-ta." And he thrust his missive into Fisher's hands.

It was just as easy to hand Rollitt two letters as one. So Fisher proceeded on his errand.

Rollitt was writing a letter, which he hurriedly put aside when the messenger entered.

"Get out!" he said, looking up. But when he saw who the intruder was his tone relaxed a little.

"Fisher minor? Better?"

"Yes, thanks. I had a cold, but that was all. I say, Rollitt, you were an awful brick helping us down that night."

"Nonsense!" said Rollitt, pulling out his paper and going on writing.

"Here are two letters for you," said the boy.

Rollitt motioned him gruffly to lay them down on the table and depart—which he did gladly.

Rollitt went on writing. It may be no breach of confidence if we allow the reader to glance over his shoulder.

"Dear Mother,—You ask me if I am happy, and how I like school. I am not happy, and I hate Fellsgarth. Nobody cares about me. It's no use my trying to be what I am not. I am not a gentleman, and I hope I never shall be, if the fellows here are specimens. Just because I'm poor they have nothing to do with me. I don't complain of that. I prefer it. I'd much sooner be working for my living like father than wasting my time at a place like this. If those ladies would give the money they spend on keeping me here to you and father it would do much more good. There is only one boy I care about here, and he is a little fellow who was kind to me of his own accord, and doesn't fight shy of me because I've no money and live on charity. I would ever so much rather come and live at home at the end of this term. It would be even worse at Oxford than it is here; and the ladies, if they want to be kind, will let me leave. I know you and father want me to become a grand gentleman. I would a hundred times rather be what I really am, and live at home with you.

"Your loving son,—

"Alfred."

This dismal letter concluded, the writer produced his books and began work, heedless of the two letters on his table, which lay all day where Fisher minor had deposited them.

He went in and out to class, and those who watched him saw no signs of trouble in his demeanour. In the afternoon he stole up to the river with his rod; and any one who had seen him land his three-pounder, and leave it, as he left all his fish, at Widow Wisdom's cottage, would have been puzzled by his indifferent air.

That evening, as he was about to go to bed, he discovered the letters.

Dangle's letter, which he opened first, he scarcely seemed to heed. The sight of the name at foot was sufficient. He crumpled it up and tossed it in the corner.

But Yorke's aroused him. He read it through once or twice, and his face grew grim as he did so. Presently he went to the corner and picked up Dangle's letter and once more read it. Then he crumpled up both together, and instead of going to bed sat in his chair and looked at the wall straight in front of him.

The next day those who watched him saw him go into school and out as usual, except that he seemed less listless and more observant. He glanced aside now and then at the groups of boys who stood and looked after him, and his face had a cloud on it which was almost thunderous.

"Did you give my letter to Rollitt?" said Yorke to Fisher minor.

"Yes, yesterday; and one from Dangle too," said the junior.

"Dangle!" said the captain to himself; "he'll think we are in collusion. Why ever didn't I leave it alone?"

He felt thus still more when later on in the day Dangle came over.

"I hear you have written to Rollitt for an explanation. It was about time. What does he reply?"

Yorke's back went up at the dictatorial tone of the inquiry.

"If there is anything to tell you, you will hear," said he.

"That means he hasn't replied, I suppose. I have taken care that he shall reply. I have told Forder all about it."

"You've told Forder? You cad!" exclaimed Yorke, in a tone which made Dangle thankful he was near the door.

"Yes," snarled he. "It may be your interest to shield a thief, but it's not in the interest of Fellsgarth. You won't take the matter up; Forder will. I've told him you know about it, and will give him all the particulars. Hope you'll enjoy it."

And he disappeared, only just in time for his own comfort.

Yorke's rage was unbounded. Of all the masters, Mr Forder was the one he would least have chosen to take up an affair of this kind. He was harsh, unsympathetic, hasty. And of all persons to prime the master in the circumstances of the case, Dangle was the least to be trusted.

His temptation was to go at once to Rollitt, and force the matter to a conclusion before Mr Forder had time to interfere. Things were going from bad to worse. Would they never come right again?

Next morning, before he could decide what to do, a message came from Mr Forder, requesting him and his fellow-prefects to come across to the master's room.

In no amiable frame of mind they obeyed. As they expected, Clapperton, Brinkman, Dangle, and Fullerton were also present.

"This is a most serious case," said Mr Forder. "Yorke, I understand you know more about it than any one. Will you kindly say all you know?"

"I know nothing," said the captain, "except that I believe the story is groundless."

"That is unsatisfactory. In a matter like this, there must be nothing like sheltering the wrong-doer."

"It's because we were afraid of that, sir," said Clapperton, "that we thought it right to tell you about it."

"Of course. Fisher major, perhaps you will tell us about the missing money."

Fisher major briefly related his loss and the efforts he had made to discover it.

"And what are your grounds for suspecting Rollitt?"

"I don't suspect him, sir; or rather I should not if it were not for what Dangle has said about him."

Thereupon Dangle was called upon to repeat his accusation.

"It seems to me," said the master, "we require two important witnesses to make the case clear. I believe Mrs Wisdom is in the house at present. Will you inquire, Fullerton, and if so, tell her to come here? And will you, Fisher major, fetch your brother?"

After a painful delay, in which the rival seniors sat glaring at one another, and the master made notes of the evidence so far, the two witnesses were forthcoming.

Widow Wisdom had nothing to say except in praise of Master Rollitt, and was glad enough in support of it to relate the incident of the boat, and even produce the receipt, which she carried about like a talisman in her pocket. She had no idea that her glowing testimony was to be used against her favourite, or she would have bitten off her tongue sooner than give it:

As for Fisher minor, confused and abashed in the presence of so many seniors, he blundered out his story of the eventful half-holiday, looking in vain towards his brother to ascertain if he was doing well or ill. He blabbed all he knew about Rollitt; the condition of his study, the nature of his solitary walks, the poverty of his possessions—everything that could possibly confirm the suspicions against him; and forgot to mention anything which might in the least avail on the other side.

At the close of the court-martial Mr Forder summed up.

"I am afraid it is a very clear case," said he. "It is very painful to think that a Fellsgarth boy should come to such a pass. The matter must be reported to the head-master. But before doing so it would be fair to see Rollitt, and hear what he has to say. We have no right to condemn any one unheard. If he is innocent, it will be easy for him to prove it. Fisher major, will you tell him to come?"

Fisher major reluctantly obeyed. It was nearly half an hour before he returned, and then he came alone.

"I cannot find Rollitt, sir. He is not in the house. He was absent from morning call-over. And the house-keeper says he was not in his room this morning, and that his bed was not slept in last night."

Chapter Twenty One
Bolted!

However slowly the rumour of Rollitt's dishonesty had spread through the School, the news of his disappearance spread like wildfire.

Mr Forder's desire to keep the matter from being talked about was eminently futile, for Wally and Percy Wheatfield both knew all about it five minutes after Fisher major had discovered the absence of the "suspect."

By everybody except a very few infatuated persons, such as Yorke and Fisher minor, Rollitt's flight was taken as conclusive evidence of his guilt.

"If he hadn't done it, why shouldn't he stay and face it?" asked Clapperton.

"The wonder to me is," sneered Dangle, "that he brazened it out as long as he did."

"Suppose you were in his shoes," said Yorke, "suspected by every one, with the evidence black against you, and Dangle in charge of the prosecution, how would you like it?"

"If I'm in charge of the prosecution," said Dangle, colouring up, "it's because *you*, whose duty it was to see the matter put right, were doing all you could to shield the scoundrel."

"I did nothing because I didn't believe him guilty, and I don't yet," said the captain hotly; "and if you call him scoundrel again in my hearing, I'll knock you down."

"Keep your temper," said Dangle, glad, all the same, that there were one or two fellows between him and the captain. "*You* may not care about the credit of Fellsgarth. We do."

"You!" retorted Yorke, with such withering contempt that Dangle half wished he had left the matter alone.

"The thing is," said Ranger, "what is to be done!"

"Nothing," said Yorke. "Forder has gone to tell the doctor all about it. They'll take it into their own hands to hunt him down—perhaps with Dangle's assistance. All we've got to do is—"

Here Fullerton interrupted—

"—is to say all the evil we can about a fellow who is down and can't defend himself."

"What's the matter with Fullerton?" said Clapperton, with a sneer; "surely he's not become one of Rollitt's champions?"

"If it matters specially to you what I think," said Fullerton, "I don't believe a word of your precious story. First of all, Fisher major's such a fool at accounts that it's not at all certain the money is lost; secondly, Dangle is the accuser; thirdly, Rollitt is the accused; fourthly, because if a similar charge were made against me, I should certainly disappear."

"Ha, ha!" snarled Brinkman, "they've got hold of poor Fullerton, have they? I wish them joy of him."

"Thanks very much," said Fullerton; "I don't intend to desert the dear Moderns. You will have a splendid chance of taking it out of me for daring to believe somebody innocent that you think guilty. I shall be happy to see any three of you, whenever you like, I can hit out as well as young Corder, so I hope Brinkman won't come. But Dangle now, or even Clapperton, I shall be charmed to see. It's really their duty as prefects to suppress any one who dares have an opinion of his own. I simply long to be suppressed!"

This astounding revolt for the time being diverted attention from the topic of the hour. The laughter with which it was greeted by the Classics present did not tend to add to the comfort of Clapperton, Brinkman, and Dangle, who very shortly discovered that it was time to go to their own house.

"Wait for me," said Fullerton; "I'm coming too."

And, to their disgust, the rebel strolled along, with his hands in his pockets, in their company, whistling pleasantly to himself and absolutely ignoring their unfriendly attitude.

Meanwhile the question, "Where is Rollitt?" continued to exercise Fellsgarth, from the head-master down to the junior fag. Bit by bit all that could be found out about his movements came to light. His study was visited by the masters. It disclosed the usual state of grime and confusion. His fishing-rod and tackle were there. There had been no attempt to pack his few belongings, which lay scattered about in dismal disorder. The photograph of the pleasant, homely-looking woman on the mantelpiece, with the inscription below, "Alfred, from Mother," stood in its usual place. His Aristophanes lay open in the window-sill at the place for to-day's lesson. Everything betokened an abrupt and hasty departure.

Among the papers on his table was a fragment of some accounts recording the outlay of little more than a few pence a week since the beginning of the term.

When inquiry came to be made, it was found that he was last seen after afternoon class yesterday, when he unexpectedly went to the School shop and purchased from the attendant there (who had been put in charge of that establishment during the indisposition of the managing directors) half a dozen Abernethy biscuits.

The matron at Wakefield's remembered that only a day or two ago a parcel had arrived for Rollitt—another unusual circumstance—containing a ham. Of this possession no sign was now to be found in his study.

The inference from all these circumstances of course was, that however abruptly he had departed, he had not gone home, but somewhere where food would not be easy to procure in the ordinary way.

Messengers were sent to Penchurch to acquaint the police and inquire at various places on the way for news of the missing boy. But no one had seen him "out of touch" for several days—since his last fishing expedition.

His home address was of course on the School books, and thither a telegram was sent. But as the place was beyond the region of the wire, no reply came for a day, when in answer to the doctor's inquiry if the wanderer had returned home, there came an abrupt "No."

Meanwhile the doctor had had another conference with the seniors of both houses, and inquired with every sign of dissatisfaction into the merits of the suspicions which were the apparent cause of Rollitt's disappearance.

To his demand why the matter was not reported to him, Yorke replied that as far as he and Fisher major were concerned they did not suspect Rollitt, and therefore had had nothing to report. The Modern seniors, on the other hand, put in the plea that they had looked to the Classics to take the matter up, and when they declined to do so, had reported the matter to Mr Forder.

Then the doctor went into the particulars of Dangle's feud with the missing boy, much to the embarrassment of the former.

"He insulted you by turning you out of Mr Wakefield's house, you say. Why were you there?"

"I went to speak to some juniors."

"About what?"

"Clapperton wanted them—"

"No, I didn't. You went—" interrupted Clapperton.

"Silence, Clapperton. What were they wanted for, Dangle?"

"They had cheated at Elections."

"What was your object, then?"

"To punish them."

"Are you not aware that the captain of the School is the only prefect who is allowed to punish?"

"Yes, sir, but—"

"Well?"

"We were not sure that their own prefects were going to take any notice of it."

"I caned all four of them for it, and you saw me do it," said Yorke.

"Humph. And as to Rollitt, how came he to be present?" asked the doctor.

"He came in."

"What were you doing when he came in?"

"There was a scuffle."

"You were striking those boys? What did Rollitt do? Did he strike you?"

"No, sir."

"What then?"

"He—he," said Dangle, flushing up to be obliged to record the fact in the presence of the other seniors, "he dragged me across the Green."

"Then you say he attacked you on another occasion on the football field?"

And Dangle had to stand an uncomfortable cross-examination on this incident too.

"What had it all got to do with Rollitt?" asked every one of himself.

"I ask you all these questions, Dangle," said the doctor, when he had brought this chapter of history up to date, "because it seems to me you are Rollitt's chief accuser in this matter. I wish I were able to feel that you were not personally interested in your charges proving to be true. That, of course, does not affect the case, as far as Rollitt is concerned. The evidence against him is merely conjecture, so far."

"But I met him at Fisher's door that afternoon," said Dangle, determined to make the most of his strong points.

"Why," said Fisher, "you told me you didn't know which my door was, when you first spoke about it."

"I found out since, and it was the same door."

"Was he coming out of the room or going in!"

"Coming out."

"You are sure of that?"

"Yes, I remember because the door nearly struck me as he opened it."

"However could it do that!" exclaimed Fisher. "My door opens inwards!"

Dangle coloured up with confusion and stammered —

"I—I thought it—I suppose I was wrong."

"I think so," said the doctor frigidly. "Thank you, boys, I needn't keep you longer at present."

"You idiot!" said Clapperton, as he and the discomfited Dangle walked back to Forder's. "You've made a precious mess of it, and made the whole house ridiculous. Why couldn't you let it alone? You've mulled everything you've put your finger into this term."

"Look here, Clapperton," said Dangle, in a white heat, "I've stood a lot from you this term—a jolly lot. I've done your dirty work, and—"

"What do you mean? What dirty work have I asked you to do?"

"Plenty that you've not had the pluck to do yourself."

"I dare you to repeat it, you liar!"

"You shall do your own in future, I know that."

"Dangle, hold your tongue, you cad!"

"I shall do nothing of the kind, you snob!"

Whereupon ensued the most wonderful spectacle of the half, a fight between Clapperton and Dangle. It was nearly dark, and no one was about, and history does not record how it ended. But in Hall that night both appeared with visages suspiciously marred, and it was noted by many an observant eye that diplomatic relations between the two were suspended.

But while old friends had thus been falling out on Rollitt's account, old enemies had on the same grounds been making it up.

The juniors having recovered of their colds, and finding themselves once more in the full possession of their appetite, their liberty, and their spirits, celebrated their convalescence by a general *mêlée* in Percy's room, under the specious pretext of a committee meeting of the shop-directors. This business function being satisfactorily concluded, they turned their attention to the condition of things in general.

That Fellsgarth should have got itself into a regular mess during their enforced retirement caused them no surprise. What else could any one expect?

But that any one should dare to suspect and make things hot for a fellow without consulting *them*, caused them both pain and astonishment. It quite slipped their memories that not long since some of them had been glad enough to listen to disparaging talk about the School hermit. That was a detail. On the whole they had stuck to him, and they meant to stick to him now!

Many things were in his favour. He had won a goal for the School. He had dispensed with his right to a fag, and had let the juniors of all grades generally alone. He was on nodding terms with Fisher minor, one of their lot. He had come up Hawk's Pike at much personal inconvenience to look for them. And he had been a customer to the extent of six Abernethys at the School shop.

For all these reasons (which were quite apart from party considerations) it was decided *nem. con.* that Rollitt was a "good old sort" and must be stuck by.

Whereupon the nine of them sallied out arm in arm across the Green, on the look-out for some one who might hold a contrary opinion.

After some search they found a Modern middle-boy, who, catching sight of Fisher minor, shouted, "How now! Who nobbled the Club money?" which made Fisher minor suddenly detach himself from his company, and shouting, "That's him!" start in pursuit. What a bull-dog it was getting, to be sure!

The whole party joined in the hue-and-cry, and might have run the fugitive down, had not the head-master stalked across the Green at that moment on his way to Mr Wakefield's.

At sight of him they pulled up short, looked unutterably amiable, doffed their caps, and made as though they were merely out to take the air on this beautiful November afternoon.

To Fisher minor the interruption was a sad one. That fellow was the borrower of his half-crown; for weeks he had lost sight of him. Now, suddenly, chance had seemed to bring both man and money within reach, when, alas! the Harpy swooped down and took off the prize from under his very nose.

The doctor having passed, they continued their search for any one who had a bad word to say for Rollitt.

But as it was nearly dark, and rain was falling, the craven maligners kept indoors, and would not be caught.

So the juniors relieved themselves by giving three cheers for Rollitt under every window round the Green, and then fell to abusing Fisher minor because his brother, Fisher major, had lost the money which Rollitt was said to have stolen.

"There's no doubt that kid's at the bottom of it," said Percy. "First of all, he's a Classic cad."

Here the speaker was obliged to pause, on a friendly admonition from the boot of his brother Wally.

"He's a Classic kid," continued he.

"You said cad."

"I said cad? do you hear that, you chaps? Thinks I don't know how to spell."

"You said he was a Classic cad."

"There you are; you've said it now. Kick him, you chaps. How dare he say he's a Classic cad?" said Percy.

This verbal squabble being settled at last, Percy proceeded to explain Fisher minor's position.

"If he hadn't come to Fellsgarth, Rollitt would have been smashed to bits over the falls. And if Rollitt had been smashed to bits—"

"He couldn't have bought six Abernethys at the shop," suggested D'Arcy.

"Right you are! And what's more, he couldn't have eaten them if he had, and he couldn't have run away. There you are, I said this kid was at the bottom of it."

"But who'd have collared the money in that case?" asked Ashby.

Percy reflected. This was a decided point.

"Well, you see," said he, "it's this way. If young Fisher minor hadn't been born, he wouldn't have had a governor and a mater, and if he hadn't had a governor and a mater, no more would Fisher major. And if Fisher major hadn't had a governor and a mater he'd never have been elected treasurer, and if he'd not been elected treasurer he wouldn't have lost the money. So you see the young un's at the bottom of it again."

"I know a shorter way than that," said D'Arcy. "If young Fisher minor hadn't fetched Rollitt up to vote that day, Fisher major wouldn't have been elected, and then he couldn't have lost the money."

"Isn't that what I said?" said Percy, indignant to be thus summarily paraphrased.

"Are you going to lick me for being born?" inquired Fisher minor.

"Good mind to. It's all your fault good old Rollitt's gone."

"Those six Abernethys won't last him long," suggested Cash.

"No. We must keep a stock of them now, and call them 'Rollitt's particular.' I fancy they might fetch three-halfpence each."

"I say," said Wally, "I vote we find Rollitt. He's not a bad sort, you know."

"All very well," said Percy, "if one only knew where to look."

"It's my notion he's either gone home or to the top of Hawk's Pike. I don't well see where else he could be."

"London?" suggested Cottle.

"Not got the money."

"Walked there?"

"Not got the boots."

"He can't be hanging about near here. Everybody knows him. No; you bet he's gone to the top of Hawk's Pike, and he's going to stay there till the clouds roll by."

This brought up a painful reminiscence. None of the party, except Wally, exactly favoured the idea of another attempt on the great mountain.

"Tell you what," said Percy, "those biscuits will last him over to-night. We'll see if there's any news of him in the morning, and if not we'll organise an expedition to find him. I say, let's go and have another shop committee somewhere."

"Where?"

"Suppose we have it in Rollitt's study. He was a jolly good sort, you know. It would please him."

The logic of this proposition did not detain the meeting.

They decided to go in the usual way. That is, the four Classic boys boldly marched into their house together, and the five Moderns dropped in one by one artlessly and quite by accident.

As Fisher minor passed his brother's door he thought he would just look in. At the same moment the house matron, with a very important face, was bounding into the room.

"Master Fisher," said she, "Mrs Wisdom's just sent back that flannel shirt of yours."

"Oh! At last. She's only had it six weeks. About long enough," said Fisher major. "I'd given it up for lost."

"It got left at the bottom of the bag, and she never noticed it till last night. And what do you think, Master Fisher! there was *this* in the breast pocket." And she handed him a little brown paper parcel.

Fisher major snatched at it with an ejaculation more like horror than anything else, and tore the paper open.

Four sovereigns and some silver dropped on to the table.

"Why," gasped he, "that's it! I remember now. I got it on the field just before the Rendlesham match, and stuck it in that pocket, and it went clean out of my head. Oh, my word, what *have* I done? What an awful mess I've made!"

Not even Fisher minor stayed to dispute this statement, but hurried off with the great news to the shop committee next door.

Chapter Twenty Two
Coming to

Fisher major's discovery put the finishing touch to the discomfiture of the Modern seniors.

And the manner in which they came by the news of it by no means tended to salve the wound which it inflicted.

The shop committee was so convulsed by the intelligence which Fisher minor brought, that they then and there promised themselves the pleasure of conveying the good news to Rollitt's accusers in person. They accordingly adjourned in a body to the Modern side.

"Won't Clapperton grin!" said Percy. "I say, you chaps, we may as well let him have it one at a time. Then he'll hear it nine times over, do you see? I'll go first."

The idea seemed a good one, but risky. Cottle calculated that after about the fourth time Clapperton would be a little riled. He therefore modestly proposed to follow Percy. Cash and Lickford competed smartly for the third place, the former being successful. Ramshaw, having to come fifth, had decided misgivings as to the fun of the thing; while the Classic juniors declined to play unless all the others remained on the spot ready to back up in case of emergency.

It was also decided that, for precautionary reasons, the key of Clapperton's door should be removed for the time being, lest he should try to lock the good news out; and that an interval of two minutes should be allowed to elapse between each messenger's announcement.

Little dreaming of the exquisite torture being prepared for him, Clapperton sat in his study engaged in the farce of preparation.

He had plenty to think of besides lessons. Things had all gone wrong with him. Dangle and he had fought. Brinkman, after his thrashing by Corder, no longer counted. Fullerton had rebelled, and was taking boys over every day to the enemy. Corder had successfully defied his—Clapperton's—authority, and the juniors snapped their fingers at him.

And yet Clapperton had come up this term determined to lay himself out for his side, and be the most popular prefect in Fellsgarth!

His one comfort was that the Classics were under a cloud too. One of their number was a runaway thief; and a stigma rested on their side worse than any that attached to the Moderns.

He was trying to make the most of this questionable consolation when the door opened, and Percy bounced in.

"I say, Clapperton; Fisher's found the money. Rollitt's not a thief. Ain't you glad? Hurray!"

And, without waiting, he retired as suddenly as he had come.

Clapperton gaped at the door by which he had gone in amazement. He had never calculated on this. This was the worst thing yet. It showed Yorke had been right, and that he and Dangle—

The door opened again, and Cottle ran in. "Hurray, Clapperton! The money's found. Rollitt's no thief. Ain't you glad?" And he, too, vanished.

There must be something in it. What a fool he would look to all Fellsgarth! Perhaps it was only a plot, though, to shield Rollitt. Perhaps—

The door once more swung open, and in jumped Cash.

"Clapperton, I say—Hooray! That money's been found. Rollitt's no thief. Ain't you glad?"

Hullo! At this rate he would get to know the news. How they would crow on the other side! He wondered if Fisher major had done it on purp—

Again there was a scuffle of feet at the door, and Lickford stepped in.

"Oh! Clapperton," he said. "Hooray, Clapperton! The money's turned up, and Rollitt's no thief. Ain't you glad?—and, oh, I say, Clapperton—hooray!"

"Come here," said Clapperton, sternly.

But, oh dear no; Lickford was pressed, and couldn't stay.

"The young asses!" growled Clapperton. "Why can't they keep their precious news to themselves? If they'd tried, they couldn't have made bigger nuisances of themselves. I suppose, now, Yorke will—"

The door swung open again, and Ramshaw, hanging on to the handle, swung in with it.

"Hooray, Clapperton! Rollitt's no thief. That money's turned up. Ain't you glad? I am—good evening."

This final greeting was cut short by a ruler which Clapperton sent flying at the messenger's head. Ramshaw dodged in time, and the ruler flew out into the passage, where it was promptly captured by Fisher minor, whose turn came next.

"Thank goodness that's the end of the young cads!" growled Clapperton. "They've done it on purpose; and I'll pay them out for it. That ass, Fisher major, he's bound to—"

Here there came a modest tap at the door, and Fisher minor peeped in, apologetically.

"Well, what do you want? You've no business on this side; go to your own house."

"All right, Clapperton," said Fisher, speaking with unwonted rapidity. "I only thought you'd like to know my brother's found the money. Hurray! Rollitt's no thief; ain't you glad?—Yeow!"

This last exclamation was in response to a grab from the enraged Clapperton, which, though it failed to catch the messenger, clawed his face.

"I've had enough of this," said the senior. "I don't care—. Hullo! where's my key?"

The key was not to be seen. He looked out into the passage; it was not there. No one else was in sight.

He returned viciously to his seat at the table, and began to read again.

The door had opened, and Ashby, on tip-toe, was in the room before the senior noticed the fresh intrusion.

"Rollitt's no thief; ain't you glad? The money's found. Hurray, Clapperton!—done it!" exclaimed Ashby, all in one breath, dancing out of the room in conscious pride at his exploit.

"All very well," said D'Arcy, whose turn came next; "how am I to do it?"

"No shirking," said Wally; "I come after you."

"Look here," said D'Arcy; "if you chaps give me a leg-up, I'll let him have it through his window. I can reach round from this passage window to his if you hang on to my legs."

"Good dodge," said Wally, admiringly, "but we'd better turn the key on the door first. If he came out and spotted us holding you, we might have to drop you."

So the key was quietly put in the lock and turned; and D'Arcy, firmly held by the heels, wriggled himself out of the window, and, with the aid of a pipe, pulled himself up, with his face to the window of Clapperton's study.

That worthy was beginning to congratulate himself that he would be spared a further repetition of the uncomfortable news that night, when a sudden, loud voice at one of the open lattice panes almost startled him out of his skin.

"Oh, Clapperton! Ain't you glad? Rollitt's no thief. The money's found. Good evening—have you used our soap? Haul in, you chaps! Sharp!"

The persecuted senior, after the first surprise, made a frantic rush, first at the window, and then, finding the bird flown, at the door. The latter was locked. He could hear a scuffling and scrambling in the lobby outside, followed by a stampede; after which dead silence prevailed, save for the vicious kicking of the imprisoned hero at his own door.

"Whew!" said Wally, fanning himself when the juniors were safe back in Percy's study. "That was a squeak, if you like. How on earth am I to do it?"

"Better let him off," suggested some one.

Wally resented the suggestion as an insult.

"Not likely," said he. "I'll do it. I don't care, if you all back up."

And in a minute, when the sound of the kicking had ceased, and Clapperton had apparently retired once more to his work, he crept out into the lobby, followed stealthily by the whole band.

As they passed the head of the stairs, whose voice should they hear below, inquiring of a middle-boy if Clapperton was in the house, but the doctor's?

"Yes, sir; shall I tell him you want him?" said the boy.

"No, I'll go up to his room," said the head-master.

"Whew!" said Wally, "what a go! and the door's locked on the outside!"

"I'll go and turn it quietly," said Percy, "if you back up in case he flies out."

But the precaution was not needed. Percy, who luckily had just taken off his boots, slipped up silently to the door, and the others from their lurking-place saw him quietly turn the key and then walk back, evidently unheard by the prisoner within.

He passed the stair-head just before the doctor came up, and to their great relief ran into the arms of his friends unchallenged.

The doctor, indeed, was too pre-occupied to dream that, as he went to Clapperton's study, nine small heads were craning out of a door at the end of the passage, watching his every step.

"I say," whispered Ashby, in tones of horror, "suppose Clap thinks it's one of us, and goes for him!"

"My eye, what a go!" ejaculated Cash.

They saw the stately figure stand a moment at the door and turn the handle.

Next moment he reeled back with an exclamation of amazement, nearly felled to the ground by a bulky dictionary hurled at his head!

The nine lurkers fairly embraced one another in horror at the sight of this awful outrage; and when, a moment after, they saw the doctor gather himself together and return to the charge, this time closing the door behind him, they did not envy the unlucky Clapperton the awkward five minutes in store for him.

How the two arranged matters no one could say. But as no sounds of violence issued, and the doctor did not summon any one to fetch his cane, they concluded Clapperton had offered a sufficiently humble apology for his mistake.

"Hold on, now," said Wally, after three minutes had passed; "I'll try it now—it's my only chance. You Classic kids be ready to cut home with me as soon as I come back."

So, starting at a run like one who had come a long distance and expected to find the senior alone, he dashed unceremoniously into Clapperton's study, of course not appearing to notice the distinguished company present, crying—

"I say, Clapperton. Hooray! The money's found. Rollitt's no thief. Ain't you glad! Oh, the doctor! I beg your pardon, sir."

The next moment he, D'Arcy, Ashby, and Fisher minor were descending the stairs three steps at a time on the way back to Mr Wakefield's as fast as their legs would carry them, and with all the righteous satisfaction of men who had done their duty at all costs.

"I reckon," said Wally, "he pretty well knows about it now—and if he don't, the doctor will rub it in."

The unfortunate Clapperton, indeed, required no one to "rub in" the fact that he had made a mess of things.

The doctor did not attempt to do it. He merely carried the news of the finding of the money, and desired Clapperton, as the head of the house, to make it known as widely as possible.

"I say nothing now of the cruel wrong which has been inflicted by hasty suspicion on Rollitt. That shadow is still on the School. But the worst shadow, that a Fellsgarth boy was a thief, is happily removed, and I wish every boy in this house to hear of it at the earliest possible moment."

And the doctor went, leaving Clapperton to gulp down the bitter pill as best he could.

Why should he have the job to do? He had not been the first to start the suspicions. Dangle had done that—Dangle, with whom he had fought. Why should not Dangle be called upon to put it right? Unluckily, Dangle was not the captain of Forder's. He was not as responsible in starting the rumour as Clapperton, in his position, had been in adopting it.

It was more than he could bring himself to, to summon the house and announce the news publicly. If Dangle and Brinkman had been with him still, the three of them together might have brazened it out. But his colleagues were sulking in their own quarters, and whatever had to be done must be done singlehanded.

He therefore sat down in no very happy frame of mind and wrote out the following curt notice for the house-boards.—

"Notice.

"The head-master wishes it to be known that the Club money supposed to be missing has been found by the treasurer.

"Geo. Clapperton."

This ungracious document he copied out three times, and taking advantage of every one being in his study for preparation, affixed with his own hand on the notice boards at the house-door and on each landing.

"There!" said he, with a sneer of disgust, as he returned to his own room, "let them make the most of that."

An hour later the dormitory bell sounded, and he could hear the scuffling of feet on the lobby outside, and the clamour of voices as boys hustled one another in front of the boards. Evidently the majority regarded the announcement in a jocular manner; and when a distant shout of laughter came up from the passage below, and down from the landing above, it was clear that Forders did not take the matter very much to heart.

"It was ridiculous, when you come to think of it," soliloquised Clapperton, "that a blundering ass like Fisher major should have brought the School into such a precious mess."

The noise gradually died away as fellows one by one dropped of to bed.

Clapperton waited till they were gone before he followed. As he passed the notice board he glanced at the document which had lately cost him so much pain. It was still there; but not as he left it. A sentence had been squeezed in between his own words and his signature at the bottom of the sheet, which, as it was a fair imitation of his back-sloped handwriting, had all the appearance of forming part of his manifesto. Clapperton gasped with fury as he read the amended notice:—

"Notice.

"The head-master wishes it to be known that, the Club money supposed to be missing has been found by the treasurer, and that I am a beast and a sneak to have accused Rollitt of stealing it.

"Geo. Clapperton."

He tore the paper from the board, and stamped on it in his rage. Then he went downstairs to look at the notice on the school-door. It read precisely like the other, the imitation being perhaps better. He stayed only to tear this down, and proceeded to the other landing, where the same insult confronted him.

Who the author might be he was free to guess.

As he lay awake that night, tossing and turning, he racked his brain to devise some retribution.

And yet, his more sensible self told him, hadn't he been leading up to this all the term? What had he done to make the fellows respect, much more like, him? He had bullied, and swaggered, and set himself against the good of the School. The fellows who followed him only did so in the hope of getting something—either fun or advantage—out of the agitation. They didn't care twopence about Clapperton, and were ready enough to drop him as soon as ever it suited their turn. The one or two things he could do well, and for which anybody respected him—as, for instance, football—he had deliberately shut himself off from, leaving his authority to depend only on the very qualities he had least cause to be proud of.

It was easy enough to say that Brinkman and Dangle cut even a poorer figure over this wretched business than he. But who troubled their heads about Brinkman and Dangle? The former had already been snuffed out hopelessly, and dared not show his face. Dangle, as everybody knew, had a personal grudge against Rollitt, and was unhampered by scruples as to how he scored. But he—Clapperton—he had always tried to pose as a decent sort of fellow, with some kind of interest in the good of the School and some sort of notion about common honour and decency. Ugh! this was what had come of it! As he lay awake that night, the sound of the laughter round the notice boards and the "Ain't you glad?" of the juniors dinned in his ears, sometimes infuriating, sometimes humiliating him; but in either case mockingly reminding him that Clapperton's greatest enemy in Fellsgarth was the captain of the Modern side.

Next morning brought no news of the missing boy, and a vague feeling of anxiety spread through the School. Boys remembered how proud and sensitive Rollitt had been, and how dreadful was the accusation against him. Suppose he had done something desperate? He had cared little enough for danger when all went well. Would he be likely to care more, now that the School was in league against him, pointing to him as a thief, and hounding him out of its society?

All sorts of dreadful possibilities occurred both to masters and boys; and all the while a feeling of fierce resentment was growing against the fellows whose accusations had been the cause of all the mischief.

Dangle, as he crossed the Green to class, was hooted all the way. Brinkman was followed about with derisive cheers, and cries of "Look out! Corder's coming"; and Clapperton, when he appeared, was silently cut. Fellows went out of the way to avoid him; and the chair on either side of him was left vacant in Hall.

"Did you hear," said Ramshaw to his neighbour at the prefects' table at dinner-time, "that they've begun to drag the lake to-day?"

A grim silence greeted the question. Fellows tried to go on with their meal. But somehow Ramshaw had destroyed every one's appetite.

"Nonsense!" said Yorke. "He took food with him. You forget that."

"That looks as if he'd gone off the beaten track somewhere," said Fullerton.

"It does—and Hawk's Pike is as likely a place as any other," said Yorke.

"Whew! there was frost on it the other night," some one said. "I wish the doctor would let us go out and look for him. We've a much better chance of finding him than police and guides."

Here the signal was given to rise, and every one dispersed. Yorke stayed—one of the last. As he went out he caught sight of a solitary figure walking moodily ahead, with hands dug in pockets and head down, the picture of dejection.

Yorke could hardly recognise in this back view his old rival and enemy, Clapperton. Yet he it was. A few weeks ago, and he always marched to and from his house in the boisterous company of friends and admirers. Now he was left alone.

A flush of something like shame mounted to the captain's cheeks. He had no love for this fellow. He owed him little gratitude. And yet the sight of him thus solitary, cut off from the stream, stirred him.

Did he not try, in his humble way, to follow in the footsteps of One Who said, "Love your enemies, do good to them that hate you"? And was not this an opportunity for putting that faith of his to the test of practice?

He quickened his pace, and overtook Clapperton. The Modern senior wheeled round half-savagely.

"Clapperton," said the captain, "we've been enemies all this term. I've thought harshly of you, and you've thought harshly of me. Why shouldn't we be friends?"

"What!" almost growled Clapperton; "are you making a fool of me?"

"No—but we've tried hating one another long enough. Let's try being friends for a change."

They stood facing one another; the one serene, honest, inviting; the other dejected and doubting. But as their eyes met the fires kindled again in Clapperton's face, and the cloud swept off his brow. He pulled his hand from his pocket and held it out.

"Done with you, Yorke. You're the last fellow in Fellsgarth I expected to call friend just now."

Chapter Twenty Three
The Voyage of the Cock-House

Yorke was roused before daybreak next morning by a voice at his bedside.

"Is that you, Yorke?"

The voice was Mr Stratton's. The captain bounded to his feet at once.

"What is it, sir? Has he been found?"

"No," said the master; "no news. Every place has been searched where he would be likely to be, except the mountain. It seems a very off-chance that he has gone up there; still, it is possible. He has been on it once or twice before. I am going there now. Would you care to come too?"

The captain gratefully acquiesced. For a week he had been chafing at the doctor's orders that no boy should go beyond the bounds. His request to be allowed to undertake this very expedition had been twice refused already.

"The doctor has given you an *exeat* if you wish to go," said Mr Stratton. "We are to take a guide, and it is quite understood we may be late in getting back. I shall be glad of your company."

Yorke was ready in ten minutes—thankful at last to be allowed to do something, yet secretly doubting if anything would come of this forlorn quest.

Apart from Rollitt, however, good did come of it to Fellsgarth. For during the long walk master and boy got to understand one another better than ever before. With a common ambition for the welfare of the School, and a common trouble at the dissensions which had split it up during the present term, they also discovered a common hope for better times ahead.

They discussed all sorts of plans, and exchanged confidences about all sorts of difficulties. And all the while they felt drawn close to one another, exchanging the ordinary relations of master and boy for those of friend and friend.

Some of my readers may say that Mr Stratton must have been a very foolish master to give himself away to a boy, or that Yorke must have been a very presuming boy to talk so familiarly to a master. Who cares what they were, if they and Fellsgarth were the better for that morning's walk?

"In many ways," said Mr Stratton, "a head boy has as much responsibility for the good of a school as a head-master—always more than an assistant master. You could wreck the School in a week if you chose; and it is in your hands to pull it together more than any of us masters, however much we should like to do it. And you'll do it, old fellow!"

And so they turned up the lane that led round to the back of the mountain.

The news that Mr Stratton and the captain had gone up Hawk's Pike to look for Rollitt soon spread through Fellsgarth that morning. The souls of our friends the juniors were seriously stirred by it.

Their promise—or shall we say threat?—to organise a search-party up the mountain on their own account had been lost sight of somewhat in the exciting distractions of the last twenty-four hours; but now that they found the ground cut from under their feet they were very indignant. Secretly, no doubt, they were a little relieved to find that they had been forestalled in the perilous venture of a winter ascent of the formidable pike they had such good cause to remember.

It was a mean trick of Yorke's to "chowse" them out of the credit, they protested. Now he would get all the glory, and they would get none.

"I tell you what," said Percy. "It's my notion Rollitt's not gone up the mountain at all. It's just a dodge of those two to get a jolly good spree for themselves. Pooh! They'll get lost. We shall have to go and look for them, most likely."

"And then," said Lickford, "somebody will have to come and look for us."

"And Rollitt's not here to do it," said Fisher minor.

This cast the company back on to their original subject.

"It's my notion," said Wally, "he's got on the island in the middle of the lake, like Robinson Crusoe."

"Rather a lark," said Ashby, "to get up a search-party and go and look for him there."

The idea took wonderfully. To-day was "Founder's Day," a whole holiday. They would certainly go and look for Rollitt on the island.

The preparations disclosed an odd conception on the part of the explorers of the serious nature of their quest. Their stated object was to rescue a lost schoolfellow. Why, therefore, did they decide to take nine pennyworth of brandy-balls, a football, a pair of boxing-gloves, and other articles of luxury not usually held to be necessary to the equipment of a relief expedition?

As regards food, they possessed too keen a recollection of the straits they had been put to up the mountain a few weeks ago to neglect that important consideration now.

Naturally, ham and Abernethys were the victuals selected. Had not Rollitt made these classical as the staff of life during voluntary exile from school?

They were compelled to put up with a very small sample of the former. Lickford had been bequeathed a bone by his senior yesterday, to which adhered a few fragments of a once small ham. Possibly it might, with careful carving, furnish nine small slices.

It was better than nothing. They would make up for its deficiency by a double lot of Abernethys.

So they trooped off to the shop.

According to their own rules, this establishment was only open between 11 and 12 in the morning, and not at all on holidays.

But another rule said that the committee might in certain cases suspend or alter the rules.

Whereupon Percy moved, and Ashby seconded, the following resolution: "That this shop be, and is, hereby opened for the space of five minutes." The motion was carried unanimously.

D'Arcy and Cottle, whose turn it was to be on duty, solemnly took down the shutters, and ranged themselves behind the counter.

"What can I do for you, my little dears?" said the former, encouragingly. "Money down. No tick. Try some of our Rollitt's particular—three-halfpence each."

"No, they're not, you cheat!—they're a penny. We'd better have two each," said Wally.

"Hullo! I say," exclaimed D'Arcy. "Look here, you fellows."

He pointed to the heap of Abernethy biscuits, on the top of which lay a sixpence.

"That's what you call looking after the money," said Wally. "Left that there all night."

"No—not a bit of it. But I tell you what," said D'Arcy, who had rapidly been counting the pile of biscuits; "there were twenty-four biscuits there when we left last night. I'm certain of it; weren't there, young Cottle?"

"Yes. I remember that," testified Cottle.

"Very well; then some one's been here in the night, for there are only eighteen biscuits now, and this sixpence."

"Perhaps Yorke got some before he started?"

"How could he? No one can get in here without the latch-key; and only the two chaps who are on duty keep that."

"Perhaps it's the owls in the belfry?"

"They don't generally pay ready money for what they take."

"I say!" exclaimed Wally; "I expect it's Rollitt. He'd have finished his others by this time, and he sneaked back in the night for some more. Good old Rollitt!"

Wally did not stay to explain how Rollitt could have got in any more than any one else. His suggestion made a deep impression. It touched them to feel that, amid all his distresses, Rollitt was loyal to the School shop; and if anything was needed to spur them on to his rescue, this did it.

They bought up the remaining eighteen biscuits between them, and sallied forth.

"You see," said Wally, "it's much more likely to be the island than the mountain. There's water there, for one thing."

"There's water on the mountain," said Ashby; "plenty."

"But not good to drink, you ass!" argued Wally.

"And there's that old broken boat-house to live in, and lots of wood to make fires, and ducks to bag and fish to catch. I say! I expect he's having rather a lark."

The prospect of sharing in his wild sports urged them on still faster.

At the lake-side a new problem arose. If Rollitt was on the island, how had he got there? And, still more important, how were they to get there? Widow Wisdom's boat had already been laid up for the winter; and the few others, which in the summer were generally kept at the river-mouth for the use of the boys, had been taken back to Penchurch. The only craft available was a flat-bottomed punt used by fishermen, and at present moored to a stake at the river-bank. It was capacious, certainly, but not exactly the sort of boat in which to get up much pace, particularly as its sole apparent mode of propulsion was by means of two very long boat-hooks, one on either side. These details, however, presented few obstacles to the minds of the enterprising explorers. The punt was in many ways adapted for a voyage such as they proposed to take. There was room to walk about in it. Nay, who should say the boxing-gloves and football might not have scope for themselves within its ample lines?

The one question was whether the boat-hooks were long enough to touch bottom all the way from the shore to the island. Wally paced one, and found it measured eighteen feet.

"Ought to do," said he; "it's bound not to be deeper than that."

So the punt, which was christened the "Cock-house" for the occasion, was loosed from her moorings, the Abernethys and knuckle-bone and other stores were put on board, the boat-hooks, by a combined effort, were got into position, and the party embarked for the rescue of Rollitt.

Thanks to the stream, their progress at first was satisfactory. They were delighted to find how easily they went. Wally with one boat-book on one side, and Percy with the other on the other side, had comparatively little to do except to prevent their hooks getting stuck in the mud at the bottom, and refusing to come out. Any one watching them would have said these boys had been born in a barge. They carried their long poles to the prow, and plunged them in there with a mighty splash. Then they shoved away, till the end of the poles came within reach of their hands. Then, in perfect step and time, they started to march, each down his own side of the boat, calling on their friends and admirers to get out of the way. Then, as they neared the stern, and the prospect of pulling up their hooks and returning fora'd for another "punt" loomed ahead, their faces grew anxious and concerned. They began to hold on "hard all," a yard from the end of the walk, and tug frantically to get themselves free. Sometimes the hook came out easily, in which case they fell backwards into the arms of their friends. At other times it stuck, and they had to detain the progress of the boat a minute or more to get it out. And sometimes it all but escaped them, and continued sticking up out of the water while the barge itself floated on. Happily, the last tragedy never quite came off, although it was periodically imminent.

When, however, the stream opened into the lake, the progress became much less exciting. The water was a little lumpy, and had a tendency, while they were walking back at the end of one punt in order to start another, of jumping the "Cock-House" back into precisely the same position from which she had lately started.

After about half an hour's fruitless efforts the twins were seized with a generous desire not to monopolise the whole of the fun of the voyage.

"Like to have a go!" said Wally to D'Arcy.

"You may have a turn if you like, Lick," said Percy.

Whereupon D'Arcy and Lickford took up the rowing for the "Cock-House," greatly assisted and enlivened in their operations by the advice and encouragement of the late navigators.

"Two to one on Lick," cried Wally, as the two started their mad career down the boat. "Look out! he's gaining."

"You've made her go an inch and a half," said Percy.

"Hang on tight now, and pull it up," said Wally, as Lickford, red in the face with excitement, was straining himself to release the hook from the mud.

"Keep her trim," said Percy, laying hold of D'Arcy's feet, as the latter was gradually letting himself be hauled out of the boat by his refractory pole.

In due time D'Arcy and Lickford unselfishly gave up the poles to Cottle and Ashby; and they, after a reasonable season of struggle and peril, nobly ceded them to Ramshaw and Cash, Fisher minor waiving his claim, and electing to sit "odd man out" and steer.

As at the end of an hour and a half's manful shoving the net progress made was a yard back into the stream of the river, the talents of the helmsman were not put to a very severe test.

"I say, it's rather slow," said Wally; "let's have some of Rollitt's particular."

So while Percy with a small pair of scissors—none of the party, marvellous to relate, had brought a knife—was carving the remnant of ham, and Ashby was counting out nine brandy-balls from the bag, each member of the party produced one of his Abernethys, and fell-to with all the appetite that waits on hard and honest toil.

"Not much of a pace yet," remarked D'Arcy. "Why, we're going better now we've stopped rowing than we were before."

"That's because the wind's changed," said Wally. "If we'd only got a sail we could make her go."

"Why not stick up the two poles, and fasten our coats or something between for a sail!" suggested Percy.

"Good idea! the poles are long enough for all the nine. One of 'em can go through right sleeves, and the other through left. It'll make a ripping sail."

So, despite the season of the year, the nine voyagers divested themselves of their coats, which were industriously threaded by the sleeves on either pole. The top coat was spiked by the hooks, and those below were ingeniously buttoned one to the other to keep them up.

Every one agreed it made a ripping sail. The difficulty was to hoist it. There were no holes in which to fix the parallel masts. They would have to be held in position, as the breeze was stiffening, and it required all hands aloft.

At length, by superhuman exertions, the complex fabric was slowly hoisted to the perpendicular, looking very like a ladder, up which nine scarecrows were clambering. However, no matter what it looked like now, as Wally predicted, they'd spank along.

"We're going already," gasped he, panting with the exertion of holding up his mast. "Look out now! here's a nice breeze coming."

He was right. Next moment the vast foresail fell with a run by the board, and the nine athletes below were nearly shot into the air by the force of the collapse. The coats, fortunately, held together sufficiently well to enable them to be hauled on board in a piece; but as they were soaked through, they afforded very little comfort to the distressed seamen, who decided forthwith to shorten sail at once, and take to the poles once more.

But by this time the "Cock-House," thanks to the tremendous impetus it had just received, was twenty yards from the shore; and Wally, when he put down his pole, nearly went after it, in the vain search for a bottom.

"Here's a go!" said he; "I say, you chaps, I almost fancy, after all, Rollitt must be up the mountain. What do you say?"

"I thought so all along," said Fisher minor. "If he is, Yorke and Stratton will find him."

"Good old Yorke! I say—we may as well back water a bit."

Easier said than done. The old punt, now she was once out on the vasty deep, behaved pretty much as she and the wind between them pleased. For a time it looked very much as if, after all the explorers would reach their destination.

But presently—just, indeed, as the explorers had started a small football match (Association rules), Classics against Moderns, to keep themselves warm, the fickle breeze shifted, and sent the "Cock-House" lumbering inshore a mile or so north of the river-mouth. The Classics had just scored their 114th goal as she grounded, and it was declared by common consent that the voyage was at an end.

Luckily, she came ashore near to a little creek, into which, by prodigious haulings and shovings, she was turned; and here, in a rude way, they succeeded in mooring her until a more convenient season.

The call-over bell was just beginning to ring when the nine mariners got back to Fellsgarth.

Great cheering was going on on the Green, and boys were crowding together discussing some great news.

"What is it?—Rollitt turned up?" asked the juniors.

"No; haven't you heard? Yorke and Stratton went up to look for him on Hawk's Pike. They didn't find him, but *they got to the top!*"

"Got to the top! One of our chaps got to the top of Hawk's Pike. Hurroo. Yell, you chaps. Bravo, Yorke! Bully for Fellsgarth!"

"I wish they'd found Rollitt, all the same," said Fisher minor; "I'm afraid he's gone for good."

"Not he. Didn't we nearly find him to-day, you young muff?" retorted Wally. "Besides, a fellow who's gone for good wouldn't come and buy sixpenny-worth of Abernethys at our shop in the night, would he?"

Fisher minor took what comfort he could from the assurance, and trooped in with his fellow-adventurers to call-over.

Chapter Twenty Four
"Bury the Hatchet!"

Notwithstanding Yorke's exploit, and the prevailing hopefulness of the juniors, the feeling of gloom deepened on Fellsgarth when another day ended, and no news was forthcoming of the lost boy.

To a great many it was a shock to hear he was not on the mountain. From what was known of his eccentricities and recklessness, it seemed as likely as not he would retreat up there and remain till he was fetched down.

When it was found he was not there, there seemed to be nowhere else left to look. The lake (quite independently of the eventful cruise of the "Cock-house") had been thoroughly searched; Penchurch had been ransacked; every cottage and home in the neighbourhood had been called at. The river-banks, up and down stream, had been searched too, and daily communication with Rollitt's home made it increasingly clear he had not gone there.

The incident of the six Abernethys and the 6 pence was not seriously considered. There was no evidence that Rollitt had effected the mysterious purchase, and the eccentricities of the young shopmen left it very doubtful whether more than half of that story was not a sensational fiction of their own.

Masters and boys alike went to bed full of trouble and foreboding.

Fisher major, more perhaps than any one, took the situation to heart. He had never ranged himself with Rollitt's accuser; yet, had it not been for his bad management and stupidity, all the trouble would never have come about. Now, if anything grave had happened to the missing boy, Fisher major felt that on his shoulders rested all the blame.

But his misery was turned into rage when, just before bedtime, a fag came over with the following letter from Dangle:—

"I am not surprised you should be so ready to be imposed upon. You have done mischief enough already; but you have been robbed all the same. Any one but a simpleton would see that the turning up of the money just when it did was a suspicious coincidence. What could be easier than for the thief either to impose on Widow Wisdom, and get her to bring back the money with the story about the shirt; or else, during one of his frequent visits there, as soon as he saw that he was found out, to slip it into the pocket himself! Where he got it from I don't pretend to guess; but I don't mind betting that somebody in the School is poorer by £4 10 shillings for this tardy act of restitution. It deceived no one but you. 'None are so blind,' etcetera.

"R. Dangle."

Fisher fairly tore his hair over this scoundrelly document. His impulse was to go over then and there, drag the writer out of his bed, and make him literally swallow his own words. He might have done it, had not the captain just then looked in.

"Why, what's up?" said the latter, who seemed none the worse for his big climb. "What's the matter?"

"Matter? Read this!" shouted Fisher.

Yorke read the letter. An angry flush spread over his face as he did so.

"He shall answer for it to-night!" said Fisher. "No, not to-night. Let the cad have a night's rest. He shall answer for it to-morrow, though, before the whole School. Let me have the letter, old man."

"If you'll promise to make him smart for it."

"You can make your mind easy about that." Next morning, to the surprise of every one, a notice appeared on the door of each house.

Notice.

"A School meeting is summoned for this afternoon at 3.

"(Signed) C. Yorke (Wakefield's).
G. Clapperton (Forder's).
P. Bingham (Stratton's).
L. Porter (Wilbraham's)."

"What's up now?" said Wally, as he read it. "Like Clapperton's cheek to go sticking his name under our man's—and old Bingham, too! What right has he to stick his nose in it?—and, ha, ha, Porter! that's the green idiot in specs, who calls himself captain of Wilbraham's! Well, I never!"

"Shall you go?" asked D'Arcy.

"Rather! Wonder what they're up to, though?"

"Perhaps Rollitt's found, and they're going to trot him out."

"Perhaps they're going to have an eight-handed mill, those four—you know—like what we had."

"I know, when you rammed me below the belt," said Cottle.

"Crams. You know I played on your third waistcoat button. I was never below it once."

"Perhaps Yorke's going to give a lecture on the ascent of Hawk's Pike."

"I know what it is. They're going to give the chaps back their subscriptions. What a run there'll be on the shop directly after!"

This last rumour was industriously put about by the juniors, and was believed in a good many quarters.

A new diversion, however, served to put aside speculation for a time.

"Hullo, who's that lout?" asked D'Arcy, as he and Wally, having shaken off the others for a season, were "taking a cool," arm in arm near the playing-field gate.

The object of this remark was a stalwart, middle-aged, labouring man, who carried an American cloth bag in his hand, and, to judge by the mud on his garments, had travelled some distance. He was trying to open the gate into the field, and on seeing our two juniors beckoned to them inquiringly.

"You can't get in there," said Wally. "You'll have to go to the other gate at the Watch-Tower."

"Is this here Fellsgarth School, young master?" said the man.

"Rather," replied Wally.

"Is the governor at home!"

"Who—Ringwood? I don't know; they'll tell you at the gate."

"He's come to mend the door of your young brother's room, I expect," said D'Arcy. "I hope he won't bung up the squirt-hole while he's about it."

"No. I say, carpenter," said Wally, as the man was about to turn off in the direction of the other gate, "when you mend that door in Forder's, make it strong, do you hear? It gets kicked at rather by fellows. And don't bung—"

"Carpenter? I ain't no carpenter. I want to see the governor."

Gruffly as the man spoke, he evidently regarded the two young gentlemen as persons of some distinction, and lingered a moment longer to ask another question.

"Beg your pardon, young gents," said he; "but you don't chance to know if Alf Rollitt has come back?"

They gazed at him in amazement.

"Rollitt? no. Do *you* know where he is, I say?"

"Not come back?" said the man, hoarsely. "I made sure as he'd be back afore now."

"Do you know where he is?" repeated Wally.

"Not me—he's bound to be somewheres. But the missus, she wouldn't rest till I come and see."

"The missus! I say, do you *know* Rollitt?"

"Well, they do say it's a wise father as don't know his own child."

"What! Are *you* Rollitt's father?" asked they, glancing involuntarily at the shabby clothes and rough, weatherbeaten face.

"Nothing to be ashamed of, are it?" said the stranger. "'Tain't my Alf's fault I ain't in gents' togs."

This rebuke abashed our two juniors considerably.

"Rather not," said Wally. "Our lot's backing Rollitt up, you know. We've been out to look for him, haven't we, D'Arcy?"

"Of course we have; good old Rollitt," said D'Arcy.

"Thank you kindly, young gents," said Mr Rollitt, who seemed rather dazed. "I ain't no scholar, nor no gent either. But my boy Alf's a good boy, and he don't mean no disrespect to the likes of you by running away. He's bound to be somewheres."

"I say," said Wally, "if you come round to the other gate, you can get in—we'll show you where Ringwood's house is."

"Tell you what," said he to D'Arcy, as the two boys went back by the field to meet him, "he doesn't seem a bad sort of chap—it won't do to let my young brother Percy and those Modern cads get hold of him. I vote we nurse him on our side while he's here."

"All serene," said D'Arcy. "Ask him to tea after the meeting."

"I suppose we shall have to let those other chaps be in it too," suggested Wally dubiously, after a moment.

"Better. We'll all see him through together."

The spectacle of two juniors, looking very important, carefully conducting an anxious-faced labouring man across the School Green, was enough to rouse a little curiosity. And when presently the bodyguard, after sundry whispered communications, increased from two to nine, who marched three in front, two behind, and two on either side of their celebrity, speculation became active and warm.

The escort glared defiantly at any one who ventured to approach the group; but when it was observed that they made straight for the doctor's house, and one by one shook hands with the visitor on the doorstep, there was very little doubt left as to who the stranger might be.

"Mind you come to tea," said Wally, as they parted.

"Don't you make no mistake, I'll be there," said the guest.

Work in school that morning dragged heavily. The impending meeting was perplexing the minds of not a few. The phenomenon of Yorke's and Clapperton's names appended to the same document puzzled boys who still kept alive the animosity which had wrecked the School clubs earlier in he term and brought the sports to a deadlock. And the addition of the names of the captains of the other two houses made it evident that the whole School was concerned in the business. This, coupled with the mystery of Rollitt's disappearance, and the now notorious internecine feuds of the Modern seniors, gave promise of one of the biggest meetings ever held in Hall.

As to the juniors, they had a treble care on their mind. First, the meeting, and the expected refunding of the Club subscriptions; second, the consequent run on the shop; and third, the "small and early." in Wally's study afterwards to meet A. Rollitt, Senior, Esq.

However, despite all these cares, the morning's work was got through, the dreaded impositions were avoided, and when the midday meal was ended a general rush was made for the familiar benches in Hall.

The state of doubt every one was in operated adversely to the usual cheering. Fellows didn't know whom they were expected to cheer. Dangle, for instance, pale and sullen,—were the Moderns expected to cheer him? The Classics hissed him, which was one reason why his own house should applaud. But then, if they cheered Dangle, how should they do about Clapperton, who had fought Dangle a week ago? They got over the difficulty by doing neither, but starting party cries which they could safely cheer; and chaffing everybody all round.

Punctually at three, Yorke rose and said they no doubt were curious to know what the meeting was called for. It was called for one or two purposes. The first was to see if they could revive the School clubs. (Cheers.) He wasn't going to say a word of ancient history. (Laughter.) But as they stood now, they had a lot of fellows anxious to play, they had the materials for as good a fifteen this winter, and as good an eleven next spring (cheers), as any school in the country; and yet the playing-fields stood idle, and the name of Fellsgarth was dropping out of all the records. They had had enough of that sort of thing. Every one was sick of it. Fellows had agreed with him when it was proposed to disband the clubs; he hoped they would agree with him now that the time had come for reviving them. But there was to be a difference. The clubs were not to be open to everybody, as heretofore. They didn't want everybody. (Hear, hear, from Wally, D'Arcy, Ashby, and Fisher, as they pointed across to the Modern juniors.) They only wanted fellows who would play and *could* play; as to the former, that of course would be decided by the fellow himself, who would send in an application to the committee. As to the latter, that would be decided by the captain. (Oh!) Yes, by the captain. What's the good of a captain if he's not to decide a matter like that? And if the fellow is not satisfied with the captain's decision, he may appeal to Mr Stratton, the new president of the club. (Cheers.) There's nothing to prevent any one who plays his best joining—there's nothing to prevent those youngsters at the end of the room, who are kicking up such a row, joining the clubs, as long as they work hard in the field. (Cheers and laughter.) The fellows who won't be eligible are the louts, and those who can play but won't. (Loud cheers.)

Clapperton rose to second the motion. He had lost a great deal of his "side" during the last few days, and though he looked in better tiff than he had done lately, the present occasion was evidently an effort. He said: "Yorke has made a generous speech. He avoided ancient history, and therefore did not go into the reason why the clubs were dissolved and the School sports came to smash. I could tell you—but what's the use? You all know. Yorke said to me before the meeting, 'Let bygones be bygones, old man—we were all to blame—bury the hatchet—let's get right for the future.' Gentlemen, there was one fellow who was not to blame. His name was *not* Clapperton. It was Yorke." (Loud cheers.) "But I say with him, if you let me, 'Bury the hatchet.'" (Cheers.) "And to prove it, I beg to hand in my name to the committee for election. I answer for myself that I am willing to play; and if the captain decides that I can play," (laughter), "why, I will play." (Loud applause.)

Fullerton and Corder both sprang up to support the motion. The former made way for Corder, who merely wished to say how delighted he was. He also voted for the burying of the hatchet. He had minded being stopped football more than anything else. He gave in his name. He would play, and he might tell them that the captain had already told him he could play. (Laughter, and cries of "Blow your own trumpet.") All right—it was the only thing he had to be cocky about; and he meant to be cocky. He supported the motion. (Cheers.)

Fullerton handed in his name, and was very glad to think that he and his old friend Clapperton would have a chance of running up the field again together. ("If you're elected!" from the end of the room, and laughter.) Oh, of course, if he was elected. He hoped when the gentleman down there was captain, fifty years hence, he would deal as liberally with candidates as he was sure Yorke would deal now. (Laughter, at Wally's expense.)

The other prefects followed suit, and gave in their allegiance to the new clubs. Curiosity was alive to see what attitude Brinkman and Dangle would adopt. For a while it seemed as if they would take no part; but at length, when Yorke was about to put the motion, Brinkman rose and said, "I made up my mind when I came here I'd have no more to do with the clubs. But Yorke's 'Bury the hatchet' gives a fellow a chance. If you mean that," (Yes, yes), "if this is a fresh start, here's my name!" (Loud cheers.) "You needn't cheer. I didn't mean to give it—but now I have, I—I—won't shirk it," and he sat down hurriedly.

Then Dangle rose, with a sneer on his face.

"This sort of thing is infectious. I can't feel quite so sure as some of you about burying the hatchet; but, not to be peculiar, you may put me down—"

"And I can tell you at once, and before all these fellows," said Yorke, rising hotly, and interrupting, "that we won't have you! And that brings me to the other business—and that's about Rollitt. We can't bury the hatchet so easily, as far as he is concerned. For he is still absent, and no one knows what has become of him. I'm not going to say a word to make little of Fisher's major's mistake. It was bad enough, in all conscience, for Rollitt. But it was only a mistake. But what do you fellows say of the cad who deliberately gets up a story about him; and, even when he finds out there is not a shadow of truth in it, repeats it in a worse form than before? There are some here who believed the first report and joined in the suspicions. That was hardly to be wondered at. But every one of them had the decency, as soon as the money was found, to admit that they had been wrong, and to regret their unfair suspicion of a Fellsgarth fellow. All but one—this cad here! Only last night, you fellows, he wrote the letter I hold in my hand. I mean to read it to you, and I hope you won't forget it in a hurry."

"You shan't read it; it wasn't to you!" said Dangle, making a rush at the paper; "give it back!"

"You shall have it back," said Yorke in a warmer temper than any one had seen him in before, "when I've read it. Stop, and listen to it. It'll do you good."

"Read away!" sneered Dangle, giving up the contest. "It's the truth."

Yorke read, and as he proceeded, shame and anger rose to boiling-point in the audience, so that towards the end the reader's voice was almost drowned in the hisses.

"There," said the captain, crumpling up the paper in his hand and flinging it at the writer's feet, "there's your letter; and until you apologise to the whole school you have insulted, you needn't expect we'll bury the hatchet!"

Dangle scowled round and tried to swagger.

"Is that all the business?" he sneered.

"No!" shouted some voices. "He ought to be kicked."

"Wait a bit," cried Wally, excitedly, standing on a form, "there's Rollitt's governor just come. Some of our chaps have gone to fetch him. He'll—"

Here the door opened, and, escorted by half a dozen of the juniors, Mr Rollitt, looking more bewildered than ever, walked in.

He looked apologetically from one side to the other, saying, "Thank'ee kindly," and "No offence, young gents," until he found himself at the end of the Hall among the prefects.

Then Yorke got up again, still hot with temper, and a dead silence ensued. Dangle smiled at first. But his face gradually blanched as he looked round and found his retreat cut off, and guessed what was coming.

"Mr Rollitt," said Yorke, "we are your son's schoolfellows. A great wrong has been done him. He has been suspected of being a thief, and has run away. We all now know that he's not a thief; and we are ashamed that he has ever been suspected. We hope he will come back, so that we may tell him so. But there is one fellow here who still says your son is a thief, although he knows as well as we do he isn't. What shall we do to him?"

Mr Rollitt looked up and down, casting a glance first at his young protectors at the end of the Hall, then scanning the benches before him, then running his eye along the row of prefects, and finally taking the measure of Yorke as he stood and waited for an answer.

Then suddenly the question seemed to come home.

"My son Alf a thief? There's one of 'em says that, is there? My son Alf a thief? Do to him! Why, I'll tell you. Just keep him till my son Alf comes back, and make him go and say it to his face. That's what *I* should do to him, young gents."

"That's what we will do," said Yorke. "The meeting is over."

And amid the excitement that ensued, the rush to put down names for the new club, the cheers and hootings and hand-shakings of old enemies, Mr Rollitt was carried off in triumph by his nine hosts to high tea in Wally Wheatfield's room.

Chapter Twenty Five
The Watch-Tower

Wally's study—he always liked to call it a "study," but his friends preferred to call it a den—could comfortably accommodate six. The juniors had frequently to own that nine, the normal size of the party, was a jam. When, in addition to that, a big, brawny man was thrown in, it came to be a serious question as to how the four walls would sustain the strain.

Wally, however, was determined to manage somehow. He indignantly rejected Percy's offer to his more spacious apartment over the way. No. He had captured the lion—he and D'Arcy—and they would entertain him in their own den.

After all, it was not so bad. It only meant letting the fire out and putting one chair in the fender, and shoving the other end of the table (which had been doubled in length by the addition of the table out of a neighbouring room, that was within four inches of the same height) close up against the door, which it was just possible to shut. As, however, the door opened outwards, it was necessary for the gentleman occupying the foot of the table to sit out in the passage, much to the inconvenience of the casual passers-by.

To a shy man like Mr Rollitt, it was a difficult position to find himself the honoured guest of nine young gentlemen like these.

"Thank'ee kindly, young masters," said he, when Ashby relieved him of his hat and Fisher minor of his bag, and Percy undermined him with a chair, and Cottle handed him the *Boy's Own Paper*, and Cash came in with a hassock, and D'Arcy put a railway rug over his knees.

Wally, whose ideas of hospitality were of the old school, deemed it expedient, while tea was being served, to engage his guest on the subject of the weather.

"Rather finer the last few days than it was the other week when it rained?" said he. "Rollitt's having fine weather for his trip."

This was an artful way of introducing the topic of the hour.

"Thank you kindly, yes. He's bound to be somewheres, is my Alf," replied Mr Rollitt.

"It's all right; we're backing him up. He made a ripping run for the School against Rendlesham. He bashed the ball through the scrimmage, you know, and then nipped it up right under their noses and ran it through. They couldn't collar him, he bowled 'em over right and left, and danced on 'em, and landed the touch clean behind the post."

"He meant no harm, young gents, didn't my Alf. He ain't often wiolent, he ain't. There's no offence, I hope?" said the father, quite overwhelmed by this alarming recital.

"No; it was a jolly good run. You ought to have seen it; I and my lot were up the oak, you know; we could have tucked you in. My young brother Percy and his Modern cads—k-i-d-s (I never can pronounce it)—were on the steps."

"Oh," said the poor guest, feeling he ought to reciprocate the civility of his entertainers. "Steps is nice things to be on when you ain't got nowheres else."

"Tea!" shouted Fisher minor, who with Ashby had been busily charging the table.

It was now the turn of the hosts to be shy. At this late period of the term funds had run low, and extras were at a premium. A busy hour had been spent during the forenoon in both houses collecting outstanding debts, contracting loans at the point of the sword, and laying out the contents of the common purse at the shop in delicacies suitable to the occasion. Abernethys and ham, of course, figured prominently. The cake and jam was rather a "scratch lot," as they mostly consisted of "outsides" and "pot-ends" collected from various sources and amalgamated into one stock. But, to compensate for this, Wally had managed to get round the matron, and by representing to her the delicate nature of the entertainment, wheedled her out of a pot of "extra special" tea, and a small jug of cream. For the rest, there were the relics of the "Cock-House" commissariat, a cocoa-nut, generously contributed by Fisher major, and the usual allowance of bread and butter.

The principal delicacy of the feast, however, was contributed by a fair lady, and to Percy belonged the honour and glory of its acquisition.

On his way from Hall he had run flop into the arms of Mrs Stratton, who was carrying in her hands a small basket of hothouse grapes.

"I'm awfully sorry, I say, Mrs Stratton," said the culprit, as the basket and its contents fell to the ground. "So am I," said Mrs Stratton. "There's two bunches out of three not bashed," said Percy, on his knees picking up the ruin. "I say, Mrs Stratton, if you'd let me pay for the other I can give you twopence a week, beginning next week. I'd rather, you know."

Mrs Stratton laughed pleasantly. It was always a satisfaction, she told her husband, to come into collision with a junior. He always got the best of it.

"No, thank you, Wheatfield. But I tell you what you must do."

"All serene, Mrs Stratton," said Percy submissively, preparing himself for a hundred lines at least.

"One of the bunches is damaged. You must take it and get your friends to help you eat it. Good-bye."

On the whole, therefore, the spread provided for Mr Rollitt was a respectable one, and not likely to do discredit to his entertainers.

He was installed in the place of honour in the fender, Wally occupying the seat in the passage, the others ranging themselves on either side of the board. They watched their guest's eye somewhat anxiously, to detect in it any signs of predilection for any particular dish. But he, poor man, was too bewildered by the novel experience he was undergoing to betray any symptoms of appetite.

"What'll you have?" said Percy, presently.

"Well, if you've got a bit of bread and cheese and a drop of something, I don't mind, thank you kindly."

This was rather a damper; but Wally was equal to the emergency.

"Have an Abernethy—that's what Rollitt's been living on. You'll like it. We keep a stock in our shop."

"Only a penny each," said Ramshaw, explanatorily.

"Better have some jam with it," said Cottle.

"Like some tea?" inquired D'Arcy, who had charge of the pot, beginning to fill up a mug the size of the slop-basin with the matron's "extra special."

"The cake's not so bad—there's several lumps not a bit stale," said Ashby.

"If you like cocoa-nut," said Fisher minor, "my brother's lent us one, and I'll cut you a chunk."

"And there's some grapes for you, when you're ready," said Percy, proudly; "a present from a lady."

The awkward thing was that, in their eagerness to see their guest eat, none of the juniors took anything. They continued to pile up the good man's plate till he didn't know where to begin, and fairly bewildered him by each commending the excellence of his own particular delicacy "Thank'ee, young gents. I ain't much of a eater when I'm away from home; no more ain't my Alf. But I'll take a snack, anyhow."

Whereupon, to their delight, he commenced an onslaught on the viands before him, every morsel he ate being followed by eighteen admiring eyes into his mouth. He made short work of the Abernethys and cake, tossed off the tea as if it were a thimbleful, jerked down the hunk of cocoa-nut, gulped the grapes, and generally gave the spectators an admirable and comprehensive performance.

They were charmed. So much so, that out of sheer pleasure they began to eat too. The meal, if brief, was a merry one. Mr Rollitt took a special fancy to the Abernethys—a choice which of course put the shop-directors in an ecstasy. They only reproached themselves that they had not provided twelve instead of six.

At length, partly because there was nothing left but lukewarm water and the toughest crusts of the cake, and partly because the guest's appetite was beginning to flag, the solid portion of the meal came to an end, and the social began.

After sundry nudgings and whisperings and signals among the juniors, Wally filled up his cup with warm water and rose to his feet.

"Ladies and gentlemen," he said, "I—you know—that is—shut up, young Cash, unless you want to do it—instead of me—it's this way, you see, you chaps: I sort of think we ought to drink the health of Rollitt's governor. He's a good old sort, and we're backing up old Rollitt. It wasn't a very grand spread. There'd have been some sardines if you'd come last week; but that greedy pig D'Arcy—"

"Go on; it was *you* finished them, three in two gulps," protested the outraged D'Arcy.

"Look here, young D'Arcy," said Wally, seriously, "am I making this speech, or are you. If you don't shut up, I'll jolly well make you.—We hope you've liked it, and don't mind our drinking your health, you know. It'll be jolly when old Rollitt turns up. We'd ask you again to-morrow, you know, only the grub's run short. Therefore, I have much pleasure in proposing your health."

The toast was drunk with acclamation, the party joining in "For he's a jolly good fellow," much to the alarm of the occupants of the neighbouring studies, who flocked out in the passage to see what the noise was about.

Wally assured them there was no grub left, so they needn't hang about; but a good many of them remained all the same, to hear Mr Rollitt's speech.

"Thank'ee kindly, young masters," began he, with his usual formula; "I ain't no schollard like my Alf is. He could talk to you straight. I'm sorry he ain't here, gents. He's bound to be somewheres, and I'm sure it's no offence meant, his going away. I likes your style, and I hopes that young fly-by-night who says my Alf's a thief will tell him so to his face. My Alf'll settle him proper. Them as pays for my Alf's schooling—which it's two kind ladies, masters, as my missus was kinder foster-sister to—means to make a gent of my Alf. But, bless you, he'd sooner be along of me in the building trade. Not that my Alf ain't a schollard, and can't behave himself. He do behave beautiful to his mother, does Alf, and ain't nothink of a fine gent at home. So there, I tell you straight, and no offence meant, young masters. I like your style, I do. Don't you take on about my Alf bein' a-missing. He's bound to be somewheres. I know'd him do it afore, when things went contrairy. But he wasn't fur off, and come back. On'y don't let 'im cop hold of that there jumper as says he's a thief, or there'll be a row in the 'ouse. Why, my Alf's that straight he wouldn't rob a dog of his bone, not if he was starving. That's flat. So here's to you, young gents; and if you happen to be passing near Crackstoke way, me and my missus'll be proud to see yer. Here's luck!"

The speech was rapturously applauded, not only by the party present, but by the knot of fellows in the passage, who were taking advantage of the necessarily open door to join in the proceedings as outsiders.

Wally, however, resented the intrusion, and as soon as the speech of the evening was ended, ordered one of the tables to be cleared, and placing his chair upon it, made room for the door to be closed on the intruders, much to their disappointment.

After the favourable reception of his speech, Mr Rollitt became very much more at home, and produced a pipe from his pocket, which he proceeded in the most natural way to light. His hosts gazed in a somewhat awe-struck way at the proceeding, but Wally gave the right cue.

"That's right, Mr Rollitt; make yourself at home."

"So I are. You see, in my days, schooling worn't what it is. Now this here school must be a topper."

"It's not bad," said Percy. "You see there was a jolly row on this term between the Classics and our lot, and they had to be taken down a bit."

"*Did* they?" retorted Wally, very indignant; "how many pegs did *you* come down? Who had to get our chaps to come and give them a leg-up every other day?"

"Who swindled at Elections and got licked on the hands, eh!"

"Who got their football bagged, and couldn't get it back?"

"Who got kicked out of the front row at the Rendlesham match?"

"'Armony, gents, 'armony," said Mr Rollitt, waving his pipe encouragingly.

The rebuke was opportune. It wasn't fair to the guest to squabble before him.

"We've stashed all that," said Percy, presently; "they got civil to us, so we got civil to them, and we're all in the shop together. And we're all backing up old Rollitt, ain't we, you chaps, and we're going down in a lump for the clubs; and we all shelled out for this do; so it's all right now. See?"

Mr Rollitt thought he did, and nodded amiably.

"You see, it's not much larks unless we're all in it. We went up Hawk's Pike, you know."

"No," said Mr Rollitt. "How did that happen?"

"Well, it was this way, you see," began Percy, taking up, as was his wont, the narrative at a remote period. "After those Classic cads—k-i-d-s, you know, had—(Shut up, Wally, I said k-i-d-s; can't you spell?) had caved in."

"Who caved in!" expostulated the Classics.

"Well, after Stratton's, you know, when we started the shop—I say, you'll have to come and see the shop—well—it was before that, though; it was when the row began about Corder not being stuck in—that was before that, you know—Brinkman screwed his foot, so there was a man short for the team, so Clapperton—that's our prefect, you know; he's all right now, but he—hullo, I say, he's gone asleep!"

Sure enough Mr Rollitt, weary with his long journey, with the excitement of the day, and with the excellence of the tea, had dozed off comfortably, on his chair in the fender, with his pipe in his mouth.

Percy felt it unnecessary to pursue his lucid narrative, and the nine hosts sat watching their man as his head nodded forward, and the urgent necessity for a snore presently rendered the position of the pipe no longer tenable.

It was a triumph! No man could have gone off like that unless he had felt thoroughly comfortable. The railway rug was again produced and laid over his knees, and his feet were gently lifted on the hassock, and a pillow was neatly inserted at the back of the chair; and all looked so snug, and the hospitable juniors were so pleased with the result, that they had the vanity to let the door stand open, so that all who passed by might see how comfortable they could make a guest when they liked.

To heighten the effect, they decided to do their preparation on the spot, and so not only impress the sleeper when he awoke, but advertise themselves to the outside world as boys who by no means neglected the serious side of school life for its lighter functions.

It must be owned that next day when the work thus accomplished was subjected to the microscopic test of the master's eyes, it was not any better—some said it was even worse—than usual. That had nothing to do with the present.

Wally, who put his chair out again in the passage, had most of his time occupied in making pantomimic appeals for silence from passers-by, to whom he pointed out the figure of the sleeping Mr Rollitt as a justification. The others, debarred from speech (for it was considered that even a whisper might awaken the sleeper, although the violent process of tucking him up just now had failed to do so), were reduced to communication with one another in writing, which took up so much time and paper that very little of either was left for lessons.

At last, after half an hour's suspense, the clang of the house-bell for call-over broke the spell. Mr Rollitt grunted and yawned and opened his eyes, looked about for his pipe, inspected the rug on his knees, took his feet off the hassock, and finally realised where he was.

"I was nigh 'andy asleep that time," said he, rummaging in his pocket for a lucifer.

"It's all right; we were doing our prep, you know. Now we've got to be called over. If you stick here, we'll be back in a jiffy, and then we'll take you to see the shop," said Wally.

"Thank'ee kindly," said the guest; "don't put yourselves about for me. Take your time, young gents."

"We shan't be long. I say, wait for us, won't you? Don't you go out with any other chaps. They ain't in it, you know."

"I ain't a-going with nobody, don't you make no mistake," was the visitor's satisfactory assurance.

They had some thoughts about locking him in, to make sure of him, but decided to trust his parole, and trooped down impatiently to call-over, binding one another to assemble at the shop immediately afterwards, whither Wally and Percy were to conduct their guest.

To the satisfaction of these young gentlemen, the bird was safely in his cage when they returned, dimly visible through the smoke, looking at the pictures in the illustrated paper. He meekly obeyed their summons, relieving their embarrassment somewhat by putting his pipe away in his pocket as he rose.

"Where's the rest of the pals?" asked he.

"Down at the shop. It's not the regular hour, you know. But we can get in with the key. Come along, Mr Rollitt."

The old Watch-Tower, which, as the reader knows, is the oldest remaining portion of Fellsgarth, was rather an imposing-looking edifice for so mundane an establishment as the School shop. The shop, indeed, occupied only a small apartment on the ground floor, which had previously been used as a porter's lodge, the remainder of the structure, including the disused belfry and watch-turret, being abandoned to the owls and ghosts and ivy, which accorded best with the ancient traditions of the place.

Mr Rollitt, whose profession sharpened his observation for specimens of bygone achievements in his own line of business, noted the venerable exterior before him with admiration.

"That there bit of bricks and mortar," said he, "warn't built yesterday."

"Oh, it's millions of years old," said Wally; "but our shop, you know, has only just been started."

"They don't make copin's like them to-day," repeated Mr Rollitt.

"We go in for good grub cheap," said Percy; "no shoe-leather, like Bob used to sell."

"I reckon them top courses is a hundred year after this here bottom part. Not much jerry there neither."

"We boss it among us, you know," said Wally, "and take turns to serve. We don't get a bad profit either."

Here they were joined by the rest of the party. But to their disappointment Mr Rollitt's interest in the shop was small compared with that he showed in the lay of the bricks, the run of the beams, and the hardness of the mortar.

"They knowed their way about, straight, those days," said he, picking away between two of the bricks with his nail.

"Try one of our 'Rollitt's particular,'" pleaded D'Arcy, in the hope that this invitation at least would interest him.

But no. He went "nosing round," taking no notice of the stores, and putting off all invitations with a "Thank'ee kindly, not to-day."

It was a sore blow to his hosts. After what they had done for him, after the way they had nursed him all day, after the tea they had given him, and the pipes he had smoked in their study! They could have thrown him overboard in their mortification. But the dread lest some one else, some of the middle-boys, for instance, should get hold of him and "run" him, decided them to pocket their feelings and back him up still.

"No offence, young gents," said he presently; "but if you've a ladder 'andy, I'd like to take a look up there."

"Oh, there's nothing up there—only bats and owls," said Wally, "and there's no ladder."

But Mr Rollitt pointed out in a corner, behind the back of the shop, some protruding bits of stone let into the brick, evidently with a view to form a rude ladder or stair to the chambers above.

This promised well. An exploration of the Watch-tower offered some little compensation for the slight put on their shop.

"I never saw that before," said Wally. "I vote we go up."

Mr Rollitt led the way with all the agility of a practical hodman. The steps ended with a trap-door in the ceiling, which he pushed up before him.

"Mind how you go, young gents," said he to his followers; "one at a time on them stones."

The trap-door opened into a sort of passage, at the end of which was a narrow brick corkscrew staircase.

It was too dark to do anything but feel their way up; Mr Rollitt leading, and testing every step as he went along.

"Why," said Wally suddenly, and with a touch of alarm in his voice, as they were halting a moment to allow Mr Rollitt to inspect with the end of a lucifer one of the loophole windows, "why, look up there—there's a light!"

They looked. And there, struggling apparently from under a door which closed the head of the stairs, came a streak of light.

"I say—it's ghosts," said Fisher minor. "Let's go back."

"More likely it's my Alf," said Mr Rollitt. "I know'd he was somewheres not fur off."

He went up, followed at a more respectful distance than before by the boys, and pushed open the door.

They heard the sound of an exclamation within, and a noise as of some one starting to his feet. Next moment, as the light streamed down the staircase, they heard a familiar voice say—

"Father!"

"That's me, Alf, my boy; I know'd you was somewheres 'andy."

"I say," said Wally, in an excited whisper to his followers, "we'd best cut back, you chaps. They don't want us up there."

The delicate suggestion was appreciated by the party, who forthwith made a precipitate retreat.

"We as good as found him, that's one thing, and nobody else was in it," said Percy triumphantly.

"Rather not. Keep it mum. Let's go and light the fire in his room, and have some grub ready for him. Good old Rollitt, I'm jolly glad he's turned up!"

"That's how he got the Abernethys," said D'Arcy. "Jolly honest to pay for them."

"You don't suppose anybody would collar things out of the shop and not pay for them, you lout, do you?"

Whereat, leaving the door on the latch, they marched arm in arm across the School Green kicking every junior they met, and mystifying everybody by whistling at the top of their voices, "See the conquering hero comes."

Chapter Twenty Six
The Final Kick

Rollitt's return to Fellsgarth was almost as mysterious as his disappearance. He answered to his name at call-over next morning as if he had never missed a day this term. And as Dr Ringwood and the other masters were present, and made no remark, it was generally concluded that the truant had turned up over-night, and had had it out with the authorities before bedtime.

Mr Rollitt, Senior, had departed. He had looked into Wally's study after the owner and his crew were in bed to get his bag, and had been driven down in the doctor's fly to Penchurch.

It was also understood that most of the Classic seniors had dropped into Rollitt's study early that morning. To some he had said, "Get out"; with others he had shaken hands. The captain had evidently been among the latter; as, on the notice board that morning, among the names of the fifteen who were to play the first match for the new clubs on Saturday against Penchurch, was that of Rollitt. The excitement caused by this discovery almost put into the shade for the time the equally remarkable fact that Clapperton and Brinkman were included in the same team.

Where Rollitt had been, and what he had been doing, remained a mystery. It was, of course, out of the question to ask him. Conjecture was rife, and was greatly assisted by the juniors, who hazarded all sorts of plausible explanations for the general benefit.

"Think he's been to Land's End?" said Wally. "I hear you can do it in a week—sharp walking."

"You can get to America in that time," said Lickford.

"Yes—he does seem to have rather a twang on him. Perhaps that's where he's been to," remarked D'Arcy.

"Penny bank coal-mine's only fifty miles away," said Percy. "It runs under the sea ever so far. I should say it was a ripping place to hide in."

From which and other similar remarks it was concluded that the juniors had a much better notion as to where Rollitt had been than they chose to admit.

They eagerly embraced the first opportunity of going to the shop, and investigating the scene of the mystery for themselves. They carefully locked the outer door against possible intruders, and then in Indian file ascended the stone ladder, and after it the corkscrew staircase.

The room in which they found themselves was pretty much as Rollitt had left it. It had evidently been made use of by a former lodge-keeper as a dwelling-room, for there was a ragged paper on the wall, and an attempt here and there to board over dangerous holes in the floor. Besides which there was a rude shutter to the tiny window, by means of which no doubt Rollitt had succeeded in concealing his presence at night. The remains of a wood fire were on the hearth, and a candle-end showed (what they already knew) that the hermit did not spend all his evenings in darkness.

More than this, in one corner still lay some of the wraps which he had evidently used to extemporise a bed. And an empty box on end in the window convinced them he had sat down during part of his residence. There was also a leaf of exercise paper and a Horace lying on the floor, which evidently had not been brought there by the owls. Altogether, as they looked round, they concluded that, but for the cold, he might have had worse quarters during his temporary exile.

But the discovery that delighted them most was a fragment of a newspaper in which were wrapped the not yet exhausted end of a ham, and half a biscuit!

Over these relics they dwelt with quite an affectionate interest, till somebody said—

"What did he have to drink? He didn't take any of our ginger-beer, and there's no water here."

"Why, you duffer, of course he could get out any time he liked. It's only a latch on the door; any one can open it from inside. He could easily get down to the river in the night, and have a tub, and fetch up some water."

They decided that in future the shop committee, except when Mr and Mrs Stratton were present, should meet nowhere but in "Rollitt's chamber," as they forthwith named the room, and proceeded to dedicate it to that use there and then.

"Do you know," said Wally, "that after we pay back Mr Stratton what he lent us to start with, there'll be a clear £5 to give to the clubs out of the profits?"

"Not bad," said Percy. "They ought to put us in the first fifteen for that."

"Never mind," said D'Arcy; "they've got a jolly hot fifteen for Saturday, Rollitt and all of 'em. We ought to put the Penchurch chaps to bed for once, I fancy."

This was the general impression throughout the School; and, as if to make up for the abstinence of the past few weeks, the fervour of the athletic set waxed high as the eventful day drew near. Yorke had out his men once or twice, practising kicks, and selecting where in the field each player could work to best advantage.

Rollitt, of course, did not attend these practices; but Clapperton and Brinkman did, and soon lost the embarrassment with which they first faced their old rivals and enemies. Corder was down too; dreadfully afraid lest by *some* mishap he should discredit himself, and so be knocked out of his coveted place in the team. Mr Stratton was on the spot also, advising and admonishing—as no one knew better how to do. Even the doctor showed his interest in the new departure of the clubs by coming down too, and by giving directions to reserve seats in the pavilion for a party of his friends.

The only unenthusiastic person, except Rollitt, was Dangle. He tried at first to brazen it out, and came down to the field with a sneer on his face to look, so he said, "at the good boys exercising themselves." But the juniors soon routed him out of that attitude.

"Booh, hoo! Rollitt's coming! Wants to hear you call him a thief. Run—he'll catch you! Put it on, well run, Dangle, you've missed him this time. Coast's clear, now; you can come back. We'll protect you," and so on.

These attentions made Dangle's visits to the field less frequent. In school, he kept the swagger up still longer.

"So," said he one day to Clapperton, "I thought you didn't approve of cutting fellows dead?"

"No more I do."

"Why do you do it, then?"

"Have you apologised to Rollitt?"

"No."

"Has Rollitt thrashed you?"

"No."

"When one or the other has happened, I shall be delighted to shake hands," said Clapperton.

The alternative was a dismal one, but Dangle saw no third way. Which course was least to be desired he could not for the life of him decide. A fight with Rollitt he knew would end disastrously. But to apologise—and in public!

The reader has already had two football matches in the course of this story. He shall not be wearied with a third.

Suffice it to say the Penchurch men—men, not boys—presented themselves on the appointed day, and all Fellsgarth turned out to see the battle.

Fisher minor scored one more triumph by bringing Rollitt up to the scratch, and so completing as sound and taut a team as Yorke had ever led on to victory.

Mrs Stratton was there, wearing the School colours round her hat; and the doctor was there with his field-glasses, pointing out the heroes of the School to his distinguished visitors.

This time, by much squeezing and mutual accommodation, the oak tree was made to hold nine persons. Who those nine were none could guess, unless indeed they happened to be standing within a hundred yards of the spot without cotton-wool in their ears.

From the first it went hard with the Penchurch men. The School had never played up better. The scrimmages were beautifully packed, and the quarter and half-backs were never off the spot. Only when, above the crowd, Rollitt's head was seen to be at work, and it was apparent he had waked up for a time, was there any risk of confusion. But Yorke's "Play on Rollitt!" generally pulled the scrimmage together again, and warned friend and (after a time) foe what to expect.

There was no holding Rollitt back when he once made up his mind to get the ball through; and no stopping him when once he got fairly started on a run. Twice before half-time and once after he scored a touch-down. Twice Yorke did the same, and once Clapperton.

Corder discovered that a fellow does not always score, and yet may play a steady, useful game. He was disappointed that it was only left him to do the latter; and he set himself down as a failure. But Mr Stratton put him on his feet wonderfully at the end.

"You've improved, Corder. You never played as well."

The others worked well, and contributed to the great result, and perhaps, better still, grudged no one his greater glory. It was Fellsgarth that was playing, not Fullerton, Ranger, Brinkman, Fisher major, or anybody else.

The final goal was Clapperton's. It was an historic event. For the first time in the match the Penchurch men had worked the ball up into the boys' quarters, and fears were being entertained lest, after all, they would save their "duck." The half-backs and quarter-backs of the School were squeezed in, all of a lump, between touch and goal; and those who looked on noticed with alarm that, as matters now stood, an easy drop-kick from any of the enemy's forwards might capture the goal.

Rollitt was the first to put an end to this dangerous state of things. He bore down the scrimmage after his usual fashion, and succeeded, as he broke through, in getting the ball into his hands. But for once he could get no further. Twenty hands seized him and carried him to the ground, but not before he had sent back the ball into Fisher's hands.

"Back up now—hard and fast!" cried Yorke.

Never was order more beautifully carried out, Fisher minor held the leather long enough to pass it to Brinkman. Brinkman staggered on a yard or two and slipped it back to Denton. Denton made a yard or two more and passed it to Corder. Corder fell back with it into the arms of Ranger. Ranger let Corder drop, but captured the ball, and with one of his lightning swoops carried it out of the ruck for twenty yards, when, as he fell, Yorke came up and captured it. Yorke, alas, was cut short in his career before he had gone ten yards, but Clapperton was there to take it. Away he went, shaking off the nearest of his assailants and distancing others, till he too fell gloriously, with his body in play, and his hands in touch, thirty yards from the enemy's lines. The serried ranks formed up on either side. Clapperton, as he stood, ball in hand, ready to throw in, passed his eye along the line of his friends, and stopped short of Yorke. Yorke understood. He caught the ball, and quick as thought, returned it to Clapperton, who, swooping round behind the line, got clear with it once more, and crossing the field, curving in all the way, carried into the enemy's lines at their far corner, whence with a wide sweep he brought it round right behind their posts, a beautiful climax to a beautiful piece of co-operative play.

As Mr Stratton said, nothing all that term had been more hopeful of the new spirit of mutual confidence and support in the School than this triumphant rally.

But the goal was yet to be kicked. To Yorke, of course, belonged the honour.

But Yorke, to every one's surprise, stood out.

"No," said he. "It's Clapperton's goal; he shall kick it."

So Fellsgarth, perhaps for the first and only time in its records, stood by and witnessed the phenomenon of its captain carrying out the ball and placing it for the vice-captain to kick.

It needed all Clapperton's nerve to save him from flurry and failure even over an easy task like this. But he pulled himself together and kicked the goal.

And with that kick he sent flying into the air the last remnant of the bad blood and jealousy which had marred the term and all but wrecked the good old School.

Here let us say good-bye—perhaps not for good. For Yorke and Rollitt, and Clapperton and Fisher, and all of them, are still alive and kicking.

Rollitt, to the general regret, but to his own satisfaction, left Fellsgarth at the end of the term for the more congenial course of a school of engineering. Before he left he invited Fisher minor to tea in his room, and alarmed that young gentleman by sitting for a whole hour without uttering a word. At length, when the guest had to leave, he said—

"Thanks, Fisher minor. Thank those fellows of yours. Tell Yorke the money that bought the boat was what I had been saving for something else. I'll write to you. Get out, now."

That was the last of Rollitt.

Dangle never made up his mind either to apologise or take a thrashing. He never met Rollitt after the return of the latter. When breaking-up day came, he got an excuse to go home earlier than the general crowd; and when School reassembled in January it was known he had left Fellsgarth for good.

The two events of the breaking-up "Hall" were—first the announcement by the doctor that, at his request, Yorke would stay on another term at Fellsgarth; secondly, the presentation of a purse containing five pounds to the School clubs by the nine juniors, as the profits for the term on the business of the School shop.

Which of these two events produced the more terrific cheers the reader must take upon himself to decide.

An hour later, Messrs Wally, D'Arcy, Ashby, Fisher minor, Percy, Cottle, Lickford, Ramshaw, and Cash, limited, walked arm in arm across the Green, after a farewell call on Mrs Stratton, on their way to the School omnibus, which waited at the Watch-Tower. Their progress was temporarily interrupted by the sudden bolt of Fisher minor in pursuit of a lank, cadaverous figure, wearing the Modern colours, who was strolling innocently off in the direction of Mr Forder's house.

"The young un's got 'em again," said Wally. "Here, come back, young Fisher minor, can't you? We shan't wait."

Fisher minor pulled up. He looked wistfully first at the retreating figure in the distance, then at his eight friends. With a sigh he decided on the latter; and for that term, at least, finally abandoned the quest of his unlucky half-crown.

It took some little time to arrange matters on the omnibus, as one or two innocent middle-boys had had the audacity to occupy the box-seat and the row behind, and had to be cajoled or pulled down. How could any one dare, when those two seats just held nine, to imagine that they were not sacred property?

"That's better," said Wally, when at last the party were safely up, with two rugs over their eighteen knees, and a gross of brandy-balls circulating for the common comfort. "Touch 'em up, driver. Give 'em their heads! I tell you what, you chaps, this has been rather a slow half. I vote we have some larks next term."

"Rather!" chimed in the chorus.